Break *the* Skin

Also by

LEE MARTIN

Such a Life
River of Heaven
The Bright Forever
Turning Bones
Quakertown
From Our House
The Least You Need to Know

Break *the* Skin

a novel

LEE MARTIN

Broadway Paperbacks   New York

This is a work of fiction. Names, characters, places, and incidents either are the product of the author's imagination or are used fictitiously. Any resemblance to actual persons, living or dead, events, or locales is entirely coincidental.

Published in the United States by Broadway Paperbacks, an imprint of the Crown Publishing Group, a division of Random House, Inc., New York.
www.crownpublishing.com
www.broadwaypaperbacks.com

Originally published in hardcover in the United States by Crown Publishers, an imprint of the Crown Publishing Group, a division of Random House, Inc., New York, in 2011.

Library of Congress Cataloging-in-Publication Data
Martin, Lee, 1955–
Break the skin: a novel / Lee Martin. —1st ed.
p. cm.
I. Title
PS3563.A724927B74 2011
813'.54—dc22
2011003329

ISBN 978-0-307-71676-7
eISBN 978-0-307-71677-4

Printed in the United States of America

Book design by Lynne Amft
Cover design by Jennifer O'Connor
Cover photograph by Lyn Hughes/Corbis

1 3 5 7 9 10 8 6 4 2

First Paperback Edition

For Baby, who spoke to me from her heart

My steel toes start kickin'
My new tattoo just ain't stickin'
You've got to break the skin
Take the needle just stick it in

—WATERSHED, "Black Concert T-Shirt"

Break *the* Skin

LANEY

December 2009

MT. GILEAD, ILLINOIS

The police came for me in the middle of the night. Two officers: one tall and slope-shouldered, the other big-bellied. They walked into the Walmart where I worked, and after speaking to the shift supervisor, they came to my register and the tall one said, "You're Elaine Volk, aren't you? We asked you a few questions once before. Remember?"

Of course I remembered. Questions about where I was on a certain morning in May. *Home, asleep,* I'd told them, and *No, I didn't hear any shots.*

Now a few customers who had been about to push their carts to my checkout line were hesitating. I gave them a grin in hopes that they'd think everything was all right, but I knew it wasn't. I said to the officers, "I'm Laney."

My voice sounded strange to me, too loud for my soft-spoken nature. I was the sort most folks didn't give a second look—a scrawny thing with short curly hair, a nothing kind of girl with no hips to speak of and arms and legs as thin as ropes. I looked like I might turn to dust, which is what I wished I could have done just then. I was nineteen, and as I stood there waiting to see what was going to happen next, I felt how far I was from the girl I'd always been—Little Laney Volk, as ordinary as bread from the wrapper, nothing to take note of at all unless, that is, you could get her to sing. Then, my mother said, the angels would fall from the sky, struck dumb with envy. As a favor to her, I sometimes sang at the

New Hope Free Methodist Church, and my senior year in high school, I played Marian Paroo in *The Music Man*. I didn't know what to say when after performances people told me I'd put a lump in their throats and tears in their eyes with my renditions of "Goodnight, My Someone" and "Till There Was You." My director said I should go on to college and study voice and musical theatre. *There were prettier girls I could have cast,* she told me, *but none of them could sing like you.* Much to my mother's disappointment, I was too shy, too afraid to leave New Hope, too worried that in a bigger place I'd find out I was what I'd suspected all along—no one, no one at all. *Oh, Laney,* my mother said. *That just breaks my heart.*

Sometimes, like that night when the police came, I felt that girl—that Laney I'd been, scared and shy—watching me, hoping beyond hope that I might find my way back to her. That night, though, I knew I was leaving her behind. I knew she couldn't save me.

The police officers wanted me to come with them. They said they had more questions. "Let's go back to wherever it is you keep your coat and purse," the big-bellied officer said. "Then we'll drive uptown to the station."

It was snowing outside, a hard, wet snow slanting down through the sodium lights in the parking lot, but I could still make out the flash of the red lights on the police car. I felt a shiver go up my spine.

"All right," I said, because there was nothing else I could say, at least not to the police officers who were waiting for me to come with them. I wouldn't say, *I know why you're here.* I wouldn't tell them that my boyfriend, Lester, after a summer of fretting, had taken off. He was somewhere I didn't know—him and that silly derby hat he always wore; him and his gap-toothed smile that could melt my heart. His house on Route 130 was locked up tight. He'd left everything behind in September, and I hadn't heard from him, not a word. I wouldn't tell the police officers that. I wouldn't say, *Go talk to Delilah Dade.* They'd already done that once. They'd come to her and said they'd heard she had a pistol and people had seen her wave it about once in a public place. Did she still have that gun?

"No," she told them. "That gun belonged to my old boyfriend, Bobby May. He took it with him when he left me high and dry." Would she mind if they searched her trailer? "Look all you want," she told them, "but you won't find any gun." And, indeed, their search didn't turn up a thing.

That was back in the summer. Now it was almost Christmas, and here they were again. This time I was afraid they wouldn't stop asking questions until they had what they needed to know.

I did what they said. I let them follow me to the break room at the back of the store, and I picked up my coat and my purse. Then I had to walk back through the store, all the way down that long aisle, my head bowed, a police officer on either side of me, the wet soles of their shoes squeaking on the floor. I knew everyone was watching—the other Walmart associates and the shoppers—but I didn't raise my face to look at them or make any attempt to say this was all a mistake. I just kept walking.

Then, at the front of the store, I glanced up and saw Delilah, who had taken over at my register. We'd sworn we'd never say a word, and now she was giving me a hard look—a look to kill.

She was the pretty one, the one with the curve to her hips and that ash-blond hair that fell to her shoulders in soft waves. She was nearly twice my age, the big sister I'd never had. Since Daddy died when I was twelve, it'd just been Mother and me, and as I got older and it became clear that I had this gift for singing but was afraid to do anything with it, we'd lived with the tension of her wishing I'd be more forward and have more confidence in my talent, until finally I couldn't take it anymore, the little ways she had of making it plain that I was disappointing her.

When I went to work at Walmart and fell in with Delilah, I didn't think twice when she asked me to move in with her at the Shady Acres Trailer Park in Mt. Gilead. It was only eight miles up Route 50 from New Hope, but it was far enough from my mother to convince me I could make a life of my own and not have to spend my time feeling all down in the mouth because I couldn't live up to what she wanted for me. *All right, then,* she said when I told her I was moving out. *You just go.*

I wanted to be like Delilah—independent and tough as nails—but that was no excuse for what I'd done to make the police have an interest in me. The time had come when I'd have to give them answers.

The police car was parked at the curb, its lights still swirling. I hunched my shoulders and stepped out into the snowy night. I let the officers lead me to the car. The slope-shouldered one opened the door to the backseat, and I got in. The snow was coming so hard I could barely make out the shapes of people moving inside the store. Just a few minutes before, I'd been one of them, but now there wasn't a sign, no sign at all, that I'd ever set foot in the place.

I closed my eyes, and I let myself be scared. Scared to death.

AT THE POLICE STATION, I sat across a table from the big-bellied officer in a room with no windows. From time to time, I could hear footsteps in the hall outside the closed door. The fluorescent lights hurt my eyes. Not long ago, someone had eaten fried food in this room, and the hot-grease smell turned my stomach.

The tall, slope-shouldered officer paced back and forth behind me, calling me "honey." "Honey," he said, "why don't you tell us what you know?" He reminded me of my daddy and how, when he was still alive, he'd say something in a way that suggested he loved me and yet was disappointed at the same time. "We'll call your mama," the slope-shouldered officer said. "Maybe that'll make it easier for you."

It pained me to think of Mother, rousted from bed in the middle of the night to come to the police station. I knew how she'd look at me, her face all caved in and sad, and I could hear her say, *Oh, Laney.* I shut my eyes and saw the bright lines sizzling at the edge of my vision, a migraine coming on. I thought I'd put them behind me for good, but now they'd come back.

"No, don't call anyone," I said. "Can I have some Tylenol? My head hurts."

Sometime later, Mother would raise a stink because the police had no right to question me like that, not without a lawyer being there, but at the time I didn't think of that. I was thinking instead about something else Daddy had told me when I was a little girl: Eventually everybody had to answer for the things they'd done.

I knew it was true, but I couldn't bring myself to start at the beginning with the story of how Mother and I had a falling-out last year in January because after *The Music Man,* when she was all excited because my director said I was so talented and I should go to college, I dropped out of high school. Just stopped going and wouldn't go back no matter how much Mother yelled and cried and told me I was throwing away everything God gave me. Just couldn't take the pressure of having to meet all those expectations, which seemed beyond my reach.

Working at Walmart seemed like something I could handle while I figured out what else I wanted to do—and then Delilah said, "Why don't you come and live with me?"

There we were, two women who'd never found a happy place to be until we had each other. When I was with her, I felt like anything could happen and it'd be all right. She even let me shoot that pistol she had—yes, it was hers, and not Bobby May's like she'd told the police—just target shooting out in the country, and I thought, Okay, then. I never thought I'd do something like that, but just look at me. I had no idea who I was becoming, but I was willing to find out.

Delilah was on the other side of Bobby May and trying to figure out whether he'd been her last chance at love, or whether he'd been someone she had to get past so she could better know the kind of man she was looking for, a man who would treat her fine forever, a man who would make sure she had a good life.

Sometimes at night we sat out on the deck in front of the trailer and looked up at the stars, and before too long, she started in with the story of how her daddy left when she was just a little girl, and then a year later, her mother's car got stalled one night on the B&O Railroad tracks on Whittle Avenue in Mt. Gilead, and the train that was coming couldn't stop. An eyewitness came forward, the owner of the B&L Liquor Store at the corner of Whittle and Cherry. He was looking out the plate-glass window about the time that freight train was coming into town from the east, curling past the International Shoe Factory, cutting its speed but still coming at a pretty decent clip. "I saw a Chevy Impala," the man said when he testified at the coroner's inquest. "Yes, that one," he said when the coroner showed him a picture of a mangled white Chevy Impala. "I saw that woman drive it down Whittle, and she got up on the crossing, wedged in between the guard arms, and she just stopped. Then she cut the engine. I saw that plain as day. She shut off the engine, and she let go of the wheel. She didn't look one way or the other. She just stared straight ahead. The engineer blasted his whistle again and again. I heard the wheels screeching on the rails as he tried to shut that train down, but it was too late."

That's what people could do, Delilah told me. Think so much of themselves that they could do something like that—just go away—no matter how much they knew it would end up hurting you. Her voice was a whisper in the dark, as if she could barely make a sound, but I could hear the misery in it, the heartache she still carried from her years of moving from foster home to foster home, the same sorrow that filled our trailer some nights when I heard her crying in her bedroom. "I never really had a mother," she told me. "Never had any brothers and sisters, either, just the other foster kids, and you don't want to know how they treated me." She reached over and found my hand, and she twined her fingers around mine. "Everyone ought to have at least one person they can count on." She squeezed so hard, I could barely stand it, but I let her. "I can always count on you, can't I?" she asked, and because I wanted to be that person—the sort a woman like Delilah, older and more experienced, could value—I told her, yes, absolutely, yes, she could. "We're like sisters," I said, and she put her arms around my shoulders and hugged me.

All this seemed too private, too much a thing that only belonged to Delilah and me, sisters at heart, so instead I told the story of the day we shot the gun, which was almost a year after I'd moved in with her. By that time, I'd gone back home to live with Mother, thinking Delilah and I were done for good. But we made up, and one day we went down into the country to shoot her gun. I told the officers about that, and then I went backwards from there, working my way to where everything—though we didn't know it—pointed us down a road toward trouble.

Delilah had a .38 Special, a five-shot pistol with a two-inch stainless-steel barrel and Pachmayr grips. Mama's Little Helper, she called it, something to keep around, *just in case.*

One night, back in April, I cleaned and oiled it, and the next day she showed it to Lester. We were in the kitchen of the trailer. She let him heft that .38, let him pop out the cylinder and take a gander at the shiny heads of the copper XPB bullets I'd slipped in after the cleaning was done. He snugged the cylinder back into place, and with the tip of the barrel he pushed his derby hat off his forehead. He was wearing a gray T-shirt and a black vest, and it was easy for me to believe he'd stepped out of some old-time shoot-'em-up. He wrapped his left hand around his right wrist, extended his arm, and sighted down the barrel.

"It's going to be loud," he said. "You got a silencer?"

The trailer windows were cranked open, and there was a breeze and birds singing. The hyacinth bulbs Delilah had planted in the fall had sent up green shoots and now the pink and purple flowers were in bloom. First-year blooms were always the sweetest, but the hyacinths' smell wasn't enough to cover the stench from the poultry house down the street.

"Never needed a silencer before," Delilah said.

It was that word, *silencer,* that put me on edge, made me understand that what we were doing was real. All along, I thought we were just talking big, but now I took in the sight of Lester holding that pistol, and I was scared.

Delilah drove us out of Mt. Gilead in her Malibu. She brought an empty plastic milk jug and a pillow to see if either one of them would help silence that .38.

We left Route 50 and drove through New Hope, that itty-bitty town where I lived with my mother. I'd gone home because of what had happened between Delilah and me and a woman named Rose MacAdow. She's the other part of my story and the reason I was talking to the police.

In a snap, I told the officers, we were curving out into the country. We took a gravel road and then another until we were back in what Daddy always called "the trashlands": run-down farmhouses, and front yards with junk cars up on blocks. Then there was nothing but the gravel road running past field after field where the wheat was still green. Every once in a while we passed a lane trailing back into the brush, most likely to a caved-in house or maybe only a set of cement steps where that house used to be.

"All right, all right," I said. I was so on edge I felt like I might jump right out of my skin. "You don't have to keep going all day."

Delilah pulled down an oil lease road that carried us into the woods. She shut off the Malibu and the three of us sat there, no one moving, as if we were suddenly paralyzed with the thought of what we'd come to do. A breeze set the branches of a sassafras sapling to twitching. Somewhere farther back in the woods, a woodpecker drummed against a trunk, the *knock knock knock* echoing in the still air.

Finally, Lester said, "A man could get away with anything out here."

Then the three of us got out of the car.

We tried the milk jug first. Lester stuck the barrel of the .38 down through the mouth and pulled the trigger. The noise made my ears hurt.

"That's no good," Delilah said. "The whole town would hear that."

So we tried the pillow, hoping it would muffle the shot, but all we ended up with was a pillow shot to hell and our ears still ringing.

"We'd never get away with it, anyway," I finally said, and to my relief, Delilah agreed.

"It was a crazy idea," she said.

We couldn't get out of there fast enough. We drove back to Mt. Gilead, and then I got into Lester's truck. We drove all the way back out to New Hope, neither of us saying a word.

Then, when we were parked in Mother's driveway, I opened the truck door. Before I could get out, I turned to him and I said, "We shouldn't talk about any of this."

"You're right." The brim of his derby hat was slung low to his eyes now, as if he didn't want anyone to get a good look at him. "We shouldn't. If people got wind of what we were scheming, it could only be bad for us."

Mother stepped out the front door and shook something from a towel. She had no idea what'd gone on down that oil lease road. To her, it was a regular Saturday, and everything was as ordinary as could be. That's what I wanted more than anything—that feeling of everything being exactly what I'd expect. No surprises. Just the regular come and go.

"I got carried away," I said to Lester. "We all did."

"It's all right, Laney." He took my hand and squeezed it. "We just lost our heads. Now, forget it. I mean it. Let it go."

But I couldn't forget how a few nights before, we'd gathered at Delilah's trailer. We sat around the kitchen table—Delilah and Lester and me. I took a paring knife, and along the length of a black candle I etched the name *Rose*.

Then I set the candle in the brass holder and put it in the middle of the table. I lit it, and as it burned, I reached out and took Delilah's hand with my right and Lester's with my left. I told them to close their eyes and to concentrate on calling forth the dark spirits. I closed my own eyes, and for a good while there was only the sound of our breathing and the candle wax dripping.

Then, for no apparent reason, the fluorescent light above the sink came on. I heard it crackle and hum, and when I opened my eyes, there it was, bright and with the slightest tinge of violet.

"Jesus, God," said Lester.

"Has that ever happened before?" I asked Delilah.

"Never." She squeezed my hand. "He's here, isn't he? The devil."

I stared into the candle flame. "Can you see him?"

I knew that she wanted to, and that made me want it just as bad. I wanted to be able to say to her, *See what I brought you.* So I kept quiet, letting her look and look.

"I do," she finally said in a whisper.

"Me, too," said Lester.

Then it happened, the thing that scared me to death. I saw the wax dripping down the length of the candle, taking away the letters of Rose's name, one at a time, and I started to cry a little, not making any noise, just letting the tears leak from my eyes and run down my cheeks.

I didn't say anything. *You have to believe me,* I told the police officers. Not a word. I let Delilah and Lester do all the talking, and that's what I'm guilty of—that silence.

"Look at her name," Lester said in a whisper. "Look at it going away."

I saw the last letter disappear, and I choked down a sob.

Delilah squeezed my hand. "Shh, Laney. Don't cry. She's hurt you long enough. She's out to get all of us. We have to stop her. That's what the devil's telling us, isn't he, Laney?"

I should have called an end to it. I should have said we were fools. I should have walked away. I should have called the police. I should have gotten out. I should have been the girl Mother wanted me to be, the girl with a singing voice so sweet and pure the angels had no hope of matching it. I should have been that girl with all her life ahead of her, a pretty life full of music and joy.

But I couldn't stand to see the pain in Delilah's broken heart, so I said, "Rose has hurt you, too." I nodded my head toward the candle. "Take a good long look at that flame. Tell me what you see."

I'll admit I said that, and then I let the candle and what was already inside Delilah do the rest. The way the flame waved and danced, it was easy to see whatever someone wanted to see.

"We have to put her away," Delilah said, and still I thought we were only talking big. "She's put a hex on us. A death hex. It won't stop until she's gone. We have to open the gates of hell and put her away forever."

We swore we'd never tell anyone. Not a soul. Not to save our lives.

WE WERE SCARED. You have to understand what happens to people who start to believe they have no choice—people like us. We had so little—or in my case, I'd thrown too much away—and we were fierce to protect what was ours. Enough things had gone wrong that we'd begun to believe that evil was stalking us, and it was up to us to find a way to stop Rose MacAdow.

That's who we were the night I lit that black candle. By then I felt like I was in a current of time that I couldn't stop even if I wanted to, a current that began when Delilah called to say someone had broken into her trailer and left a mess. "Come over here, quick, Laney, I'm scared to death."

When I walked into the trailer—it would be a few more days before I lit that black candle—my heart started pounding. Whoever had come to do this had been out of control: kitchen drawers yanked out, their contents dumped onto the floor; broken dishes; slashes in the couch upholstery so the stuffing stuck out; glass picture frames cracked; clothes cut to rags; the toilet stopped up and flushed so it overflowed; a symbol drawn on the bathroom mirror in lipstick: a circle with a pentagram inside it. I'd seen that symbol before, and it always put me in mind of the star I'd learned to draw in grade school from one continuous line, only this star was turned so two of its points touched the top arc of the circle that contained it.

An inverted pentagram, I told Delilah when the two of us walked through the trailer, overwhelmed with the destruction. We stood before the mirror, the pentagram seeming to fall across my face. It was meant to conjure evil spirits, to call them into the trailer where they'd feast off whoever lived there.

"It was Rose, wasn't it?" Delilah said.

I nodded. "Who else?"

We set about cleaning up the mess, talking as we worked, wondering what might be about to happen next and what we could do to stop it.

THE NEXT DAY, Lester came home from work and found that someone had been out to his place. They'd spray-painted those same inverted pentagrams on the front of his house.

"Rose shouldn't get away with this," he said, and I told him we wouldn't let her.

That night, when I was driving to work, a car came up behind me, so close its headlights filled my Corolla. Whoever was in that car had the high beams on. I looked in my rearview mirror, but the lights were so blinding I couldn't make out anything about the car that was following me and I couldn't see anyone inside it. I hunched over the steering wheel, trying to get out of the glare.

Finally, the car fell back. I took another glance at the mirror, but I still couldn't make out a thing about that car.

"It could have been nothing," I said when I told the story to Delilah. "Maybe it was a drunk, or some kids out joyriding."

"You know exactly who it was. It's a wonder you weren't killed."

When she said that, I felt my knees go weak. I put my arms around her and pressed her to me. "What in the world have we got ourselves into?"

She let me hold on to her like that. Then, finally, she pulled away. She said, "We better get out of it quick." She used the back of her hand to caress my cheek. "Right, Laney? We better get out before someone gets hurt."

I nodded. I'd figure out something, I told her. "Don't worry," I said. "I will."

IT WAS UP TO ME, I told the police officers, on account of Rose had taught me how to cast spells. "I've been doing them a long time now," she told me, "and I swear, Laney, they really work. Just put the right energy out there, and, trust me, you'll get what you want."

At one time, she and I and Delilah lived together at the trailer park. It was there, one March morning toward dawn, more than a year before we'd test-fire that .38, when Rose cast the first spell, a spell for love. Now that what we started is done, I can own up to the fact that, yes, I stood as witness, and yes, Delilah was there. She was there, and she said, "It's just for fun, right, Rose?"

Rose wouldn't answer. She just went on with what she was doing, her small hands—pretty little hands for a woman her size—busy with the candle and the match. She set the taper—red, to represent the heart, she told us—on Delilah's night table and lit it. Rose had the blackest hair, cut in a bob and parted in the middle. When she leaned over the candle, the ends of her hair came close to the flame. Her face was so pretty in the light: pale skin, button nose, dainty mouth, red lips. Her mouth looked like it should have belonged to a smaller woman. Not that she was sloppy fat. Fleshy, I guess you'd say. Hips a little too wide, bottom a little too round. Sometimes she tried to make herself feel better about her weight by saying there was more to her to love than a skinny thing like me could put in front of a man. I never took offense. I understood she wanted to be thin. Maybe not as thin as me, but still.

The smoke curled up from the match when she shook it out, and somehow it found me and I had to fan it away from my face. She spread a white handkerchief on the bed. It was early in March, and Venus was rising in the morning twilight. The time Rose had waited for, the perfect time, she said, because the goddess of love was riding on that morning star.

"I call thee, beloved ones," she whispered, "to love us more than anyone."

The curtains at the bedroom window were open, and over her shoulder I could see the sky just beginning to brighten in the east along the edge of Mt. Gilead and the far reaches of the trailer park. The three of us filled that trailer with our longings for love. Would any man ever have us? That's what Delilah wanted to know. "Jeez, Laney. Look at Rose and me. Two gals on our way to being old maids." I was young, and Delilah said there was time left for me. She was thirty-five, the same as Rose, and they were desperate. They'd had men to love them, only they were the wrong kind of men, not the kind to make a life with. Me? I'd never even been close to knowing what it was to be in love. So that morning in March—*Yes, it was 2008,* I told the police officers—when I had no way of knowing that Lester was in my future, I was enchanted with the idea that Rose could cast a spell to bring us the men of our dreams.

That's how everything started—with this ache for love. We didn't want our lives to be ugly. Really, we didn't. We wanted what everyone wants—a pretty life, the sort that makes you want to get out of bed each day, excited to see what wonderful something might be waiting for you. We might have had that—I guess we'll never know—if we'd only been more patient and not so certain that we were at the edge of last chances.

Birds were coming up from sleep in the woods behind the park, and they filled the air with their chatter. The trees were still bare, and their black limbs stretched across the sky. Soon there would be daffodils and hyacinths and the smell of the earth thawing and grass going to green and sunshine warm on my face when I stepped outside, but on that morning, we still hadn't left winter behind. A little hoarfrost laced the grass, and it was cold in Delilah's bedroom. I rubbed my bare arms to keep off the chill.

Rose had gathered seven straight pins from her sewing basket, and as she chanted the spell, she stuck each pin into the handkerchief. "Seven times I pierce thy heart," she said. "Today the magic of Venus starts." She reached out her arms and took Delilah and me by our hands. We were a sisterhood of lonely hearts. Rose's eyes were closed, and she was still chanting in that whisper that made a shiver go up the back of my neck. "I bind thy heart and soul to me. As I do will, so let it be."

I closed my eyes, too. It makes me sad now to think of the girl I was in that room, to know my life was such that I had to believe in magic. What was the harm in believing in Rose? At least that's what I thought then. I didn't stop to wonder why, if what she claimed was true about spells getting you what you wanted, she was who she was—a woman sharing a trailer with the likes of Delilah and me, which was surely not what she hoped for herself.

She chanted a whisper of promise, and I let it take me outside myself until it felt like I was looking down from a distance on that white cloth and Rose bending over it with her pins.

Then I heard her whisper my name, heard her call me back to my body. "Laney, you're trembling," she said. "You poor thing." I couldn't speak. Rose's chant had swallowed up my voice. I didn't know how to say that I'd seen all the way to the deepest part of me—I guess it was the little girl inside me who came out every time I sang, the little girl who was bruised and aching because her father, a kind and decent man, had gone away and she had no way to get him back. "It's just for fun, Laney." I let Delilah put her arms around me, let her hold me close. She said, "Tell her, Rose. Tell her we're just fooling around."

Rose bent close to the candle and blew it out. The light dimmed all around us.

I won't speak for Delilah, but I suspect, like me, she felt her heart open to what might be possible, even for the likes of us. We didn't know what was about to happen, or how we'd let it sweep us along once it did.

Rose's voice came from the darkness. "I guess we'll just have to wait and see, now, won't we?"

* * *

WHEN WE LIVED together that spring, Rose had a doll, a poppet she'd made from black cloth and stuffed with birch bark, garlic, and rue. Mr. Mank, that's who the doll was meant to represent. The manager at the Walmart where we worked the night shift, eleven to seven. For whatever reason, he was always giving Rose a hard time. She claimed it was because he tried to kiss her one night in the break room and she slapped his face so hard his glasses flew off, but Delilah told me that was only wishful thinking. Mr. Mank wasn't chasing Rose, not a heavy girl like her. At any rate, she decided she wanted him out of her life, so one afternoon, not long after she cast the love spell, the three of us drove out into the country near New Hope and she tossed that poppet into the Bonpas Creek.

"Bum-paw," we all called it, which was as close to the original French pronunciation as we could manage. The word, I'd learned in school, meant "Good Path," and that's what Rose said she needed, a good path for Mr. Mank's exit from her life. The spring rains had come and the creek was up. We watched the poppet doll twist along with the current as it headed downstream. Eventually, the Bonpas would empty into the Wabash River and then the Ohio and finally the Mississippi, and carry that poppet all the way to the Gulf of Mexico.

"Bye-bye." Rose waved at the doll as it moved away from us. She blew it a kiss. "Good-bye, Mr. Mank, and good riddance."

The next night, she called in sick, as she was apt to do whenever she just didn't feel like working, and when she came into the store the night after that, Mr. Mank told her he was letting her go.

"How about that?" she said to me after she grabbed her jacket and purse from the break room and was heading out the door. Her big bottom made an angry little jostle inside her khaki pants. She threw her hands up over her head, disgusted. "Fired," she said, and then she was gone. I watched her swinging her arms as she marched across the parking lot. The last glimpse I had of her was when she made it to Highway 130 and turned south, stomping away, as pissed off as pissed off can be, walking home.

"Well," Delilah said when I found her in Electronics and gave her the news, "looks like that's one spell that worked. She wanted Mank out of her life, and that's exactly what she got."

I felt sorry for her, tossed out like that, so our next night off I said it was time we painted the town. "Get slinky, ladies," I said. "It's our night to howl."

"Laney, you're bad," Delilah said with a laugh.

She always thought it was a riot when I put on my vamp act, because I was about as unvampish as a woman could be. Little slip of a thing, straight up and down like a boy, a mess of dark curls that looked like a nest of snakes. But, like I said, I could sing better than the angels, and Mother called me "Little Bit," her little bit of heaven. She'd always told me my good heart and my voice would take me places, but here I was, nothing down the road except my job at Walmart and my life with Delilah and Rose.

I sucked in my cheeks and made my lips all pouty. I put a hand on my hip and flounced across the room. I got up close to Delilah's face and batted my eyelashes. "Hey, baby, was that an earthquake, or did you just rock my world?"

I had a list of pickup lines I'd overheard in bars, none of them directed at me. They cracked me up, and I used them from time to time to get a chuckle out of Delilah and Rose.

"Men," Rose said with a roll of her eyes.

Why did we want them so much when they were so stupid? Just couldn't stop ourselves, I guess. Couldn't stop wanting them even if they rarely paid us any mind, or else gave us the sort of horndog going-over—*Ooh, you fine thing*—that we didn't really want.

"We'll change our luck tonight," Delilah said. "Maybe even you, Laney."

I had to turn my face away so she wouldn't see how much that stung. I wanted to toughen up, to be as full of vinegar as she was. I wanted to prove that I could be more than Little Bit.

Truth be told, I guess I was more than a little in love with her, too, and I needed her to love me back. Not that I wanted to love her *that* way—you know, the way a woman can love another woman with her mouth and her hands—but more that I wanted to have her with me always, have the company of her. That's what I wanted most of all. Daddy was gone, and Mother was crosswise with me. I needed Delilah and me to be enough for each other. Maybe we would have if I hadn't had a soft spot in my heart for Rose, too—if I hadn't got myself caught between them.

I'd had a big fight with Mother in January when I told her I was dropping out of school and going to work at Walmart. Soon I was getting cozy with Delilah, and Mother said that I was hiding my light under a bushel and letting my singing talent go for nothing. "You're better than that, Elaine MaryKatherine Volk," she told me, "and you're better than that gal you run with. You could be somebody. She's on a fast track to nowhere."

Trashy, she said. Just look at Delilah and those short skirts she wore, and those men she took up with, doing God knows what, though it wasn't hard to imagine.

I packed a duffel bag and walked out.

It was Delilah who gave me a place to sleep, who made me feel good. Delilah who called me "'Lil Sis." Delilah who sometimes stole cosmetics from work and showed me how to put on lipstick and eyeliner and shadow and blush. It was a delicate balance for her. She'd spent too much time in the sun, and it was starting to leave crow's-feet at the corners of her eyes. She needed just the right concealer and moisturizer and foundation. "You could be pretty, Laney," she said once, "if you'd try."

It wasn't long after this that Rose started working nights with us at Walmart. That's how we met her and how all of us came to live together in the trailer that spring.

Late in the afternoons, when we were just waking up from a day's sleep and Rose was still snoozing, Delilah turned on *Oprah,* and we watched it together. " 'Lil Sis," she said from time to time, "you get me, you really do."

That's who I was, the one who got Delilah, and trust me, sometimes she was hard to get. She could be all lovey-dovey one minute—oh, she knew how to flirt—and then hard to the core the next. She'd set her jaw and purse her lips, and little wrinkle lines would flare under her nose. At work she could tell Mr. Mank to fuck off and leave her be and never catch his shit the way the rest of us did. Maybe it was because she kept that pistol in her purse and showed it to him one night.

"You're going to get in trouble with that thing," Rose told her.

"I'm not looking for trouble," Delilah said, "but I'll be ready for it if it comes knocking."

Rose's problem, according to Delilah, was she needed to grow a set of balls and grab what she wanted instead of relying on wishes. That was Rose's way. She thought she could make the world to her whim by thinking what she wanted. Her energy would create what was best for her, and if she needed a little help, she had her poppets—poppets for healing, poppets for charms, poppets to sweep the ugly out of her life, and poppets to bring her joy.

Delilah called her "Mary Poppets," but that was just a joke between her and me, and I felt guilty every time I laughed about it on account of I loved Rose, too—loved her because she was a big woman with a big heart, and because she loved so hard and felt so deeply, she always had a long fall to make whenever things didn't work out to suit her. I was afraid life would always be hard for her, and that made me love her even more.

I was afraid to tell Delilah that those poppets intrigued me, made me think about how we might be able to have power over someone else. Maybe it happened, and we didn't even know it. Maybe there were people in the world—strangers—and every little thing we did in our own here and now shot through space and tapped their hearts.

The night we were heading out, Rose got all excited, the way she could when she was convinced something good was just around the corner.

"Tonight's the night," she said. She'd curled her lashes, and they swept up from her big eyes.

"For what?" asked Delilah.

"True love."

So there we were strutting into the South End Tavern, a rough-and-tumble joint on Whittle Avenue just up from our trailer park. It was where the line workers from the poultry house went after their shift, where anyone underage could get served with no questions asked, where someone was sure to be gearing up on crank in the bathroom, where the bartender cracked heads with his ball bat if things got out of hand. Why in the world did we think we'd find the right kind of man there? I guess that was a sign of how desperate we were.

How ridiculous, too. From where I sit now, I'd laugh if I could. Just the picture of the three of us all glammed up—at least we thought we were. Rose in tight jeans and a cropped top, her bare belly rolled up around her belt line. Delilah in a snug wife-beater to make her chesticles stand out, and me, Little Bit, my own beestings two bumps in a T-shirt that said *Does This Shirt Make My Tits Look Big?*

"It's ironic," I told Rose the first time she saw it and gave me a puzzled look.

"But, Laney, you don't have hardly anything at all."

"That's the joke."

"I don't get it."

"It's ironic," I said.

"Okay."

And we were. Ironic, I mean. Just like Rose, who had no idea why my shirt was funny, we didn't know how far we were from the sultry, on-the-make women we were pretending to be. I can see that now. One of us too big, but with a beautiful face. One of us too slight and boyish. One of us, the one closer to "just right," too rough and hard. Yet all of us as needful and as deserving of romance as any woman, no matter how beautiful, how average, how plain.

It was a Friday night, the best night because we were all jazzed up and there was a live band, a local group called Helmets on the Short Bus. The front man was a tall, lanky redhead, his hair in dreadlocks, a splatter of freckles across his face. When we came in, he was singing the opening verse of "Stairway to Heaven"—"There's a lady who's sure all that glitters is gold"—and Delilah stopped walking all of a sudden, her eyes on that man, as if she couldn't look away even if she wanted to.

I bumped into her back. "Keep moving," I told her.

The wood-plank floor squeaked as Rose came up behind me. "Would you look at that?" she said, and I knew he'd caught her eye, too.

Finally, we got to a table off to the side, but down front, so I could watch the way that man's fingers flew over the frets of his electric guitar. They were long fingers, and I liked the way his wrist curved and how he wore that guitar on his pelvis and how he made it talk.

We ordered our drinks—Jack and Coke all around—and we watched that man. Mmmm...mmmmm...mmmmm. I sat up straight and pushed my shoulders back so if he looked my way, he'd be able to read my T-shirt.

Don't get me wrong. He wasn't a beautiful man, not one of those drop-dead gorgeous men, and maybe that's why he charmed us so. We could imagine that if the cards fell just right we could have a life with him. He was too tall and gawky, and all those dreads made his head seem too big to be held up by that long, scrawny neck, but Lord, God, those hands and the way they played that guitar and that voice, just enough of a rasp to make a girl think of dark rooms and whispered I-love-you's. By the time that song really got going, we were love-struck, riding the wave of the guitar solo to its climax, and then falling into that man's smoky voice, nearly whispering the last line—"And she's buying a stairway to heaven"—in a way that made us think of his arms around us, rocking us, making us feel cared for and loved.

It was so quiet as the last note faded away, quiet long enough for it all to seem unnatural there in the South End, where usually you could hear the roughhousing and the loud talk and the sound of the balls clacking together on the pool tables in the back. Quiet enough long enough for everyone to hear Delilah when she said, "Oh, my. My, my, my."

Then people were clapping and stomping their feet on the floor, and the red-haired man grabbed the mic stand and swung around to face us. His shirt was open, and the stage lights made his bare chest look so smooth and pale. His jeans were low on his hips, low enough to make me think about what it would be like to unbutton them. A few red hairs in the space between his navel and his jeans looked coppery in the light.

"We're Helmets on the Short Bus," the man said. "Don't go away. We'll be back after we take a little break."

Delilah leaned over and whispered to us, "That boy better get *his* helmet on because I mean to rattle his bones."

"That's just lovely, Dee," Rose said, and I could see she was upset. "That's real romantic."

She got up and started making her way to the ladies' room.

"What's that all about?" Delilah said, and I told her I'd go see.

The ladies' room had three stalls, and there was no one there but Rose. I could see the scuffed toes of her Dingo boots under the locked door of the third stall, the one by the window, where someone had written on the sill with a Magic Marker, "Don't wish ill for your enemy, plan it."

I tapped on the stall door. "Rose, it's me."

She was sniffling, and I knew she'd been crying and was trying to stop in hopes I wouldn't notice.

"What do you want, Laney?" Her voice had that little cry quiver in it.

"Just checking on you. You all right?"

She flushed the toilet. Soon the stall door opened and she stepped out, a hard set to her eyes that told me she meant business. "Someone ought to tell her," she said, and then she scrunched her mouth up like she could barely bring herself to call Delilah by name. "Dee." she said. "She carries on like a whore."

"Oh, you know Delilah. She's just cutting loose."

"Like that man would ever have any interest in her."

Rose brushed past me and turned on the water at the sink. She looked at herself in the mirror, leaning in close, checking to see, I imagine, if her eyes were puffy from the crying.

I ducked my head and traced my finger over the letters written on the sill. "He's something, isn't he?" I said, and it was a brave thing for me to say on account of if Rose didn't think that red-haired man would have any interest in Delilah, then she'd probably hoot at the idea that he might take notice of me. I got up the nerve to lift my head. "Isn't he, Rose?"

She glanced at me in the mirror, and for just an instant her eyes opened wide and I could see the light that man had left in them. Then she looked away. She stood up straight and tugged at her crop top. She folded her arms over her bare belly, probably wishing she'd never worn such a thing, a heavy gal like her. "Men like him," she said. She bit her lip, trying to find the words to say next. She pulled a couple of paper towels from the dispenser and dried her hands with angry, jerky movements. "That man," she said. Then she wadded up the paper towels, stuffed them into the trash can, and stormed out, leaving me to fill in the rest: *That man is wonderful!*

When I came out of the ladies' room, I saw Rose at the end of the bar, her hands pressed against it, like she was hanging on to keep her knees from buckling and sending her sliding down to the floor. I saw what she was taking in, the sight of Delilah and that red-haired man getting cozy on the stage. He was talking to a bowlegged little man with a derby hat on his head, a man of an age somewhere between Delilah and me. The red-haired man had his arm around Delilah's shoulders, and she was leaning into him, her hand flat on his naked stomach, as if they'd been an item for years. She laughed at something the red-haired man said. Then he plucked the derby hat from the bowlegged man and set it on top of her head. She held it in place and came up on her tiptoes to give the red-haired man a kiss.

The bowlegged man scratched his head. Then he turned away and got busy repositioning mic stands, even though they probably didn't need to be. I knew he was one of those men who made himself feel important by attaching himself to a band, making it seem that he was part of it, when really all he did was fetch beers, fiddle with mics and amps, and peddle T-shirts like the one he was wearing, a black T-shirt with a giant red bike helmet on top of a little yellow school bus.

Rose had seen enough. She was on her way out the door. I didn't know whether to follow her or to stay. I felt the same pain in the heart that I imagine she felt when she saw Delilah with that man, a man we'd all taken to but it was Delilah who'd been bold enough to claim him.

She called to me. She took off the little man's derby hat and waved it over her head. "Laney," she said, "come meet my fella!"

Maybe it was my first mistake in the whole chain of events that would soon follow—to put on my best face and go to Delilah, to leave Rose to walk back to the trailer by herself. I took a glance out the plate-glass window, and I saw her on the sidewalk looking back toward the door, hesitating just a moment, hoping, I imagine now, that I'd be coming out soon to check on her. If I'd been a better person, I would have, because I knew what it was to be on the outside looking in, to feel lost.

I turned away from her, and maybe that's when she decided her next move, or maybe it came to her later, after Delilah said, "Rose, that spell worked. You sure as hell brought me a man."

His name was Russell Swain, but he said everyone called him "Tweet."

"Like Tweety Bird," Delilah said, and then she did something I couldn't believe. I'd never have had the nerve. Not in a million years. She put her hands on his back and turned him so he was facing away from me. Then she lifted up his shirt, hooked her finger in the waistband of his jeans, and tugged them down just enough so I could see the tattoo of that cartoon bird on his left hip. "How do you like that?" she said.

All I could think to do was to ask him a question, one that didn't have anything to do with that tattoo, or how Delilah had so quickly discovered it, or the fact that I was looking at not only his hip but to be more to the point, the swell of his butt, and I was finding it hard not to stare. "How come you're called Helmets on the Short Bus?"

He tugged his jeans back up, and Delilah smoothed his shirt down. "I used to drive one," he said. Then he told me how he drove one of those little buses for special-ed kids, the kids who had to wear helmets so they wouldn't bang their heads on something and hurt themselves.

"That's mean," I said. "Calling your band that."

He seemed genuinely hurt that I'd think that. "No, no, no. You don't get it. We're not being mean. Those kids frickin' rock!" They liked listening to him sing on those bus trips, he said. He'd get them all bobbing along to something like Ween's "Waving My Dick in the Wind." That was the one that got him fired. He shrugged his shoulders. "Go figure."

"Spilt milk," I said.

"Ancient history."

He gave me a sheepish grin. Now he was jockeying cars for the Ford dealer in town, running trades to other dealers in the Tri-State and bringing a vehicle back in return. The band played gigs at clubs in Illinois, Indiana, Kentucky, Missouri while they waited for their big break.

"Yeah, and when's that going to be, you think?" I surprised myself with how forward I was. It was easier now that I knew he'd fallen for Delilah. I could be a smart-ass if I wanted. What'd I care if I pissed him off? "When pigs fly?"

"Laney!" Delilah said.

"It's cool." He shrugged his shoulders again. "Who knows, Laney-Girl." Just like that, he gave me a nickname, something better than Little Bit, or 'Lil Sis, and I fell in love with him again. "It's a long way to the top," he said.

I couldn't help myself. I took a big breath and belted out a little of the chorus from that AC/DC song, the one about the hard road to the top playing in a rock 'n' roll band: "If you think it's easy doing one night stands / Try playing in a rock 'n' roll band."

He joined me on the last line, and even without a mic, our voices soared over the noise of the South End.

When we were done, I realized that people had stopped talking and were looking up onstage. Delilah's mouth was open, like she couldn't believe what she'd just heard. "Jesus, Laney," she finally said. "I had no idea."

Now it was my turn to shrug my shoulders. I felt the heat creep into my face. "I guess I can sing a little."

"A little?" Tweet said with a laugh. "Laney-Girl, you could sing with this band any day. Better get your helmet on."

I wanted him to mean it the way Delilah did when she said she was going to rattle his bones, but I knew he didn't. He said it the way a big brother might goof with his little sister, and there I was again, 'Lil Sis, and I was sorry that I'd sung those few lines and let my secret out: I could sing, not just singing-in-the-shower kind of sing, but flat-out touch-your-heart, rock-your-world kind of sing.

Some people clapped their hands together, and pretty soon everyone was clapping, and I knew they were clapping for me.

"Hell, damn," a man said. "That little girl can sing!"

I turned to the people sitting at the tables, and I didn't know what to do next.

Then another man shouted, "Darlin', I don't know about your tits"—he was talking about my T-shirt—"but you sure got a pair of lungs."

I couldn't believe how much it stung to hear him say that—to shout it out for everyone to hear. As much as I wanted to believe I was tough, there was still that Little Bit inside me that could hurt more than I thought possible. I felt the ache come into my throat, and I knew if I stood there much longer, I'd start to cry. I wasn't about to let anyone see me do that, so I took a bow, a grand, sweeping bow. Then I lifted my arm and folded in all the fingers except the pinky and the pointer, and I gave the crowd the devil horns, and they all went wild, shouting, "Rock 'n' roll! Rock 'n' roll!"

That's when I jumped off that stage, made my way to the door, and stepped out into the night hoping Rose was still there, but she was gone.

A goth girl came out of the South End. Her face was pale with a heavy layer of white makeup. Her eyes were lined with black, her lashes painted with mascara. She'd drawn thin black coils from the corners of her eyes onto her cheekbones.

"I saw what you did in there," she said to me. "I got it, sister."

"Got it?"

She held up her hand and gave me the devil horns. "Don't worry," she said. "I won't tell." Then she leaned in, and before I knew what she meant to do, she kissed me on the mouth. "Worship him," she said.

"Satan?" I said, and I swear this is true: I felt a shiver go up my spine. The girl laid her hand on my cheek. I wanted to look away from her, but there was something in her eyes that made it impossible. Something about the way she looked at me as if she understood exactly who I was.

I WALKED BACK to the trailer and left Delilah to do whatever it was she was going to do with Tweet. It was a nice night, one of the first warm nights of spring, and I didn't mind being alone in the dark, walking down Whittle past the B&L Liquor Store and the Sudsy-Dudsy Laundromat and over the railroad tracks into our neighborhood, that part of Mt. Gilead everyone called "Bird Town" on account of the poultry house. I didn't even mind its stink, a smell of scalded feathers and old meat. What little breeze there was came out of the west and pushed that stink a little farther away, a little closer to Route 50 that ran out to New Hope, where, although I didn't know it that night, Tweet rented a house at the edge of town just off the highway. His house and another one were out there by themselves as if they'd been picked up by a windstorm and set down some distance from everything else in town. A cornfield stretched on from those two houses to my mother's place and the other homes that started New Hope proper. "Small world," she'd say eventually, and I'd agree.

We lived in small towns in a part of southeastern Illinois that was mainly farmland, where the same families went on through generations, but, as I'd point out to Mother, there were all sorts of ways that people could cross one another's paths.

That night, as I walked into the trailer park, I couldn't get that goth girl out of my mind and the way she'd kissed me on the mouth and called me a sister of Satan as we parted. I'd never even known she existed, and all of a sudden there she was. Things could get crazy like that. Even in a small town like Mt. Gilead. Who knew, until we walked into the South End, that Tweet was out there on our horizon? And that little bowlegged man with the derby hat. Who knew about him, and whether we'd all end up meaning anything at all to one another, but there we were, coming and going in this town where hearts full of longing came together all the time because, when you got down to it, we were all looking for someone—anyone who would make us feel less alone.

I saw the lights on in the trailer windows, heard the muffled sounds of televisions, the thump of the bass on a CD player, a woman's laugh, a dog barking, and I thought of all of us in those trailers we called home and how sometimes a fight would break out and soon there'd be men outside swinging fists; or in the middle of the night, I'd hear a bottle break, the roar of a car engine, gravel spraying the side of our trailer. I thought of ragged lives and how you never knew the ways they might rub up against you, or what would happen once they did.

There'd been a time not long ago when some nights the trouble brewed up in our own trailer. Delilah had that boyfriend, Bobby May. A no-account man. Trouble from the word go. He'd even spent time locked up in Vandalia for burglary. It didn't matter to Delilah. She swore she was in L-U-V. Even when he drank too much. Even when he stole money from her. Even when he laid a fist to her face. One night, though, he went too far. He came at her with a stiletto knife. She'd called him out for stealing from her purse and he'd gone off, saying she was a lying bitch, sending her running out of the trailer and up the street. I ran with her. We held hands and ran as fast as we could. It was still winter, but we'd had no thought of grabbing coats. The cold burned my throat and lungs. We ran all the way to the police station, where we gasped for air and panted out our story. "Boyfriend . . . drunk . . . knife."

The police went looking for Bobby May, but he was long gone. Drunk as he was, he figured out that he couldn't afford to be arrested and sent back to Vandalia. He just up and went, and we didn't know where he was. For a long time, Delilah was sad. "He was just drunk," she kept saying. "He didn't mean to hurt me."

Finally, I had to tell her the truth of the matter. "Good riddance," I said. "He was no kind of man."

She sniffled a little. "He was *my* man."

"He would've ended up killing you," I said. "He's gone. Now, build a bridge and get over it."

It wasn't long before she bought that Taurus .38. She was a different woman after that mess, a little harder in the heart. "No man's ever going to pull a knife on me again," she said when she showed me the .38. "Next time, I'm not running anywhere. I'll have the answer right here."

Then Rose moved in with us. We had that double-wide trailer, one of the few in the park, and Delilah and I were glad to have help with the rent. The trailer had fake stone skirting around the bottom meant to make it look like it had a real foundation. The nicest thing, though, was the cedar-stained deck out the front door with latticework privacy screens around it.

I expected I'd see a light on in the trailer that night when I walked home from the South End. I expected Rose would be up fretting over Delilah and Tweet, but the trailer was dark. The only light was the bulb outside the front door, the one that lit up the deck and the latticework. I could hear the wind chimes Delilah had hung tinkling in the breeze.

I unlocked the front door and stepped inside, letting my eyes get used to the dark. I could smell us in that trailer, all our sprays and lotions and perfumes, as if smell alone would be enough to snag us a man. Rose's Song of India Patchouli, Delilah's spicy Euphoria, the cotton candy of my own Prince Matchabelli, the first scent Mother bought me and the one I still used.

It was so quiet in the trailer I could hear the clock on the living-room wall humming. I felt my way along that wall to the little round table by the window. I switched on the lamp that Delilah kept there and saw Rose's Dingo boots kicked off by the couch. I listened for some sound of her, but there was nothing.

I picked up the boots and moved down the hall to her room. The door was closed, and there was no strip of light in the small space below it. "Rose." I tapped on the door. "It's me."

"Go away." Her voice was dull. I heard her bedsprings creak, and I imagined she was rolling over, turning her face to the wall. "I'm trying to sleep."

"I'm sorry about tonight." I laid my cheek against the door, as if that would somehow let her know how badly I felt. "I should have come outside with you."

"I don't want to talk about tonight."

"Rose." I hoped she'd let me in so I could give her a hug.

"I mean it, Laney."

Her voice had a hard edge to it. I didn't know what else to say. "I've got your boots," I told her.

Maybe that would bring her to the door. Maybe if she opened it, she'd see in my face how sorry I was. Maybe we could be a comfort to each other because I could tell we were now going to be the ones alone. Delilah was busy with her new fella, and not likely shy about running her good luck up the flagpole. The next morning, she'd give Rose a hug and say, "Thank you, thank you, thank you. I really think he's the one. My dream man." And Rose would grit her teeth and say, "I'm happy for you, Dee. I really am."

But as I waited for her on the other side of that door, all she had to say was, "Scuffed-up old boots. Throw them in the garbage for all I care."

"They just need a little polish."

"Oh, really, Laney," she said with disgust. "Please." Her voice cracked a little. I knew she didn't mean to be sharp with me. I knew the best thing to do was to leave her alone.

"Good night," I said, but she didn't say a word in reply.

SO IT WAS LIKE THAT for a while—Delilah crowing about her lover boy, while Rose and I put on our best smiles and pretended we were happy for her. And really I was, on account of she'd gone through so much with Bobby May and she deserved a good man in her life, but I was also jealous—I'll admit that—a little jealous that she'd claimed Tweet, and a little jealous that she was spending more time with him and less time with me.

Then one night, the bowlegged man with the derby hat showed up at Walmart. I was restocking plastic bags on the carousel at the end of my checkout line when I heard someone say, "You're that girl." I looked up, and there he was, smiling at me. I thought the gap between his upper front teeth was the cutest thing. He let his smile get bigger. "That girl who sang with Tweet."

"You were with the band." I thought that would make him feel good to hear me say that, but he just shook his head. He took his hat off and twirled it around on a finger. "Not now," he said. "Tweet said I couldn't hang around anymore. He told me to take a hike."

"How come he did a mean thing like that?"

"Guess you'd have to ask him." He put the derby hat back on his head and put out his hand. "I'm Lester," he said. "Lester Stipp."

I took his hand in mine, and I was surprised by how soft his skin was, not roughed up with work the way so many men's hands were in this part of the world. Lester Stipp's hand was smooth and warm, and I can't deny it gave me a good feeling inside to have him touch me.

"Laney," I said. All of a sudden I was incapable of talking in complete sentences. "Elaine, really. Full name Elaine MaryKatherine Volk. Always called Laney."

"I like it." He smiled again. "Laney," he said, trying it out. He said it like it was the most wonderful name in the world. "It doesn't try too hard." He ducked his head, turning shy. "It's just enough pretty."

We had an awkward moment then, when neither one of us knew what to say. I got busy for a while with the plastic bags. He whistled a little nonsense tune under his breath.

Finally, he said, "Well, then. You think they got any jobs around here? Any work I could do?"

"You'd have to ask the manager, Mr. Mank."

Just then, as if I'd called him, I heard Mr. Mank say my name. "Miss Volk." I turned around and saw him pointing a finger to my register. "You have customers."

Sure enough, while I'd been talking to Lester Stipp, an old woman wearing her hair in curlers and a man with a big square bandage on his forehead had steered their carts into my line and were waiting patiently for me to notice them.

"Sorry, Mr. Mank," I said.

Mank was a scrawny man whose shirt collars were too big for his neck, and his ears stuck out from his narrow head. He had a thin mustache that looked like he'd drawn it on with an eyebrow pencil, and one time I caught him in the break room, leaning into the mirror and clipping stray hairs with a little pair of scissors. He used gel on his stringy black hair, sweeping it up from the sides so it met in a spiky ridge in the center. That was his attempt to look up-to-date, but on Mr. Mank, that hairstyle made him look like an old man trying too hard and it was just sad, if you want to know the truth.

"You need to pay attention, Miss Volk."

He gave me a hard look and then turned on his heel, hitched his khaki pants up his bony hips, and marched down the aisle. I watched him until he took a turn and disappeared into Hardware.

When I turned back, Lester Stipp was gone, leaving me to recall his smile, and that gap between his front teeth that was so adorable, and the way his hand felt when it touched mine.

"You remember that bowlegged man?" I said to Delilah at our three a.m. "lunch" break. It was just the two of us in the break room; the others who had break at that time were already done and either out on the loading dock smoking or back to work on the floor. She squinted and looked at me as if she had no idea who I was talking about. "Derby hat?" I said.

"Little fella." She nodded her head. "Tweet said he was stealing from the band, pocketing money when he sold T-shirts and CDs. You know, like that."

I didn't want to believe her. "He seems like he's a nice man."

"You see him again?"

"Tonight. He was here looking for a job."

"Looking for something to steal is more like it."

"Maybe Tweet doesn't have his facts right."

"Now, Laney. Why would Tweet make up something like that?"

I looked away from her, and I guess for just an instant, the hurt I felt must have come into my eyes, and she said, "Wait a minute. Oh, don't tell me. Little Bit's after a man?"

"Don't call me that. I'm more than a little bit."

"Sure you are, Laney. More than a little bit in love."

I tossed the last of my sandwich into the garbage can. "That man's short," I said, "and he's older than me. Probably ten years at least."

"Ah, Laney, I'm just having fun. You go get that fella. Why, I bet he's another part of Rose's spell."

The next night, when I came to work, Lester was there collecting carts from the parking lot. He had on one of those fluorescent green reflective vests the cart jockeys wore, and he was wrestling a long train of carts into the store. He gave me that grin again. "Hey, Laney," he said. "I came back and they hired me."

We got on right away. He had little ways of making me laugh. He'd come by my register in the dead hours and tell me a stupid joke—*If you were going to shoot a mime, would you use a silencer?*—and I wouldn't be able to stop myself from laughing. He'd be coming in with another train of carts, and he'd stop and give me a big wave, and, always, that gap-toothed smile. Other times, he'd come by and give me a Hershey's Kiss, or a smiley face sticker, or one of those candy Valentine hearts that said, "Be Mine" or "Kiss Me." "Just thinking of you," he'd say.

He was flirty and sweet, and it felt good to be chased after, but, jeez, he was, as I'd told Delilah, at least ten years older than me, and I kept wondering if what she said about him stealing from Tweet's band was true. All that was enough to keep me on the careful side for a while.

Then, one morning in April, when we were getting off work, he said, "Laney, you want to have breakfast?"

What could be the harm in that? I told him I guessed that'd be all right, and then I went to tell Delilah I wouldn't be riding back to the trailer with her on account of I was going with Lester to get something to eat.

"You got a date?" she said.

"No, we're just friends."

Soon enough, though, we were dating. We never called it that, but when we had nights off, we'd go to Ty's Buffet for supper or to a movie at the Arcadia Theater. Just hanging out, I guess. We never held hands. We never kissed. I told Delilah all that, but she still insisted that Lester was the man who came to me from Rose's spell.

"How about that, Rose?" she said one day. We were all sitting around the table.

Delilah told a joke about two bachelor farmers who were looking at the Sears catalog and noticing how pretty the women models were, and how inexpensive, too. "Think I'll order me one," the first farmer said. "Tell you what," said the farmer. "If the one you order is as pretty as her picture, I'll order me one, too." A few weeks went by and one day the second farmer said to the first, "Say, did that gal from Sears ever come?" "Shouldn't be long now," the first farmer said. "Yesterday, UPS dropped off her clothes!"

Delilah and I had a good laugh about that one, but Rose slapped her hands down on the breakfast table and stood up. "That's not funny, Dee. You told that just to rub it in, didn't you?"

"Honey," I said, "it's just a joke."

"That's right, Rose," said Delilah. "Just something Tweet told me."

"You're making fun of my spell," Rose said.

Delilah took her by the hand. "Now, Rosie, settle down. I didn't mean that at all. Looks to me like your spell's been working out just fine. Don't worry, honey. I'm sure your fella's coming." She should have left it at that, but then she couldn't stop herself from saying, "Or at least his clothes!"

Rose jerked her hand away and stomped out of the trailer, slamming the screen door shut so hard, the little clock on the wall fell off. It was one of those clocks that some folks around here make out of circular saw blades. They paint a background scene on the blade—this one was a beach scene with white sand and sea oats and driftwood, and then a sailboat on the horizon of the ocean and gulls in the sky above it—and then glue on numbers and rig up a motor and a set of hands on a spindle. Delilah's mother had done this one specially for her just before she parked her Impala on those railroad tracks, and it was one of the few things Delilah had to remember her by.

She picked it up from the floor. One of the hands had broken when the clock fell. She closed her fist around it and started toward the door.

"Delilah," I said, following her. "She didn't mean to break it. We can put on new hands."

Rose was on the deck, her back to us. She was playing with one of the wind chimes, pushing at the paddle with her finger to set things to jangling. Since she'd lost her job, she'd been at loose ends. Delilah and I would come home from work and see the messes she'd left in the kitchen (dirty dishes, cooked food sitting out on the counter, stains on the stove and table) and in the bathroom (hair in the sink, wet towels on the floor, hairs from her shaved legs sticking to the bathtub). She wore the same clothes, day after day—sweatpants and a T-shirt that said *I'm the Best You Never Had* in hot-pink letters. She was just scraping along, and it was starting to get on Delilah's nerves, not to mention causing a problem with our rent.

"You owe me," Delilah said when she stormed out onto the deck. "You're behind on your share of the rent, and I'm not going to let you float much longer. Are you even looking for work?"

"I'm looking," Rose said. She wouldn't turn around, and she said it in a quiet voice. It was a voice full of hurt. We knew she was lying—she was collecting her unemployment, but not chipping in much for our expenses. She was mooning around over her broken heart. I found a piece of notebook paper in the trash one day. She'd written Tweet's name over and over, had written it with hers inside a heart, like she was a schoolgirl. It was enough to make me feel embarrassed for her, and to make me swear never to be like that over a man. "Just give me a little time," she said. "Please."

It was the way she said that last word—like she was lost and needing someone to bring her back to a happy way of living—that must have grabbed Delilah's heart as much as it did mine. She didn't even mention that broken clock hand. She just turned around and went back inside the trailer.

I went to Rose and stood there beside her. It was one of those pretty days at the end of May, one of those days when the summer heat hadn't yet hit us full in the face, and it was nice there on the deck, shaded by those privacy screens, birds singing in the trees. Someone had a barbecue grill going, and the smell of the charcoal was enough to almost make me forget the stink of the poultry house. Kids were playing outside the trailer across the way, and their laughs and bright voices gave me a happy feeling.

"It's going to be all right, Rose." I slipped my arm around her waist. "You'll see."

She sort of leaned into me then, and something about her weight against my body let me feel, at least a little, what it was like to be her. I held her tight. I wished for something to do or say that would make a difference.

Finally, she broke the silence. "I'm happy for you, Laney. Really, I am."

But her voice was sad, and I felt my heart break. "I wouldn't blame you if you weren't."

"But I am," she said, and although I knew she was hurting, I could tell that she meant what she said. I'd never felt closer to her than I did at that moment, but still I couldn't find the words to say as much. All I could do was keep holding on, thinking about how Mother and I did the same in the days after my father died, and it was just the two of us, alone. Everything we carried with us got said with our bodies—a hug, a gentle touch on the back, a hand reaching out to find a hand. Until this moment with Rose, I hadn't realized how much I missed my mother, and I was sorry in a way I hadn't been before that I'd hurt her by dropping out of school and moving in with Delilah.

"I'm going to go for a walk," Rose said. "Want to keep me company?"

Delilah was slamming kitchen cabinet doors inside the trailer.

"I'm just going to sit out here a little while," I said.

Rose pulled away from me then. She glanced back at the trailer before looking me straight in the eyes. "You know she doesn't own you."

There was that part of Rose, too, the part that crowded its way into her heart from time to time, no matter how hard she tried to keep it out—the part that made her tell you exactly what she thought. It was always there alongside all that love she could feel, all that love that left her prone to disappointment and then anger.

"Go on," I told her. "It's a pretty day. I'll still be here when you get back."

I SAT OUT THERE on the deck thinking about Rose and how, out of the three of us, she was the one with the biggest heart, the one who wasn't just looking for what she could get from a man, but instead what she could give him. *I want to make a nice home for someone,* she'd told me more than once. She wanted to take care of a husband, wanted him to know every day what he meant to her, wanted to make his life easy. Do all the little things like ironing shirts and putting good meals on the table. Do all the big things like encouraging him if things got rocky, or standing up for him when he needed that. Partners. *If you love someone like that, Laney, they can't help but love you back.*

Such a different way of thinking than Delilah, who, the first time she saw Tweet, promised she was going to rattle his bones. Delilah, who wanted, wanted, wanted. And yet I loved her because I always knew the orphaned little girl she was deep down inside. A girl like me, who'd lost her father, who was on the outs with her mother. Laney and Delilah—two stray hearts looking for home.

Finally, she came out on the deck to sit with me, and at first we didn't say much at all. We sat on the steps and didn't even look at each other.

Then she said, "I didn't mean to get mad at her. She broke my clock."

"We'll fix it."

A breeze kicked up and set the wind chimes going. Somewhere across the trailer park, a car door slammed shut.

"Mama left me on a swing in the park." Delilah bent at the waist, her hands clasped between her knees. "Right before she went off and got herself killed. I ever tell you that? She had a note in my pocket that said, 'Please take care of my little girl.' "

For a few seconds, I couldn't find my voice, overcome with the thought of Delilah swinging in that park, wondering when her mother would be coming back to get her.

"I don't like that story," I finally said.

"It's not a story." She straightened and looked at me. "It's my life. It's everything about who I am."

A horn honked, and I looked up and saw the white Ford Econoline van that Tweet used to haul his band and their equipment from gig to gig turning into the trailer park.

"Didn't know he was running a taxi service," Delilah said.

I took a closer look, and I saw that Rose was riding in the van with him.

Delilah shoved up from the deck and went down the steps so she was standing on the patch of grass in front of the trailer, hands on her hips, when Tweet and Rose came out of the van.

Rose was laughing. "That is so true," she said.

Tweet clapped his hands together. "I told you, didn't I?"

"Told her what?" Delilah threw her arms around Tweet's waist. She had on a short denim skirt and an orange peasant blouse that dipped off one shoulder. When she hugged Tweet, she came up on her toes, and the muscles tightened in her calves and along the backs of her thighs. "Hey, good-lookin'," she said.

She pressed herself into him so hard, he stumbled back a step or two. "Whoa, lady," he said. "Easy there."

I felt a little embarrassed for her, the way she was hanging on to him. It was obvious how desperate she was to impress upon Rose that this was *her* fella.

"Tweet do you a favor?" she said to Rose, who was sort of hanging on to the van door like she didn't want to close it and come back to her regular life.

"I saw her walking," he said, "and I gave her a lift."

"That was sweet of you, baby." Delilah kissed him for a long time, so long that he finally pushed back from her.

"I was just coming by," he said. "You know, to say hey."

Delilah hadn't forgotten her original question. "So what were you two laughing about?"

Tweet and Rose glanced at each other and then looked away, and I knew that they were feeling guilty about something.

"A joke," Tweet said.

For the first time, Rose spoke. "That's right, Dee. Just a funny."

I could tell Delilah wasn't buying it. "You said you told her something," she said to Tweet.

"That's right," he said. "A joke."

"No, you didn't say it like that's what you were talking about. You said it like you'd been playing footsies. Getting chummy, are you? Sharing secrets?"

I could tell this was heading somewhere bad in a hurry. I came down from the deck and I said, "Hey, Rose. Hey, Tweet."

"Laney-Girl!" Tweet said. "Tell me something good."

"What can you tell me about Lester Stipp?"

Tweet glanced over at Delilah. "They're sweeties," she said.

"Now, Laney-Girl, you want to be careful with him. He's not to be trusted."

I shrugged my shoulders. "He seems all right to me."

"That dude." Tweet shook his head. "He's got bad juju following him. He was in the war, you know. Iraq." He said it "Eye-Rack."

"So?"

"He won't talk about it, but something bad went on. I felt sorry for him at first. Then he started to give me the willies. I told him to quit sniffing around the band."

"Was he really stealing?"

"Nah, that's just the reason I came up with."

"That was mean."

"Meaner than saying 'I don't want you around anymore'?"

Rose took her chance to slip inside the trailer, avoiding Delilah's questions. Delilah, though, hadn't forgotten them. "What did you tell Rose?" she asked Tweet when it was just the three of us standing there. "Was it something about me?"

"Jesus, Delilah." He slammed the door of the van. "Leave it alone, okay?"

"I most certainly will not leave it alone." She slapped him across the back. She tried to let on that she was playing, but I could tell she was serious. "You act like you're hiding something."

He spun around. "All right, you really want to know?" He gave her a chance to say no, and when she didn't, he went on. "Rose and I were talking about your wind chimes."

Delilah swiveled around to look at the wind chimes hanging from the latticework around the deck. "What's so funny about my chimes?"

"Look at them," Tweet said. "You must have a dozen of those things. I'm surprised the neighbors haven't complained." He gave a little laugh, trying to turn this into the joke he must have told Rose as they were pulling up in the van. "I told Rose we're going to have to start calling you Tinkle Bell. You know, like the fairy in Peter Pan, only instead of Tinker, we'd call you—"

Delilah stopped him. "You don't have to explain. I'm not stupid."

"I didn't say you were stupid. Who said anything about that? I was just having a little fun, that's all. No harm in a little fun, is there? I'm sorry if you took it wrong."

"Oh, I didn't take it wrong." She reached up and gave his cheek a little pat. "Like I said, I got it. Baby, I got it just the way you meant it."

She turned and walked back to the trailer, taking her time, putting more of a swish to her hips than normal. She climbed the steps, that short denim skirt inching a little higher as she went.

Tweet looked at me. He raised his eyebrows, curious about what had just gone on.

"Yes, she's mad," I told him, "and yes, you better make it up to her. She doesn't forget."

"It was just a joke," he said.

I owed him the truth. "You should have told it to her when she first asked you. That's when it was a joke. Now it's something else, something that hurts."

INSIDE THE TRAILER, he told Delilah he had to run a Mustang GT up to Terre Haute in the morning.

"You want to come along?" he asked. "I could take you to the mall, and then we could get lunch somewhere nice."

She was wiping the stove top with a dish rag. "You going early?"

"First thing."

"I work till seven."

"If you want to sleep..."

"I can sleep when I'm dead." She threw the rag in the sink and put her arms around him. "What kind of ride will we have coming back?"

"SUV."

"Oooh," Delilah said, with a flirty tone. "Sounds good. Roomy in the back? Seats fold down? Maybe we'll get lost somewhere and have a little you-know. Right, Tweet?"

He glanced at me, and this time I was the one who raised her eyebrows, telling him to say yes.

"Right, baby," he said, and that, for the time, was that.

So the next day, they went to Terre Haute and back, and then that night on our way to Walmart in the Malibu, she told me how wonderful the day had been. They hummed right along in that Mustang and had it swapped out all before noon. Their ride coming back was an Explorer. "Seats seven," she'd pointed out to Tweet. "Mom and Dad and five kids." She told him she wanted more kids than that. He didn't say anything, just reached over and took her hand. It was nice, she said, just riding along, imagining one day they'd be husband and wife with a fine ride like that, and a house somewhere nice.

"You don't even like kids," I said to her. We were driving past the city park, and through the dark I could see the gaslights along the walkways. "You've said as much a hundred times."

She gave a little wave of her hand like she was shooing off a fly. "I was just telling him what I thought he wanted to hear. Something wrong with that? We were just playing pretend, anyway."

"Don't you believe in telling the truth?"

"Only if I have to."

Much later, I'd remember this moment and I'd wonder whether she'd invented other things to tell me, lies to get what she wanted, but at the time it didn't matter to me. At least that's what I thought.

"Go on and play make-believe all you want," I told her. I couldn't get the picture out of my head of the little girl she was that day in the park when she swung back and forth and waited for her mother to come back for her. I guess she deserved a little make-believe now. "Go on," I said again. "Dream a little dream. Really, Delilah. What harm can it do?"

MISS BABY

September 2009

DENTON, TEXAS

This is the truth. Lordy Magordy. Listen. He was just there. He was standing on the corner of Fry and Oak, looking at the drum circle, a group of North Texas students who had gathered, as they usually did that time of evening, on the grass outside the Language Building across the street. It was mid-September, near dusk, and the grackles were flocking to the live oaks, screeching as they settled on the branches. Soon a campus maintenance crew would set up shop on the roof and put the propane cannons to work. Their blasts—a *boom boom boom* I always felt in my chest—was a humane way to disturb the grackles and send them off in search of somewhere else to roost.

But in the last moments before the noise came, it wasn't bad at all. It was all right. Dusk coming on, and the drum circle setting a rhythm that went through my legs. A breeze rattled the leaves on the live oaks, a little cool air at the end of the day, a blessing after that blazing North Texas sun. The sky was all different shades of purple-blue with a haze of orange down low on the horizon, and I was just a woman, almost forty, pretending I was in love with my life, pretending I didn't have a brother, Pablo Omar Maximillian Ruiz, who was in trouble and needed cash, who would eventually say to me at a time when I didn't want to think what it would cost me to help him—when I was so close to having the life I'd always wanted—"Betts, do me this favor. I'm a dead man if I don't get the money."

That's me, Betty Ruiz, but most folks know me as Miss Baby, owner of Babyheart's Tats, a parlor right here on Fry. You want barbed wire on your bicep? A rose on your ankle? A heart with an arrow through it on your forearm? I'm your gal. I'll even drill as much of the Lord's Prayer as you want across your back: *And lead us not into temptation*. But don't come asking for the nasty. No tats on your ta-tas. No rat-a-tat-tat anywhere near your bird or your back door. Go on down the street if that's your kick. Miss Baby runs a classy place.

"Betts," Pablo would finally say when he didn't know what else to do, "you know I need the cash."

Oh, but so much would happen before we got to that point. That night on the street, I had no idea what I was headed toward. I just knew it was an evening like all the other evenings ahead of me—time to pass on my own—and all of a sudden there he was, this man. Short, bowlegged man. He was wearing a derby hat, and that hat caught my eye. He took it off and fanned his face as he squinted into the last of the sun. He wasn't from here. Least, that was my guess. His skin was too fair, and he looked too fresh. He hadn't been here long enough to get beat down by the sun, to let it leather his face, dry out his lips. No, this man looked like he came from a land of water and lush green. A land of brooks and streams and shady woods. There was something about him that made me want to put my arms around him. Maybe it was the way he looked out of place, the way I'd felt nearly all my life, a Mexican girl who knew she wasn't pretty like the *gringas*.

I was short and thick-legged, and I kept my black hair cropped close to my head and spiked with gel so it wouldn't get in my way when I was drilling ink. I wasn't the girlie sort who could turn a man's head, but that never stopped me from trying. I imagined I could put my face up close to this man's, and he'd smell like pine trees, hyacinths, lilacs. Just listen to me go on.

Then he looked at me as if he'd sensed I was watching. He put his hat back on. He gave me a shy smile, took a step in my direction, and stopped. He had a little space between his front teeth, and something about the way that made him look—like a little boy, lost—caught me by the heartstrings.

Next thing I knew, I was there beside him, and I couldn't help myself. I said, "Hey, good-lookin'."

That's me. Too forward sometimes. But you have to know what happened to me just minutes before I closed my shop, stepped out onto Fry, and saw him on the corner. You have to know that the phone rang, and it was Pablo's ex, Carolyn, and she said to me, "You hootchie bitch." Said, "You cow." Said, "From the heart, Baby. From the heart."

What was her gripe? Only that she blamed me for the trouble Pablo was in. Back in the spring, I'd introduced him to Virgil Dent, a ranch hand who went by the nickname "Slam." He slammed shots of tequila, slammed his way through the world, slam-bammed-thanked-me-ma'am. From time to time, he came into the shop for some fresh ink. He favored eagles and wolves and cattle skulls, and whenever I drilled him, I could feel his eyes, deep-set and chestnut brown, taking me in. He wasn't a beautiful man—he needed more flesh, and his face was pitted with acne scars—but he was a man who knew what he wanted, a wiry man all muscle and bone, and for a while he wanted me.

Then he offered Pablo a cash-making proposition rustling cattle and selling them to auction barns in Kansas. No brand laws there, he pointed out. They'd be in and out like a fiddler's elbow. He winked at Pablo, and they both laughed. We were in Dallas one night late in April, sitting around a table at Club Dada in Deep Ellum, and under that table, Slam ran his hand up my leg and let the knuckle of his thumb press into the crotch of my jeans. He winked at me. "In and out," he said, looking right into my eyes. "Just like that."

Up to twelve hundred dollars a head for cows stolen from pastures and loaded into tractor trailers in the dead of the night. Easy money.

Then Pablo made the worst move of his life. It was sometime in the middle of June when he sold a load of cattle and instead of splitting the $36,000 with Slam, he skipped town with it, and now he was on the run. No one knew where he was—not me, who worried over him, not Slam, who was determined to find him and get his money, and not Carolyn, who was convinced that if it hadn't been for this trouble, she and Pablo would have worked things out, got married again, and lived happily ever after. "We were that close," she told me, holding up her thumb and forefinger. "Then you got him hooked up with your trashy boyfriend and look what happened."

He wasn't my boyfriend anymore, and hadn't been since well before Pablo cheated him. I was what Carolyn wasn't—a woman who could make it just fine without a man. At least that's what I told myself that night in September. Then I closed my shop early and stepped outside.

Like I said, there he was, this man, as if he'd been waiting all his life, hoping sooner or later I'd come along.

"Cutie." I tapped him on the chest with my finger. "You looking for someone?"

"I don't know." He whispered as if he thought someone else might hear, as if he wanted to tell me something he couldn't quite manage. "I'm not even sure who I am," he said, and his voice shook so badly, I was convinced he was telling me the truth. Wherever he'd come from, he was spooked by something. "Please," he said. "Can you help me?"

That's when the propane cannons started firing. Blast after blast. He covered his ears, closed his eyes, and shook his head. He clenched his teeth, and his face was a face of anguish. I put my hands on his arms. It was the thing I wanted to do, and I did it.

"Hush, sugar, it's all right," I said, and it came to me, this whole other life, as if a curtain parted—Lordy Magordy—and I could see through to the other side. For whatever reason, this man was so much in trouble, so much at loose ends, I knew I could claim him, and he'd let me.

From where I stand now, would I do it again, given the chance? Sometimes you don't have a choice. That's what I've learned. Sometimes things happen, and there you are.

"You've been waiting for me," I said, and he said yes. "You're Donnie," I told him. I grabbed the first name that came to me. "You're my sweet Donnie. Come on. Let's go home."

HE WENT WITH ME, this man I'd just named Donnie, and it suited him, that name, a name I grabbed out of the air because I thought I was doing magic—Houdini, Who-dun-it, my Donnie. Let's get this straight. He was a sweet-natured man. Granted, he was a little younger than most people would have thought appropriate for a woman my age, but I truly believe that had the circumstances been different—if we'd met each other and dated, courted and wooed and fell in love the way folks do—our life together, preceding the one we were just starting, would have been grand. It's just that now we were picking up in the middle of things. Very convenient, if you ask me. None of that awkwardness of the beginning, but with all the flash and thrill of first falling in love.

"Why don't I remember you?" he wanted to know.

"Honey, you remember me," I said. "I'm Betty."

I meant to stop it before it went too far. I want that on the record. I fully intended to stop, to take this man to the police, to get him the help he needed, but then he took my hand. A thing as simple as that. He took my hand and he said, "Betty." He said it like no man had ever said it to me. "Betty," he said, like I was an angel, and that was enough to make me crazy.

So we went on up the street. The UNT maintenance workers were still firing the propane cannons from the roof of the Language Building, and the grackles were lifting from the trees, dark clouds of them wheeling off and looking for some safer place to stay the night. Every time there was a concussion, Donnie squeezed my hand and I squeezed back, and after a while it was like our hearts were beating together, and we just kept walking down Oak where the street dipped and then, off in the distance, rose again, and at the top of the hill the neon sign outside the Civic

Theater glowed red and beyond that the dome of the courthouse sat just below the dusky sky.

I was doing it. I was taking him home the way I'd carried in stray cats when I was a kid and my *abuelita* said, "Bee-Bee, merciful God, what's to become of you and your tender heart?"

She told me I'd be a prize for any man smart enough to claim me. I'd be just fool enough to never say no to whatever he wanted. Like my *mami,* who had me and then Pablo before she was eighteen. And no man—this was her story when we grew old enough to wonder about our father—no *papi.* "As if," Mami said, "I was the Madonna." Blessed with babies and never the misery of a man. Now she'd been dead four years, her heart stopped by her own reckless living, and Pablo and I were left with no *mami* to tell us anything. We were on our own, *mami* and *papi* to each other, the way it had been, really, most of our lives.

Sometimes I thought if we'd had a *papi,* Pablo wouldn't have fallen into the trouble that he did. If there'd been a *papi* to teach him the right way to be a man in this world, maybe then he wouldn't have been where he was that evening I walked down Oak with this Donnie—*mi hermano,* Pablo, hiding on the other side of trouble so big even I couldn't see a way out for him. He had the cash from those bulls and bred heifers he'd sold in Kansas, but it was cash got with a big price attached. Not only had a Special Ranger from the Texas and Southwestern Cattle Raisers Association started sniffing around, Slam Dent was also on Pablo's trail.

I put it all out of my mind the best I could and concentrated on my own story. I was trying to convince this Donnie that we were husband and wife. Yes, it was crazy, but I didn't care. I'd stopped thinking right. Was I ever scared of him? No. Like I said, he was a gentle man, and from the start, it was like I'd known him a long, long time.

"We're going home," he said, like he was trying hard to accept that this was his life that he had stepped into, the life that had always been going on even when he didn't know it. I told him, "Yes." I reached out and touched his wrist. I stroked it the way I'd pet a stray cat, easing my way into its trust. "We're going home."

"Home," he said. He had it now. He'd given into it, the fact that he had a home and that's where we were going, and for just a moment I had a twinge of guilt because I wondered where his real home was and who was waiting for him there.

It was only three blocks up Oak, a block west on Scripture, and then we were at my little bungalow, the one with the sapphire blue gazing ball on its pedestal by the front steps, the clear glass bottles hanging from the branches of the mimosa tree, bottles meant to catch the evil spirits before they had a chance to enter my house, and for good measure a string of green chili peppers around my door frame.

Donnie touched one of the bottles on the mimosa as we came up the walk, gave it a little nudge and sent it to swaying.

"They're pretty," he said. "Those bottles. They catch the light."

It was true. The gaslight along the walk was on in the dusk, and the bottles held its glow as if a low, warm fire burned inside them.

"They keep the devil away," I told him. "Remember?"

He stood there awhile, tapping his finger against the bottle, and a pained look came onto his face as if he were close to recalling something important and if he just concentrated he could find it, something that meant the world to him.

"No," he finally said. "I don't remember, but it sounds like a good idea. Did you think of that? Did you..." His voice trailed off, and I realized then he was trying to recall my name. "Did you, Betty?" he said.

"You did," I told him, hoping that little lie would make him feel better about where he was, would give him a sense of owning the ground he walked on, the house he was about to walk into. "You hung them there to keep us safe."

My throat filled up on that last part, feeling, as I did, how desperate I'd always been for a good man to watch over me.

Just then, my neighbor, Emma Hart, came out onto her front porch and called to me. "Miss Baby, I'm home."

She'd been gone since the Fourth of July, visiting her daughter in Mississippi, and I'd looked after her house and yard.

"Did you have a good visit?" I asked.

"Humidity near melted me. I felt like I was nothing but water."

I didn't want to be rude, but I needed to get Donnie inside and out of sight. "It's been dry here." I pulled him gently up the walk toward my front door, but he paused to take a look over at Emma. "Hot and dry," I called to her.

She was an itty bit of a thing, her back all humped up from years of leaning forward as she walked through the world, and though I couldn't see her plain as she gripped the porch railing with her bony hands, I knew she'd have her face made up, the way she did every day and night until she cleaned it off and made ready for bed. She'd have those thin, arched eyebrows painted on, and those two little spots of rouge on her cheeks, and cherry-red lipstick on her mouth.

"Miss Baby, she was here looking for you tonight." Emma was trying to keep her voice low now. "That Carolyn. I told her, 'Scat. Go on now. Miss Baby don't suffer your kind.' "

"You hadn't ought to take a chance on making trouble for yourself, Emma." I took Donnie's hand and kept leading him up the walk, eager to get inside before she took a notion to ask who it was I had with me. I was standing between her and him, and I was hoping in the gathering dark, given her old eyes, she might not even spot him. "Carolyn's mad as can be. There's no telling what she might do."

Just then, a flock of grackles came swooping down to settle in the trees. The glass bottles in the mimosa clinked together, and the birds screeched.

"She's trash," Emma said. "Don't worry about me. I know her kind."

"You can stand up for yourself. I know that for sure." Donnie and I were at the front door now, and I had the key in the lock. "Good night, Emma."

I unlocked the door and swung it open. A few ticks more and we'd be inside.

Then Emma said, "Who's that with you, Miss Baby? Is that Pablo? Has he come back?"

I gave Donnie a nudge, and he stepped into my house, out of sight. I felt the burden of having to decide what to do next—to call the police and say, *I found this man;* or to say to Donnie, *Cutie, let's have some supper;* to lie down beside him in the dark and put my lips to his, to his neck, his chest, and say, *Remember this... and this... and this.*

"No, it's Donnie." What else could I do but say the story I was inventing? "I don't know where Pablo is. He's still in trouble."

"Those cows. Him and that old boyfriend of yours."

"It's late, Emma. We'll talk tomorrow."

"Donnie," she said. She was used to people coming to my house, looking for Pablo or else, drunk, wanting me to open up my shop, fire up my iron, and pound some skin because, *Miss Baby, there's this tat I just got to have tonight.* I could tell Emma was searching her memory to see whether she could recall someone named Donnie. "Little fella?" she said, and I felt it was a sign, the fact that she'd gotten this right. "Fair-skinned?"

"That's right," I said. "Donnie True."

Just like that I gave him a last name, said it before I even knew it was on my tongue, spoke that wish for how I wanted everything to turn out.

WHEN THE TROUBLE first started for Pablo and Carolyn and they filed for a no-fault divorce, I told him he could stay with me. This was just after the New Year—Happy 2009!—and on April 1, the divorce was final. "April Fools' Day," Pablo said. "Baby, I hope I haven't made a mistake."

The story was simple, as old as Moses—a man with a woman no amount of money or love could ever satisfy. A *gringa* to boot. Little, blond priss of a thing who thought a Mexican boy would be to her taste. Carolyn. A name as white as that.

She wanted too much. I can't say she's any different than the rest of us in this regard, just more insistent, more apt to pitch a fit when Pablo didn't come across with the goods. He was working an honest job then, hauling freight for Air-Ride Transport, and for a while he was flush with cash. Carolyn spent it as fast as he could bring it home, and before long he'd had enough of that.

Still, after the divorce became final, he couldn't get her out of his head. He even called her up sometimes and took her out to dinner. If he only had a way of making more money, he thought he could satisfy her and everything would be the way it was when they first fell in love.

He saw his chance when I introduced him to Slam Dent. All he had to do was haul those stolen cows to Kansas. Slam had the tractor trailer, and Pablo knew how to drive it. He'd make enough extra cash to win back Carolyn's heart.

From time to time, he sent her flowers, bought her jewelry. They swore the divorce had been a mistake. They started talking about getting back together. She said that if they did, she wanted a new ring. A Hearts on Fire diamond ring—a Seduction Solitaire. To mark her sweet surrender, she said. New day, new luck, new bride, new love.

I suppose that's why Pablo decided to cross Slam Dent around the middle of June. Maybe he was thinking about new beginnings, and he saw a chance for a bigger payday. Maybe he wanted that extra share of the profits to help buy that ring, so he took the bank draft made out to him from the auction barn in Kansas, cashed it, and instead of giving half to Slam like he was supposed to, he pocketed the whole thing. He didn't know that the Rangers would soon be on his tail, and he didn't know that Slam would be ready to get his money back by force if need be.

Now Pablo was a fugitive from the law and a target for one

pissed-off Mr. Virgil Dent. Pablo would call me once in a while, but he wouldn't tell me where he was. "Just checking in," he'd say, and I'd tell him Carolyn was still pounding on my door trying to find him. "He's my one true love," she'd say, "and now he's going to end up in jail or dead."

Pablo couldn't help it. He'd made a choice and crossed over into a world full of danger. He'd stolen for Carolyn's sake, but now he was reluctant to talk to her except through me. "Tell her I'm sorry," he said during one of his quick calls, and I could hear in his voice that he meant it. He couldn't give her much thought because she was the least of his worries. She wouldn't kill him, but Slam Dent just might.

One day in September, maybe a week before I found this man I named Donnie, Slam came into my shop. He had on his snakeskin cowboy boots, tight Wrangler jeans, and a freshly ironed white shirt with a bolo tie. He'd folded the shirt cuffs back, and I could see the last tat I'd drilled into his right forearm—the head of a longhorn bull, one eye closed in a wink. *Slam,* said one horn. The other one said, *Bam!*

"Baby, you been missing me?" he said.

"Not for a second."

He leaned over and whispered in my ear, "You can't lie to me. I remember how much you liked the old Slam-Bam. Ain't that right, Baby? You know you were crazy for it. Still are, I expect."

"In your dreams." The sex with Slam had always been rough and selfish, and nothing I ever wanted again. "You think you're a big man, but you're just dirt. That's all you'll ever be."

He closed his hand around my arm, and his nails, untrimmed and sharp, dug into my skin. "You tell your brother," he said, "we got business to finish." Then he bent down and kissed me on my earlobe, let his lips linger there, just the lightest kiss, before he took the lobe in his mouth and bit down. "I mean it, Baby," he mumbled with my earlobe clamped tight between his teeth. "You tell him I'm not to be fucked with. You tell him I got six ways to Sunday to hurt him, and, Baby, one of those ways is you." He pulled away from me then, and he used his finger to wipe a little dab of blood from my ear. He poked that finger to my lips, pressed hard until I had no choice but to open them. "Love you, Baby," he said with a laugh.

Then he left my shop and I spit the taste from my mouth.

Pablo was lucky that he was one step ahead of Slam, and I was lucky that it was a house with Pablo's things in it, but no Pablo, that Donnie and I walked into the evening I brought him to live with me.

I switched on a tea lamp just inside the door, and Donnie stood in the middle of my living room blinking his eyes. I tried to imagine what it would be like to see everything in my house for the first time and what someone would think of a woman who collected what I did: fairy figurines, some of them made from crystal, others from porcelain or ceramic, all of them as dear as the day they gave babies away with a half a pound of tea, which was something Mami used to say when Pablo and I asked who our father was. "I went down to the baby patch," she said. "Oh, that was the best day—the day they gave babies away—and that's how I got you both, and tea to boot, what a steal."

That's the way we came to think of any day, long coming, that finally arrived—the day they gave babies away—and here I was on one of those days, a man in my house, a man I'd latched on to and named.

I was glad I'd put on just a touch of lavender eye shadow that morning, that I'd had some auburn highlights added to my hair a few days before, that I was wearing the new purple Tommy Bahama halter top that made me feel sexy.

"This is something." Donnie looked all around him, and his voice was hushed. "It's like the Otherworld."

It touched me, the fact that he knew the name for the land of the fairies, and I took it as a sign that he and I were meant to find each other. I slipped my arm around his and let my hand come to rest on his so we were touching, palm to palm. For a good while, neither of us spoke. We just stood there, and I laid my head on his shoulder. The fairies were all around us in the dim, soft light: fairies on toadstools, on tree limbs, with unicorns, in snow globes; winged fairies with flowers wreathing their heads, sprites who could shake the human world in the most magical and mischievous ways. In the old stories, they could cast love spells or turn people into donkeys. Sometimes, like now, I could look around at all the figurines on my bookshelves, my television, my tables, and I could believe that nearly anything was possible.

"We've always loved them," I finally said.

Donnie laced his fingers through mine and squeezed my hand. "Yes," he said, and I knew then that he was buying what I was selling. Don't think it's so far-fetched, the fact that he could believe that he was in the right place. Maybe it's as simple as this: Maybe, no matter what had happened to throw him off his pins, to leave him mixed up and searching for someone who knew his name, he wanted, like we all do, to be home. "Yes, Betty. We have."

He believed—I wasn't about to question why or how because I wanted to believe, too. If I've done anything wrong, it was only that. I wanted him to believe in the two of us and the life we were going to have.

Oh, I know it was crazy, but I suppose I was like my *mami,* looking for the next good thing, ready to seize the day my life turned around and I stepped into a world where my brother wasn't on the run, and his ex-wife wasn't phoning to call me a hootchie bitch, where I could be who I knew I was: Betty Ruiz, Miss Baby, tender in the heart and eager for love.

I could have stopped it then and there. I know that now. All right, I suppose I knew it even then. But he kissed me. He took his time. A sweet, soft kiss, his hand a light touch against my cheek, and I let him. I kissed him back, and when we were done we held on to each other. I heard his heart beating, and I'm not ashamed now, no matter all that's gone on, to say I couldn't have let him go to save my life.

"Betty?" He kissed the top of my head. He rocked me in his arms. "Betty, I'm so sleepy."

I led him into the bedroom. "It's been a day." I unbuttoned his shirt and laid my hand against his bare chest. "It's been quite a day," I told him.

"Baby, you've got that right," he said, like we'd been together for years.

He slipped out of his shirt and jeans. Then he lay back on the bed. He closed his eyes, and just like that, he was asleep.

I picked up his clothes from the floor where he'd left them, and I felt the weight of his wallet in his jeans pocket. I sat on the window seat, where the full moon was letting in light, and I opened the wallet and took a look at what I could find. It didn't add up to much: a few bills, fifty-five dollars in all; a Greyhound ticket stub (one-way) to show he'd come from Mt. Gilead, Illinois, on September 14; a four-leaf clover, laminated in plastic; an Illinois driver's license. When he couldn't remember who he was, why hadn't he taken out that license, or even that Greyhound ticket stub, and read his own name? He just hadn't thought to do that—at least that's what I told myself at the time; I hadn't yet reached the point where I'd wonder whether he was only pretending to not know who he was.

I held the license up to my face so I could read his name—his real name and not the one I'd given him. Lester Stipp. I let it go. I didn't want it in my head, because he was my Donnie, and I didn't want any reminder otherwise. I didn't want him to have one, either. I got a pair of nail scissors from my vanity, and with great care I clipped out his name and that address, just took them away. I would have cut up the whole thing, but I couldn't bring myself to give up that photo of him looking so shy and sweet, the gap between his front teeth enough to charm me stupid. He looked a little scared and that only made him more precious to me. *Donnie,* I kept saying to myself. *He's my Donnie.* Five feet six inches tall, so the license said, 130 pounds. Hair, brown. Eyes, blue. He'd come from Mt. Gilead. He'd come down from the mountain to rescue me. That's the way I preferred to think of his appearance in my life and the fact that he was sleeping now in my bed—*our* bed—the moonlight on his face. He'd come down from Mt. Gilead to the hot, dry plains of North Texas because in the Otherworld, the world somewhere we weren't allowed to see, fairies cast their spells and he appeared, this man I needed.

Laugh if you want, but that's what I wanted to believe that night, so I got my purse, and I slipped that driver's license into my wallet so he couldn't find it and maybe start to remember. I tore the Greyhound stub into pieces and dropped them into the trash. I know now I was buying time, as much as I could, all for the sake of how wonderful it felt to have a man in my bed. I understood what had sent my *mami* out night after night looking for someone to make her feel less alone. I wanted more than she ever had. I wanted a man to stay with me forever.

Then the phone rang, and, of course, it was her, Carolyn, and she said, "Who loves you, Baby? Huh? C'mon. Tell me. Who?"

This was what she did from time to time, called me up just to stick in the knife. If she couldn't find Pablo, she'd turn her temper on me. Who was I, anyway? That's what she was really saying whenever she called. *Who are you, Betty Ruiz?*

I wasn't anything that amounted to shit to hear her tell it. If I stayed on the phone, she'd list every reason in the world no man would ever have me: too nutty—what was the deal with all that fairy crap, anyway?; too bossy—look what I'd pushed Pablo into with Slam Dent; too this; too that. My butt was too big, my arms too hairy, my hands always stained with ink. What kind of man would want a woman with tattoos, and in places best left private. "That's skanky," she said. "And you're old, Baby. You're just too damned old."

The truth was, despite what people like Carolyn believed, I had no tats. Lordy Magordy. I'd be afraid to let someone punch me with an iron. I got started in the tattoo business because I could draw, and Mami, who'd owned the shop before me, taught me how to drill the ink. She always wanted me to let her give me a tat, but I wouldn't go for it. No sir. No one, not even her, was ever going to brand me. I see these kids come into the shop, some of them on a dare, and if they're underage, I turn them away. "Come back when you're eighteen," I tell them. If someone of age wants a tat, it's just commerce as far as I'm concerned. But if you're too young, or too drunk, or not in your right mind for whatever reason, then it's on my head, and I'm not going to have that.

And sure, there's the rub. I know it. I'm not stupid. There I was, all holier than thou about not taking money from someone who didn't have sense when it came to getting a tat, but I was more than willing to take advantage of this man in my bed, this Lester Stipp, to invent a life for him, all for what I could get from the deal. It goes to show you, doesn't it—who we are under our skin? Ask any tat artist and they'll tell you about the people who come in and have to talk themselves into going through with the deal. Sometimes we tell them what we know they want to hear: *Yes, I've done it myself. It won't hurt*... not much. *You'll love it*... once it's done. *It won't get infected*... if you care for it right. And finally they say yes. They give themselves over. Who knows, I told myself that night as I watched Donnie, awakened for the briefest moment by the ringing phone, roll over and go back to sleep, maybe it was me who was saving him.

"I'm not going to listen to you," I interrupted Carolyn. "No more."

"You have to listen to me, Baby, because you know it's true."

"No," I told her. "You listen to me." I told her what it was like to be me in a world of pretty people like her. Pretty blond girl with the creamy skin. Skinny little girl with all the curves in the right places. "You're like a Barbie doll," I told her. "You're blond and white and slim and pretty, and we all want to be you. Even I want to be you, and if you want the whole truth, I can barely stand to look at you because you've got everything a woman could want."

For a good while, she didn't say anything, and I thought maybe she'd hung up. I was about to say her name, when I heard her take a long breath. Then she said, "I don't have Pablo," and her voice was all washed out. I understood then that she was more sad than anything and she'd trade all the Hearts on Fire diamonds in the world if she and Pablo could go back to where they started and stay that way the rest of their lives.

I wanted to tell her he wasn't worth it, but I could see she thought he was, and who was I to argue with the private yearning of her heart?

"Baby?" She wasn't angry now or upset. She was calm the way folks can be when they run out of ways to bend the world to fit their needs and just give in to the facts of the matter. "That man, that Slam Dent, he came to see me tonight."

The way she said it, I knew she was scared of him. By all rights, I should have been, too, but there's this thing about me—some folks call it spunk, others call it stupid—that won't let the scared show through. I just knuckle down and bare my teeth. If I could have gotten away with it that day in my shop when he said those ugly things to me and then forced his finger into my mouth, I would've scratched Slam Dent's eyes out.

Carolyn could put on the spit and sand for a little while. She got her back up with people she thought of as family—the ones who had to take it—and, for better or worse, that's what we were, former sisters-in-law. I didn't have to take it, though, and I was just about to tell her that when she began to cry. I could hear her sniffling and boo-hooing, and it should have made me laugh or else given me a high horse I could use to ride roughshod over her sniveling little candy-ass ways, but what it really did, to my surprise and dismay, was make my heart go out to her. I understood that now the tables had turned and I was the one with a man and she was all alone. What's more, I felt certain that Slam Dent had been more than just inquiring when he paid her his call.

"Carolyn, did he hurt you?"

"He made me take off my clothes. He had a gun. He made me stand there while he looked at me. Said he wanted to see what Pablo had walked away from. That's all he did. He just looked. I was naked, and he looked at me. I never felt so ugly."

She was crying hard now, not those little sniffles and boo-hoos, but throat-scraping, shoulder-shaking sobs. I let her go on awhile. Then I said, "He had no right to do that. You should call the police."

"Baby, I can't bring myself to do it. I can't tell them what he did."

I knew then she was leaving space for me to say that I'd make the call and take care of everything. But I was scared. If the police started poking around, what would they find out about this man in my bed?

"Maybe he won't come back," I said.

"He doesn't have to," said Carolyn. "He's already done me in. Shame, Baby. That's what he left behind. I can't even look at myself in the mirror."

So there it was, the way one look could make us feel ugly the rest of our lives.

"Do you want..." I meant to change my mind and ask whether she wanted me to call the police for her, but before I could finish, she took my first words as an invitation.

"Oh, yes, Baby. Thank you. I can't bear to be alone tonight. I'll be right there."

MY *MAMI* USED TO SAY, *Cada corazón tiene un hogar.* Each heart has a home. That's what I thought about as I waited for Carolyn—how there were places in the world we were meant to walk, and if we were lucky, we found them. We had people we were meant to be with, and again, if the stars lined up just right, we put on the lives we were intended to have.

I left Donnie sleeping in the bedroom, and I eased the door closed behind me, not wanting to wake him. How would I explain him to Carolyn? I sat down in the living room, in the soft glow of a fairy night-light, and I waited for her, remembering the night Pablo came to live with me. She stood on my porch that night and pounded on the door. She called his name over and over, and the name got all mixed up with her crying, and before long she was hoarse with the effort, and, finally, she did the only thing she could. She went away.

With Pablo gone, her rage built, and more often than not, I was the easy target for it. Then Slam Dent came along and showed her no one was safe. No matter how pretty you were. No matter how blessed, you were the same as the next person, even someone like me, the one Carolyn blamed for the trouble Pablo was in. Under our skins, in the echoes of our heartbeats, we were both afraid of being alone.

So she came to me. I let her into my house, and for a moment, neither of us said a word. She was at the end of things. I could see that right away. Her face was the one God had given her—the first time I'd seen her without makeup—and she'd drawn her hair back into a bun, as if she'd done everything she could to make herself plain. It was odd seeing her without lipstick and rouge and eyeliner and those false eyelashes she always wore. If I'd seen her on the street, I'm not sure I would have known her. For just a moment, I might have wondered who that Plain Jane white girl was and why she looked so washed out and down in the mouth.

"Baby," she said, in such a wretched voice, "oh, Baby," and then she told me the story again of how Slam Dent had held a gun on her, had made her strip down, had told her to turn this way and that, had watched her as cool as could be. Then, when he'd seen enough, he said to her, "I can do this to you." He used the barrel of his revolver to brush her hair back from her face. "Look at me," he said. "I can find you, and I can do this to you anytime I want."

That's what sent her to me, scared to death.

"If we call the police," she said, "I'll have to tell them all of that."

So it was "we." *We* were in this together, and yet she was giving me the chance to let it go, to not say a word on her behalf, to tell her Slam was all blow, and odds were he wouldn't bother her again. But I knew better. I knew he wasn't going to stop until he had what he wanted, and that was Pablo. He'd do whatever he had to in order to find him and get his money.

"Do you want me to call?" I asked Carolyn.

"Baby," she said, her hands trembling. "I expect you should."

* * *

A POLICE OFFICER CAME, and keep in mind, when he stepped into my house, Donnie was still sleeping in my bed.

Carolyn told her story. She told what Slam had made her do. It was a hard thing to say, but she did it. She kept her voice as steady as she could. She sat on the edge of my couch, hands clasped between her knees, her torso rocking back and forth ever so slightly, and she said it all. When she was done, she kept looking at the floor, unable to lift her head and face the police officer, a bug-eyed man with a red mustache. Although it was hidden beneath his blue uniform shirt, I knew his chest was hairless and that he had a tat in the middle of it: a big Valentine's heart, the kind that comes up on the screen at the end of that old TV show *I Love Lucy*. Inside the heart was the outline of the state of Texas, and the words, in a flowing script, *Deep in the Heart*. I knew it to be so because I was the one who'd put it there one night in my shop.

He took notes while Carolyn told her story, and when she was done, he slapped his little steno notebook closed and he said to me, "Miss Baby, I suppose this is about Pablo." I told him it was, and he nodded. "I don't suppose you're ready to tell us where he is. You know the Rangers are on this rustling case. We're all looking for Pablo and this..." He flipped his notebook open again and found the page he was looking for. "This Virgil Dent."

"He calls sometimes," I told the police officer. "Pablo, I mean." I'd never known the officer's name. I'd spent all that time staring at his chest, listening to the little whistle of breath through his nose, smelling the sweet mint of his chewing gum, but I'd never had reason to ask who he was. He paid me with cash, and then he was gone. "He doesn't tell me where he is," I said. "That's all I know. But Slam Dent—that's his ridiculous nickname. Virgil Dent, as you've just heard, is still in the area. Maybe you'd have a good chance of finding him."

Just then the bedroom door opened, and Donnie took a few shuffling steps into the living room. He was bare-chested, wearing only his boxers. His hair was mussed from sleep, and he had this dazed look on his face, like he'd just woke up in the Otherworld and was trying to get his bearings.

Carolyn said, "Oh," with a gasp, and then covered her face with her hands.

"Hold it." The police officer drew his service revolver and pointed it at Donnie. "Stay where you are."

I was already moving, not even thinking whether it was a stupid thing to do, only knowing I didn't want that gun aimed at Donnie. I stepped between him and the police officer. I said that silly thing I always say when I don't have words. "Lordy Magordy."

It worked like some sort of incantation, a little hocus-pocus. "Lordy Magordy," I said, and the police officer lowered his revolver.

He gave me a sheepish grin. "I thought at first it was Pablo."

I couldn't help but tease him. "You had your eyes checked recently?" I stepped aside so he could get a good look at Donnie. "Does that look like a Mexican man to you?"

The officer jammed the revolver back into its holster. He leaned into the dim light to study Donnie. "Who are you, mister?" he asked.

Carolyn uncovered her eyes and took a look herself. She glanced at me, her eyebrows raised as if to say, *What in the world?*

I cleared my throat. Then Donnie, bless him, said, "I'm Donnie. Donnie True. What's the trouble?"

"Do you live here?" the officer said.

Donnie chuckled. "You think I'd traipse around like this in a stranger's house? Of course I live here." He put his arm around my shoulder. "This is my wife."

I didn't think anything at the time about how easy it was for him to say this and everything that followed. I just fell into the gentle tone of his voice, gave thanks for his story. Somehow in his sleep he'd dreamed it all, or else he'd carried the truth of his real life into the one he was now making with me. I didn't care which it was. It all sounded fine, even the things I couldn't have imagined—the part about how we liked to watch old Marx Brothers movies and eat Greek food. He just yakked on and on, until the police officer held up his hand to stop him. "All right, cowboy," he said. "You're not Pablo. I got that much."

The officer left, and Carolyn said to me, "Married? My, my, when did this happen?"

I grabbed a date, my *mami*'s birthday. "We'd been seeing each other ever since June, just after Pablo left town. Then, August seventh, we decided to take the jump."

Donnie still had his arm around my shoulders. "Lucky number seven." He gave me a squeeze. "Right, Baby?"

"Count my lucky stars," I said.

He winked at me, and I got the feeling, not totally unwelcome, that he and I were weaving this story, this lie, together.

OF COURSE, CAROLYN was doubtful. I knew that right away. I let her sleep in my spare bedroom—Pablo's old room—and the next morning, when Donnie and I came out of our room, she was in the kitchen, drinking a cup of instant coffee.

"Donnie?" she said. "You think you could be a hon and fetch me a little sugar for this coffee?"

I understood it was a test. She was suspicious that we weren't really married. My husband would surely know where I kept the sugar, right? Otherwise, what would Carolyn think? That I'd brought a man home for a one-night stand. Surely not the truth: that I'd stolen him away from wherever he was headed, that I was trying to make him into someone who would believe we were in love.

"Sugar?" Donnie said, glancing at me.

"Yes, dear," I said, trying to make a joke.

Carolyn put her hands on her hips and studied Donnie. "You know where the sugar is, don't you?"

He reached into the pocket of his jeans and pulled out a pink paper packet. He held it up and looked at me with a big smile on his face as if he couldn't believe his luck. "We don't have sugar," he said, handing the packet to Carolyn. "We've got Sweet'N Low instead."

She studied that Sweet'N Low packet a good long while, and I held my breath. "It'll do," she finally said, "but, Baby, I seem to remember you always take sugar in your coffee."

"I gave it up," I told her. "I'm slimming down."

We didn't have much to say after that, or else we had the world to say, but we didn't know how to say it. Carolyn drank her coffee, and she kept her eyes on Donnie and me, looking for a sign, I'm sure, that we weren't married at all.

"Baby," she finally said, "where's y'all's wedding rings?"

She had me there. Our fingers were bare, and I didn't expect that Donnie would pull any rings out of his pockets. "We're going to pick them out real soon," I said. "We have to put some money aside first. You know how love can be." I snapped my fingers. "When it happens, it happens fast. We couldn't wait to get married."

"Oh, I'm sure." She set her coffee cup down on the counter. "Mercy, yes. Fast. I imagine your head is still spinning." She clicked the point of her fingernail against her front teeth. Then she said, "I hope you get those rings real soon 'cause I'd sure like to see them. Yessiree, Baby, I surely would."

"NOW, WHO WAS THAT?" Donnie asked me after Carolyn had gone, and I told him about Pablo and how Carolyn was his ex. I even told him about the cattle-rustling scheme and how in the middle of the summer it all came apart and left Slam Dent pissed off and on the hunt. That's all I told him about Slam. I didn't say that he'd been the last man in my bed. I didn't tell Donnie how he'd treated me like I was nothing but his whore. I wanted to get as far away from those days as I could, and Donnie, though he didn't know it, was helping me do that.

"He's trying to get to Pablo by putting the fear into Carolyn," I said, and then I told Donnie why she'd come to the house, afraid, and why I'd called the police. "There, that should just about have you up to date."

It was going to be another scorcher. I could tell that. The sun was bright through the kitchen window, spreading across the linoleum floor, falling on our legs where we sat at the table, Donnie across from me. I could hear a yard sprinkler buzzing next door at Emma's, jetting water onto her St. Augustine grass, and I imagined she'd be over soon to drink coffee and shoot the breeze with me until I had to get to work, the way she usually did when she wasn't off on a trip somewhere to visit family. She had kids and grandkids all over the South.

Babyheart's Tats opened at noon, so the mornings were always leisurely, plenty of time for Emma. I told Donnie about her. "Our neighbor," I said. "Miss Emma Hart."

He got up and went to the window and stood there, looking over the top of the privacy fence that separated my backyard from Emma's. A mockingbird was perched on the fence, singing away. "How come it is I don't know any of this?" His voice was halting, slow with the hard work of trying to understand, tinged with just enough misery to break my heart.

So I told him the first thing I could think of that might explain his predicament.

"Amnesia," I told him. "You got hit on the head just a few days after we got married. You were in a coma up until a few days ago, and since you've been home from the hospital, you've had some trouble remembering things."

"Who hit me?"

"A man." I was flying by the seat of my pants now, saying whatever came to me. "We were in Deep Ellum—we'd just left The Bone—and there was this man in an alley, and he asked you for money. You told him no, and that's when he hit you with his fist. You went down and hit your head hard on the pavement. He went through your wallet. Took your cash, your credit cards, your driver's license. Then he threw the wallet on the ground and he ran."

Donnie touched his fingers to the top of his head, feeling for any sign—a knot, or a scabbed-over gash—that what I was telling him was true.

Emma's knock on my front door was a loud *rap rap rap.* She called out, "Yoo-hoo. Miss Baby? It's Emma."

Donnie took his hand down from his head. "Emma Hart," he said, recalling what I'd told him. I'd never seen a smile like the one he gave me, such a grin of pure bliss. "I remembered, didn't I?"

"That's right, cutie." I laid my hand on his cheek. "You called it up just fine."

I would have stood there forever like that if I could have, but Emma was knocking and yoo-hooing again, and so I left him in the kitchen and went into the living room to let her in.

"Did I see the police over here last night?" She brushed past me, her head swiveling around, looking for any sign of what might have transpired when the police came to my house. She was good-hearted and nosy. Lord love her. "Miss Baby, are you in trouble?"

She swung back to look at me, and it was all I could do, I swear, to keep from laughing. It was clear she'd put on her face in a hurry, eager to get over to my place to see what was going on. She'd drawn on her eyebrows with a sharp peak in each center rather than the half-moon arc she usually used. Her lipstick strayed at the corners, as if someone had jostled her arm, and she hadn't got her hair all the way brushed out after taking it out of the curlers. She was a woman who looked startled.

"No," I told her. "No trouble." I didn't see a need to go into the story of Carolyn and Slam Dent and ruin the pleasure Emma took from hating Carolyn. "They just had more questions about Pablo and that cattle rustling."

"Did you tell them what they wanted to know?"

"I don't know anything, Emma."

"Does Carolyn? Is that why she was here last night?"

I pretended to be peeved at her. "Emma, were you snooping out your windows?"

She twisted up her mouth in disgust. "I was *not*. I saw that woman leave this morning when I was setting up my sprinklers." Emma crossed her arms over her chest and gave me a haughty look. "A body has a right to take note of a few things, doesn't she, Miss Baby Ruiz?"

"She needed a place to stay."

"And you let her?"

I tapped my chest with my fist. "What can I say? Soft heart."

"Soft head is more like it. Oh, Miss Baby. What on earth were you thinking? Lord-a-mighty. After the way that woman's treated you?"

"Things are looking up, Emma. That's all I'll say." I took her by her scrawny arm, pulled her close, and whispered in her ear, "I got married."

She tipped her head back and squinted at me. "While I was in Mississippi?"

"Justice of the peace," I said. "A courthouse wedding."

"That Donnie fella? I didn't even know you were keeping time with him."

"Well, Emma, you just don't know everything." I winked at her. "Even though you want to."

"Are you saying I'm nosy?"

"Come on in here." I took her hand and led her toward the kitchen. "I want you to meet my sweetie."

Donnie was standing just where I'd left him, as if he couldn't unstick himself from that spot.

Emma walked right up to him. "You're Donnie," she said. "Donnie True."

"True enough," he said.

She got tickled. "True enough." She cackled and swatted my arm. "Did you hear that?" she asked me. "Donnie True is true enough."

He took her hand and raised it to his lips, and that was enough to stop her from having the hysterics. She put her other hand to her mouth, amazed. I saw a little blush creep into her cheeks the way it must have when she was a girl and a boy paid attention to her. Donnie kissed the back of her hand where the veins were roped up and the knuckles were all knobby. He kissed her hand like an old-time Southern gentleman, and I knew he'd won her over.

"Charmed," Donnie said.

"Why, Mr. True," said Emma. "What a sweetie pie you are, and cute as a Kewpie. Believe me, sir, the pleasure is all mine."

WHAT CAN I SAY? We got on, my Donnie and me. Our first whole day together, after Emma had gone home, we walked back to where we'd started—the corner of Fry and Oak—and I opened up Babyheart's Tats.

"So this is our shop," I told Donnie.

He leafed through a binder full of sample tats. "I'm a tattoo artist?"

What was I to tell him? Yes? No? I wasn't sure which way to go, afraid I might scare him off.

"You've done it before," I finally said.

He slapped the binder shut. "I don't think I could do it now. I wouldn't remember how it all went."

"That's all right," I told him. "You don't have to remember everything at once. We'll take it slow."

And we did. All through the rest of September, we fell into a gentle rhythm—the easy tempo of our own fairy tale, as I came to think of it. Pablo, when he'd finally run, had left things in my house—jeans and shirts and underwear and socks and toiletry items. He and Donnie had the same build, so it was easy to convince Donnie that everything was his. While I worked at the shop, he helped out by sweeping the floors and emptying the trash. He even got good at answering the phone and writing down appointments. If someone asked something he didn't know, he put them on hold and came to find me. Sometimes, when everything was slow, he watched the television I had in the waiting area, and if I could spare the time, I sat with him and he held my hand.

He seemed satisfied to be there with me as the days got shorter and the darkness came earlier. Soon we were walking home beneath the glow of the streetlights along Oak, and there was enough of a chill that we had to wear jackets.

Those walks were what I came to love best about the time we spent together. Sometimes we talked about funny little things that had happened at the shop—the man who fainted before the needle even touched his skin, the boy who wanted lips tattooed around his belly button—and other times we didn't say much at all, and that was all right. We were both just happy to be walking hand in hand down the street in the dark, just a man and a woman going home.

One night, as we turned left on Scripture, he pulled me to a stop, and he said, "What was it that made you fall in love with me?"

The question, so sweet for the doubt behind it—as if Donnie couldn't believe he had anything to offer—nearly brought me to tears. It was like we were teenagers, amazed by the love we felt; a little scared of it, but more than a little thrilled.

"It was the way you looked at me," I said, recalling the first time our eyes met. "I could tell you needed me. I wanted to take care of you forever."

He nodded. "You take good care of me, Baby." It all seemed right to him—what I'd said—and for that I was thankful. "I can't imagine being anywhere but with you," he told me, and I couldn't have asked for anything better to hear. I started to believe that I could pull this off, that no one would ever question me, that the people Donnie had left behind would never find him.

"We're good together, aren't we?" I said.

"Thank you." I heard the catch in his voice, and I put my arms around his waist and hugged him to me. "Let's go home," he said, and that's what we did.

Night after night, we lay down to sleep, the way married folks do, and we held each other, and some nights we made love. Oh, I know it was a fool thing to do—I had no idea who this man was or who he'd been with, and these days I know a girl has to be careful—but you have to understand that by this time I was gone. I wasn't living in the sane, rational world. I was living in the world I was making up as I went along, and in that world this man was Donnie, my husband, the man I trusted and loved.

He was there in the evening when I closed my eyes to sleep, and he was there in the morning when I woke up. I came to count on the joy of his company.

Then one day he wasn't in my bed.

I rushed out into the living room, but he wasn't there. He wasn't in the kitchen or the bathroom. He wasn't anywhere that I could see. I stood in the middle of my living room and listened to the clocks ticking, and my house was so quiet without our two voices. I sat down on the floor, drew my knees up to my chest, and started to rock back and forth, the way I did when I was a girl and my *mami* went out for the night and I was afraid she wouldn't come home. *"Loquita!"* my *abuelita* told me, pointing out what a silly girl I was. "She has to come home. This is where she lives."

Words to hang on to, whether they were true or not. I believed them because I needed to believe that sooner or later, my *mami* would come to my bed and lean over to kiss me. Her hair would smell of cigarette smoke, her breath like liquor, her skin like sweat and Heaven Scent perfume. I'd wrap my arms around her neck and cling to her. This was all when I was a little girl, but now that I was a woman, I wondered whether it was true, what my *abuelita* told me, that the restless spirit always longed for home.

Someone knocked on my front door, and I ran to it, thinking it must be him, but it was only Emma come for our morning chitchat.

"Where was Donnie going?" she asked me. "I just now saw him walking up Scripture." I couldn't bear to tell her I didn't know. I wanted to brush past her, run up the street barefoot and in my panties and T-shirt if that's what it took to catch up to Donnie and bring him back. "I called his name, but he didn't even look my way." She held out her hands, palms up, and shrugged her shoulders. "It was like he didn't know me at all."

That's when it hit me, how wrong this all was. He wasn't mine to keep. He belonged somewhere else. Maybe he had a woman who was crazy with worry because she didn't know where he was, and I was partly to blame. I'd been keeping him from being where he truly needed to be, all for my own selfish ends. I was a woman who thought she'd missed her best chances at love, but what right did that give me to make this man, this Lester Stipp, believe that we were a couple?

But then, we were, weren't we? Hadn't everything been so fine between us, and not just because I suggested it had always been so, but also because the two of us clicked, because we were good for each other, because there was something between us that we both needed?

So there I was, torn in two, part of me saying it's only right that he go—what a fool I was to think my crazy scheme would work—and part of me missing him so much I couldn't live with the thought that I might never see him again.

"Oh, you know men," I said, all la-di-da, like this was nothing at all, just a little hen talk between the gals. "They always think they've got someplace they need to go."

"That's the truth, Miss Baby." Emma clucked her tongue. "Yes, ma'am, that's the God's honest truth."

IT WAS THE MIDDLE of the afternoon when Donnie came into the shop. I was in my studio with a customer, a little old man who wanted an olive wreath tattooed on his bald head.

"You know," he said. "Like Julius Caesar."

"It'll hurt like fire," I told him.

"Honey," he said, "I can take it."

I heard the bell on the front door jangle, and when I looked out through the window into the waiting area, there was Donnie.

"Oh, I know you can." I patted the old man on his slick head. "You just hang on a minute. I'll be right back."

Donnie was standing in the middle of the waiting room, his hands stuck into his pants pockets, his head down, as if he didn't know whether he should stay or go. I was afraid to touch him, afraid he'd spook, so I just went up to him and didn't say a word. When some time had gone by and he was still there, I said to him, my voice a whisper so the old man in the room behind us wouldn't hear, "Hey, stranger."

"Were you worried?" Donnie edged his foot forward and bumped it up against my toe.

"Sick," I said.

"I had some thinking to do."

He leaned down until his forehead was resting on mine. Then we talked our quiet talk, words not meant for anyone else to hear.

"Sometimes I get sad," he said. "I can't remember meeting you. I can't remember how it was when we were falling in love. It's like there's this whole part of us that I can't get at."

"It was like it is now." I tilted my head and put my lips to his forehead. I kissed him, once, twice. "It was holding hands and keeping each other company and feeling like it was decided a long way back that one day we'd be together. That's what it was like when we fell in love."

"Like the way I feel now?"

"Just like it."

"And you remember?"

"I'll always remember," I said. "I'll remember for both of us."

He nodded. "Then we're lucky."

His hands found mine, and we laced our fingers together. "Like you wouldn't believe," I told him.

"I will if you say it's true."

"It's true. Every bit."

I promised myself I'd never again doubt how right it was for the two of us to be together. I'd stop thinking about the life he had before I found him. I'd grab on to this second chance to trust in what was good and right between us, and I wouldn't look back. I'd let the story I was spinning sweep me along. I'd keep my eyes on the future.

I went back to my studio, back to the bald man, and he said with a wink, "Boyfriend?"

"He's my husband," I said.

"Nah, can't be." He waved a hand at me as if to dismiss the very idea. "You must be newlyweds."

"Sometimes it seems that way," I told him, and then I went to work on his head.

THEN, ONE DAY in December when Donnie and I had finally settled in—when it looked like Carolyn would leave us alone, when Slam Dent was just a funny name I laughed about from time to time—Pablo came home.

"¿Estas loco?" When I opened my door and saw him on my step, I asked him if he was crazy. I shoved him out into the yard, out by the mimosa tree where he hit his head on one of the dangling glass bottles, out by the gaslight, and then beyond it into the dark of night because I was afraid someone might see him, either the police or worse, Slam Dent. "Don't you know he's still looking for you? Do you want to get killed?"

It was the Christmas season, and all along the street the neighbors had strung lights around their tree trunks, hung them from their roofs, draped them over their nandina bushes. The wind came up stronger—a blue norther moving in, the first of the season—and the temperature dropped. An empty can went clanging down the sidewalk. Somewhere up the street, a car door slammed, and my heart jumped up into my throat. With Pablo back, nothing seemed safe, and though it was true I feared for his well-being, I was also worried about what would happen if he came into my house and I had to explain who Donnie was and how he came to be there.

"Quit shoving me." Pablo held his hands out in front of him to stop me from pushing into his chest. "I mean it, Betts. Don't make me ugly up on you."

This was always our story, this threat. Ever since we were kids, Pablo knew he could get me to do whatever he wanted if he mashed me hard enough. He had deep-set brown eyes, and a little half-moon scar between them where he'd fallen when he was a boy and smacked the corner of a countertop. He was a former Texas State High School wrestling champion in the 130-pound weight class, and he could still muscle up to someone if he took a notion. Sometimes all it took was a look to put me on my heels, but other times it was something he said, something to make it clear that he was disappointed in me, something he said in a wounded voice—"Ah, Betts"—and I remembered we were blood.

"I'm worn out with running," he said that night in my yard.

He told me about the close calls he'd had with Slam Dent—times he'd been in restaurants and had to sneak out men's room windows, times he'd hidden in trash Dumpsters, all the times he'd had to drive like a crazy man just to get away from Slam, who always seemed to be close to snagging him. That's all it took, those stories. I knew I'd let him into my house, invite him to hide his car in my garage. I'd do whatever he asked because he was my brother, and all our lives, we'd counted on each other.

"All right," I said. "You can come in, but first I've got to tell you something."

"Will I like it?"

"You don't have to like it. You just have to listen."

So I told him about this man, Lester Stipp, and how I found him on the street, not knowing who he was.

"You told him what?" Pablo said.

He made me repeat it, the part of how I fell in love, how I told Lester his name was Donnie, and he was my husband.

"You can't tell anyone," I said. "Pablo, I mean it. If you do, I'll call the police on you."

"You'd do that?"

"I love him," I said. "We're good together."

Pablo laughed. "So you're just like me, Betts. That's rich. You rustled yourself a bull."

It was more than that. I still believe it. I wanted to explain it to Pablo again that night. I wanted to tell him that no one should question the witchy heart or how it comes to find what it needs.

"So when did you and him get 'married'?"

"August seventh."

"Ha! Oh, Betts, that's rich. Wouldn't Mami be proud?" He used that exaggerated laugh again. "Ha-ha!" Then he fell quiet. Finally, he said, "All right. If that's your story, let's go meet the mister."

Inside the house, Donnie was finishing the dishes. For fun, I'd tied an apron around his waist, an old-timey thing my *abuelita* used to wear: a red organdy with a felt pocket in the shape of a heart.

Pablo took one look at him and said, "My, my. Do you do the cooking, too? Make the bed? Wash the clothes?"

Donnie glanced down at his apron, then over at me, his eyes narrowed with confusion. "I'm washing the dishes," he said.

"Oh, I can see that," said Pablo, "and looking so pretty, too."

I smacked him across his arm. *"Cabron,"* I said under my breath, letting him know he was a bastard for teasing Donnie.

"Huerga bribona," said Pablo, calling me a tricky bitch.

Donnie untied the apron, folded it very carefully, and handed it to me. "I'm finished," he said, and for a moment I felt a blaze of panic in my chest because I feared he was saying he was done with me. Then he picked up a dish towel and laid it over the dishes in the drainer, and I understood I was being foolish; he was just letting me know he'd finished with the dishes.

This was the time of night when normally we would have gone into the living room, switched on the fairy night-light, and sat close together on the couch, not saying much at all, just letting the day wind down. I liked looking at my figurines, imagining the fairies watching over us, sprinkling us with pixie dust to keep this love alive. But with Pablo here, everything was different. I felt like Donnie and I were on display, and I could tell he felt it, too. He didn't reach for my hand, like he usually did when the dishes were done and we were ready to relax. He stood there, filling his cheeks with air and then letting it out in little puffs. He gave Pablo a timid smile, and I realized then he had no idea who Pablo was or why he was there.

"Donnie," I said, "this is my brother, Pablo. I told you about him. Remember?"

Pablo had this knack for making everyone feel like he was their best friend. Even if he liked to stir things up from time to time, he was easy to forgive. He put one arm around Donnie's shoulders, and with his free hand he patted him on the chest. "Welcome to the family. *Una familia feliz.* We're one happy family, *sí*?"

Donnie nodded. *"Sí,"* he said.

Pablo chuckled. "That's the ticket. Now, let's you and me sit down and get acquainted." He winked at Donnie. "I've got stories to tell you, and I bet you've got some of your own."

I won't deny I felt jealous watching Pablo usher Donnie into the living room, his arm still draped over his shoulders as if he, Pablo, were claiming him for his own.

"You got beer?" he called back to me. *"Dos cervezas, pronto."* He petted Donnie's back. "Oh, my friend," he said. "We have so much to talk about."

I could see that Donnie was taking a liking to Pablo, and I imagine it was because Pablo didn't question him. Pablo just yakked about things that interested him in the here and now, and listening to him, one would easily get the notion that there wasn't such a thing as history—no past at all, only what was right there before us. I sat on a chair in the corner listening as Pablo rattled on and on. He and Donnie had their feet propped up on my coffee table, and every once in a while, Pablo's toe would tap against a fairy snow globe, and I told him to be careful.

"Chill, Betts." He hoisted his bottle of Corona toward me in a salute. "I won't break it."

He had two gold chains around his neck and what looked like a diamond stud in his left ear. His shirt was a sapphire blue Guayabera with French cuffs; the gold links sparkled in the lamplight. It was clear he'd found a way to spend some of the money he'd pocketed from that cattle sale. His ivory slacks were linen, and as he went on telling Donnie about the things that mystified him, he took some of the material and rubbed it between his fingers, appreciating the way it felt.

"How come it is," he wondered, "that birds could sit on electrical wires and not get shocked?" "And why didn't people have one big nostril instead of two smaller ones? Ever wonder about that?" he asked Donnie. "Or cereal: How come some of them make a popping noise when you pour milk on them and others don't?" "But here's the one that's been bugging me lately," he said. "How come the cashew is the only nut you can't buy in the shell?"

"Urushiols," Donnie said.

Pablo drew back his head and studied him. "Say what?"

Donnie patiently explained that the cashew shell contained the same oily chemicals that poison ivy did, urushiols. "That's why they used to call cashews blister nuts. You wouldn't want to handle those shells."

"Well, what do you know?" Pablo winked at me. "We've got a walking, talking encyclopedia here. A regular Mr. Know-it-all. I'm going to start calling you Britannia."

"Britannica," Donnie said. "It's the *Encyclopedia Britannica.*"

Pablo laughed. "See what I mean? He knows everything."

When we were finally alone in bed, Pablo settling down in the spare bedroom, I said to Donnie, "How did you know that about the cashews?"

He got a curious look on his face as if he couldn't explain it himself. "I don't know. It was just in my head."

It took me a long time to go to sleep, wondering, as I did, what else was there in his brain just waiting for him to call it up.

PABLO'S PLAN WAS THIS: He wanted to see Carolyn. He wanted to tell her he was sorry he'd gotten into trouble and ruined their plans to remarry.

"Whose fault is that?" I asked him.

It was the next morning, early, and I was outside tying another bottle to a branch on the mimosa tree. Donnie was still asleep. Even the windows at Emma's were dark. Pablo and I were the only ones up and about just past dawn, the raw wind still blowing in from Oklahoma. The bottles in the mimosa clinked and clinked, and it was a sound I'd ordinarily have taken comfort from, so merry it was, but on that morning, when Pablo started talking about Carolyn, all the noise got on my nerves. Despite everything I'd felt for her the night she told me about Slam Dent, I couldn't bear the thought that Pablo was still on her string.

"Mine," he said. "The blame is all mine. I own up to that, but gee, Betts, I did it all for her. She wanted that diamond ring."

He'd always been such a little boy around her—starstruck—and it looked like all his trouble, all his time on the run, hadn't changed that a bit. I'd told him, when he'd phoned to check in from time to time, about the things she said to me. How she called me a cow, a hoochie bitch. "Me," I told him. "Your sister."

I guess, if I wanted to take an honest look at things, I'd understand why he'd never gotten over Carolyn. She was a princess—all that blond hair, those blue eyes, her trim and curvy figure. A *gringa,* a Barbie doll, every Mexican boy's dream. But that's not being fair. It wasn't just the fact that she was white and blond and so *bonita*. She was also—deep down I knew this to be true—a good person. I'd seen the way she'd fussed over Pablo when they were first starting out and he hadn't yet got into trouble with Slam Dent. She did all the things for him that had never seemed that important to me. She kept her house in order, decorated it with little doodads from Pier 1—baskets and silk flowers and the like. She bought matching window treatments from JC Penney, sprayed the rooms with tutti-fruity air fresheners from Bath & Body Works—scents like Basil and Thyme, Lavender-Vanilla, and Cinnamon Stick—did everything she could to make that house, as she told me once, a place Pablo would look forward to being in after a stretch of days on the road, hauling freight as far as El Paso or Houston or Lubbock.

"I'm going to look her up today," he told me that morning in my yard.

"You do what you want," I said. "You're a big boy, Toots. I've got my own fish to fry."

I had that little issue of wedding rings to see to, and later that morning, I told Donnie we were going downtown.

"You going to work early?" Emma asked when I opened the front door and found her on the step about to knock.

"No, we're going downtown," I said. "We're going to First People's Jewelers."

"Ooh, lovebirds." She put her hand over her mouth and coyly turned her head as if she were shocked. "I bet someone's getting a diamond."

At the jewelry store, we sat on cushioned chairs at a glass-topped table, and a woman with black hair and pretty hands brought out rings for us to see. She laid them out on a black velvet cloth and asked me if I saw anything that caught my fancy. She even picked up my left hand and let it lie on her palm. "Something dainty, maybe," she said, and I thought she was saying that my hand was small and anything large would overwhelm it.

"No," I said. "I wanted to see the Seduction Solitaire." If it was good enough for Carolyn, then it was good enough for me.

The woman frowned at me. "That's a big diamond," she said. But she found it in the case, and she slipped it onto my finger. "What do you know?" she said. "It fits. How lucky is that?"

She'd been right, though. It was too much of a ring for my hand, and I felt ashamed to see it there on that stubby finger—so ugly mine was next to her long, slender ones. Mine were just right for curling around the barrel of a tat machine, but not so much made, it seemed, for wearing fine jewels. I noticed how the skin was starting to wrinkle around my knuckles and how there were ink stains in my cuticles. I wondered what I'd been thinking when I got the notion that I deserved this fairy tale, this chance to be a bride.

Then Donnie said, "The gold looks so perfect against your skin." He took my hand on his palm the way the woman had done, and it was like she vanished, and it was just the two of us—Donnie and me—alone. "Beautiful," he said.

I felt it then, the way the world can disappear and the only thing that matters is the person you're with, the one who knows you better than anyone else alive. That's what I felt that day in First People's, like everything could be perfect: my little brown fingers, that gold band, the Seduction Solitaire engagement ring with a diamond that was stunning in its clarity and cut—the light sparked out around it—and Donnie and I; we could be grand forever and ever.

"How much does it cost?" My voice was so small, overcome with the love I felt for my life at that moment. I still remember what it was like to be surprised by the magic lurking in the world. Donnie was right. The golden ring looked just right against my brown skin.

"A set? Wedding band, too?" The woman with the black hair and the pretty hands had a pair of black-rimmed half-glasses that she kept on a beaded chain around her neck. She looked at me over the tops of those glasses. "That diamond is a Hearts on Fire diamond, the most perfectly cut diamond in the world." She told us that less than one percent of rough diamond crystals are pure enough to become Hearts on Fire. "They're what the movie stars wear," she said. "I'm afraid these rings are *mucho dinero*."

I hated it when the *gringos y gringas* spoke Spanish to me. Whenever it happened, I felt like a little girl, a finger wagging in my face. *Mucho dinero,* the woman said, and I knew she was implying that I couldn't afford the cost of those rings.

But like I've already made clear, I'm sometimes too brassy for my own good. I didn't hesitate.

"These are the rings I want," I said, my voice strong now.

"But, Baby," Donnie said. "You don't even know how much—"

I cut him off. "It doesn't matter." I took off the set and laid the rings on the velvet cloth. "I want these rings."

The woman told me the price, a sum I could never afford in a million years, and still I didn't back down. "Is there a matching wedding band for *el caballero*?" I asked, and the woman squinted at me. If she wanted to speak Spanish, okay, we'd speak Spanish. "The gentleman," I said, hoping the woman felt stupid. I put my hand on Donnie's back. "Is there a band for him?"

"Of course," she said.

"Good. Then we'll want it, too."

The woman took off her glasses and let them dangle from their chain. She looked me square in the eye. "And how will we be paying?" she said.

That's when the door opened, and Pablo came storming in. He took me by the meat of my arm and jerked me to my feet. *"Vamanos,"* he said, hissing it beneath his breath, and before I could stop him, he was dragging me toward the door. I saw the look on the jewelry store woman's face, and I knew she was thinking, Well, of course, another squabble between hot-blooded Mexicans, just what she'd expect and a sure sign that she was right: I was wasting her time looking at that Hearts on Fire diamond ring. I tried to dig in my heels, but it was no use. Before I knew it, we were out on the sidewalk, and Donnie was with us, telling Pablo to leave me alone.

"What's your problem, anyway?" Donnie said. "How come you're making a scene?"

"You could have told me." Now Pablo had his finger up in my face. "But you didn't say a word."

I yanked my arm free. "Told you what?" I rubbed my sore arm. "How'd you even know where we were?"

"Emma," he said, then he started to calm down, and he looked all embarrassed because he'd blown up like that. "Damn it all to hell, Betts. Why didn't you let me know about what happened to Carolyn?"

Donnie was petting my arm, rubbing his hand along the place where Pablo had grabbed me. "You've got no right to treat your sister like this."

"You're right." Pablo ran his hand through his hair like he was trying to wipe the memory of what had just happened out of his brain. "Sometimes I just go a little *loco*. Hotheaded, right, Betts?"

It'd always been that way. Pablo would let his temper get the best of him, and he'd just go off. Then he'd be sorry. He'd give me the moon and the stars to try to make the two of us feel better. *I'm an idiot,* he'd say, and I'd agree. *But you love me, don't you?* he'd ask, and I'd tell him, *Sure, I love you—until next time. Until always,* he'd say, and kiss me on the forehead.

But this time, in front of Donnie, I wasn't so eager to forgive. Now that I had a man to stand up for me, I didn't have to let Pablo off the hook. I said, "You keep what's between you and Carolyn to yourselves. I've got my own life, *muchas gracias, señor*."

I said the Spanish part in a catty way, letting him know I thought his trouble with Slam Dent was the foolish game of little boys stoked with too much machismo. Think about it. How much trouble in the world comes down to exactly that? Donnie was different. He was gentle and kind and yet firm when he needed to speak up about something he knew was wrong. He'd told Pablo he should treat me with respect, and I thought, Well, he's right. It hurt me to have that woman in the jewelry store see me in the midst of something ugly like that—I knew she'd be talking about it at home that evening; "Mexicans," she'd say—and, too, it hurt me to think about that Hearts on Fire diamond ring still resting on that velvet cloth inside the store, a store I'd never go back into, not unless I could buy that ring with cash money and watch that woman's eyes pop out.

"What were you doing in there?" Pablo asked me.

"Buying wedding rings." I saw the woman in the store returning the Hearts on Fire ring to the glass case and turning the key in its lock. "You sure took the romance out of it."

"I'm sorry, Betts."

And with that, Pablo went into the store.

I watched through the window as he spoke with the woman. She had her arms crossed over her chest at first as if she feared he might do her harm. Then Pablo said something that made her laugh. She looked at the window and caught me watching, but I couldn't bring myself to look away because now Pablo was taking out his wallet and fingering out a pile of bills onto that black velvet cloth where only minutes before all those rings had rested.

The woman picked up the cash and counted it. She found an order pad, and I could tell she was getting information from Pablo. I knew he'd just put a down payment on those rings, and my heart leapt with joy, because could it be he'd just bought them for Donnie and me?

When he came out of the store, I threw my arms around his neck and gave him a hug. "No one's ever done anything like that for me before." I kissed him on the cheek. "But shouldn't you keep that money and give it to Slam Dent so he won't hurt you?"

Pablo eased himself out of my arms. "What do you think, Betts?" He lifted an eyebrow and smirked. "I'm buying that ring for Carolyn."

I felt the ground drop away from me, and I swore I was falling. I watched him walk away from me. I called his name, but in a voice so weak there was little chance that he heard me. Or, if he did, he didn't care. He didn't stop or even look back. He just kept walking like he didn't have a reason in the world to think of me.

Donnie was still stroking my arm. "Are you all right, Baby?"

"I'm fine," I told him, but, of course, I wasn't. Inside I was shaking.

"Do you want to go back into the store?"

I shook my head. Then I told him the truth, as hard as it was for me to admit. "I don't have the money for those rings." I let my breath out with a gasp, and I felt the tears start to come.

"Don't cry." He pulled me close to him, and I pressed my face into his chest and listened to his heart beating, that strong, steady beat that reminded me of the drum circle on the lawn of the Language Building the night my new life began. Who knew where it was going? I only knew I was thankful for the arms that were around me, and the beat of that heart, and that soothing voice telling me everything was going to be all right. "No worries, Baby," he said. "Rings or no rings, I'm here."

WHAT DO YOU do when you're being hunted the way Pablo was and your ex-wife, whom you still love, tells you that the man who's after you came into her house and held a gun to her head and made her take off her clothes and looked her over for a good long time?

You go off. At least that's what Pablo did. You go looking for that man, that Slam Dent, and you don't give a shit what happens when you find him.

Donnie and I hustled back to the house, but by the time we got there, Pablo and his car were gone.

I looked through the spare bedroom, and all his things were still there: gold chains and bracelets laid out on top of the dresser; a pair of cordovan loafers lined up neatly in the closet; silk shirts and dress slacks still on their hangers; a Gideon Bible, taken, no doubt, from a motel when he was on the road, open now on the nightstand to the beginning of the thirteenth chapter of the Book of Hebrews. I'd never known Pablo to be a religious man, and I could only assume that some night, when he was on the run, he'd become so frightened, he'd opened this Bible and looked for comfort. I rubbed my hand over the page—so thin and sleek it was—and then I read, the first verse, "Let brotherly love continue."

It blindsided me, that exhortation to love, and I was sorry for the anger I'd felt toward Pablo at the jewelry store. When I thought about him hunkered down in a motel room God knows where, longing for home, I couldn't help but feel sorry for him.

The second verse was one I knew, the one about how we should take care of strangers because sometimes they might be angels, and if we turned them away, who knew what might happen tomorrow. That's the thing that froze me, that uncertainty about what was coming at me from the future. I kept turning it over in my head, the fact that when we make a choice, we create a realm of possible consequences, and another collection of possibilities go zooming past us, and we never know what they were. We never know how things might have turned out differently. What was left to us, then, but, as the verse said, to let love continue? I told this Lester Stipp that he was mine, and now here I was in the midst of what I'd made. I didn't know if he was an angel come to save me, but in my heart I believed it was true.

"I have to find him," I said to Donnie. "I have to find Pablo."

But it was almost time to open my shop. "I'll take care of it," Donnie said. "You just go."

So we agreed that he'd open up Babyheart's Tats, and he'd tell anyone who came in that Miss Baby would be there shortly. He'd let them leaf through the sample tats. He'd get them coffee or a Coke. He'd shoot the breeze. He told me not to worry, and I gave him the key.

CAROLYN LIVED in the house she and Pablo had bought when they got married. She'd kept it in the divorce, but I knew it was hard now for her to keep up with the mortgage payments. It was a nice brick ranch house in the northwest part of Denton where the developers were chopping up pasture land, but still there was open range and longhorn cattle, and land with nothing taller than scrub oak and mesquite stretching out to the horizon. Not much to stop the wind, so plastic shopping bags from the

K-Mart on University Drive blew around and stuck to the barbed-wire fences. I drove out there to look for Pablo. An armadillo scooted across the road, and I had to stomp on my brakes to keep from hitting it.

When it comes to matters of love—real love, the kind that sears you; when it comes to Hearts on Fire—does the pledge ever die? With Pablo and Carolyn it was easy to imagine she was who he'd go to now because even I had to admit that it was true—he still loved her.

But he wasn't there. Carolyn let me in, and I took in the scent of fresh-baked cookies, one of the air fresheners that she used, and I have to admit it was nice to smell that, and to watch the way the sunlight streamed in through the windows and fell across the blond wood onto all the living-room furniture and sparkled in the globes of the ceiling fan lights, and put shadows on the walls. I could see the lines on the carpets from a recent vacuuming, and there was a can of furniture polish and a cloth on the coffee table.

"I've interrupted your housework," I said.

She reached behind her head and tightened the knot on a red bandanna she was using as a kerchief. Her hair was in a ponytail, and she was wearing a dark green UNT sweatshirt with a smear of white paint across the bottom. That, and a pair of running shoes left just inside the door, one shoe tipped over on its side, was enough to make the house seem more cozy, a house where someone lived with joy and sometimes loneliness and sometimes heartache, the way we all do, one day following another and us with no idea what might be just around the corner.

"Baby," Carolyn said, "you should've known Pablo wouldn't keep his mouth shut about what you've got cooking with that man, that Donnie."

"Was he here? Pablo?" I had all sorts of horrible thoughts as I imagined the harm that might come to Pablo if he found Slam Dent or if Slam found him. It seemed to me that the two of them were on a collision course, and there was little I could do to stop it. Still, I had to try. "Carolyn," I said, "tell me where he's gone."

She looked at me like I was crazy. "He went looking for you."

"Just now?"

"No," she said, "earlier."

"He hasn't been back?"

"He was just here once. This morning. He told me the truth." She put her hands on her hips. "About you," she said, "and how Donnie doesn't know who he is and you've got him thinking he's your husband."

"I imagine you're happy about that."

Carolyn shook her head. "I wouldn't say happy. No, that's not the right word. Satisfied, I guess. Satisfied, Baby, because now you can't hide." She did the most surprising thing then. She leaned over and kissed me on each cheek, and I understood she was welcoming me to the fold, to the clan of women who'd do almost anything for love. "It's all out in the open now," she whispered in my ear. "Just how much alike we are. You and me, Baby." She kissed my forehead. "We're simpatico."

She was right, of course, and, really, hadn't I known it ever since that night I told Lester Stipp his name was Donnie, and then I took him home? How could someone do a thing like that if she weren't crazy for a man to love her? And wasn't that Carolyn's story as well, she who, when push came to shove, would do practically anything to make things right between her and Pablo?

"All right," I said. "So what are you going to do about it now that you know?"

Carolyn laughed. "Maybe you should put a tattoo on that man of yours." She was enjoying teasing me, and there wasn't much I could do but take it. "Yes, sir, Baby. I'd get a brand on him pronto. Looks like he's a bull that's apt to wander away from the herd."

When the phone rang, I nearly jumped out of my skin. Carolyn didn't move to answer it. The cordless phone was right there on the end table, but she just let it ring. Finally, the answering machine picked up, and it was Pablo's voice still on the machine from the days when this was his home, and what he said was, "You've reached Pablo and Carolyn," and then I didn't really hear the rest because I was thinking how once there'd been love in that house, and maybe it would have had a chance to endure if Carolyn hadn't wanted too much and Pablo hadn't gotten into his mess with Slam Dent.

The voice that left a message for Carolyn belonged to Slam. It was raspy from too much booze and too many cigarettes. "He was lucky this time. Next time? Maybe..." For a good while, there was nothing. Then he took another tack. "Sugar," he said, and Carolyn crossed her arms over her chest. I could feel how afraid she was the night Slam Dent was in her house, how afraid she'd always be, and I sensed how this mistrust of the future was about to be mine because I knew, as soon as Slam Dent said *he was lucky,* he was talking about Pablo, and I knew, whatever the rest of the story was, it wouldn't be one we'd choose to have waiting for us on down the line. It was like Slam was here again, Carolyn naked in front of him. "Sugar, I dream about you," he said. "Better keep your door locked." He laughed. "For what good it'll do."

I couldn't take it anymore. I snatched up the phone and said, "You asshole."

That didn't faze him a bit. "Why, hello there, Baby. How's tricks?"

"Have you hurt him?"

"Hurt him? Why, Baby, don't you know who I am?" I could hear him breathing. "He had a little cash on him this time. I took that for interest on what he still owes me. Eighteen grand. I want it before the week's out. If I don't get it, I'll kill him. Plain enough for you?"

I couldn't find my voice. I couldn't say a word.

PABLO WAS AT THE SHOP—Carolyn and I went down there in my car—and Slam had beat him bad.

"I found him," Pablo said with a little laugh, and maybe he even winked at us, but it was hard to tell because Slam had left him with both eyes nearly closed and bruised up ugly in different shades of black and yellow and purple and green. Pablo was sitting on a chair, his arm in a sling that had been jerry-rigged out of a dish towel, safety pins, and a belt. "Pretty slick," Pablo said. "That asshole fucked up my shoulder, but Donnie took care of it."

"It was out of the socket." Donnie was checking the safety pins that held the belt by buckle and tongue hole to the dish towel. "The humerus was dislocated from the scapula. I put it back in place."

He said it as if it had been nothing at all, like he went around all the time fixing dislocated shoulders.

"I didn't find it very humorous," Pablo said.

"That ought to do the trick," said Donnie, "until I can get a proper sling." He looked at me. "Is there a medical supply store in town?"

"On Teasley Lane." I was having a hard time believing that he'd been able to fix Pablo's shoulder. "You just put it back into place?"

He nodded. "It's called a closed reduction. You just put the head of the bone back into the joint socket."

"Just as easy as that, huh? A snap?"

"I didn't say it was easy." He said this with a pained tone to his voice, and I could tell I'd been too flip. Pablo and I had lessened what he'd done with our play on words. I tried to make it up to him by letting him know how amazing I thought it was.

"Of course not," I said. "You're a real miracle worker. I don't know what we'd have done without you."

Carolyn was standing beside Pablo. She was petting his hair. "Ah, honey," she said. "This just breaks my heart."

"That's better than your nose or your arm," Pablo said, and he tried to smile, but his lips were cut and swollen, and the effort hurt too much.

Carolyn said, "Don't talk, hon. We need to get something on your face. Baby, do you have something to keep these cuts from getting infected?"

I had rubbing alcohol, of course, and the A+D Ointment that I gave to customers to put on their new tattoos.

"It's going to burn, isn't it?" Pablo braced himself when he saw me douse a cotton swab with alcohol. "A whole hell of a lot, isn't it, Betts?"

"Afraid so," I told him, and Carolyn let him hold her hand. "Just tell yourself that when it stings, it means it's doing what it's supposed to do."

I didn't know how he'd lay hands to eighteen thousand dollars—Slam's share of the cattle sale—by the end of the week. After making the down payment for that ring, he was close to busted. That was the problem. A huge problem, and no one had any answers. Between all of us, we didn't have that kind of cash. So there we were. Stuck, and time ticking, and Pablo trying to keep the cops from knowing he was back in town.

"All right." He nodded at me, and then braced himself for the sting of the alcohol. "Go ahead, Betts. Hit me."

LANEY

As the days went on, I thought things might work out all right. Rose found a job taking care of a shut-in woman out in New Hope, a job that came with a room of her own. She moved out of the trailer, and once she'd saved enough wages, she paid Delilah what she owed for rent. Delilah was glad to see her go, but of course it left us tight for money. We took out an ad in the paper, looking for another roommate, and even put a notice up on the bulletin board at work, but the days went by and we didn't have any takers.

When he could, Tweet stopped by late in the afternoons just as Delilah and I were getting the day started. Sometimes he brought a box of doughnuts, the kind with the white icing and the pink sprinkles that Delilah liked so much, and we all sat around the breakfast table drinking coffee and eating those doughnuts and gabbing about this or that.

"I hear you and Delilah were playing Mommy and Daddy," I said one day. "You know, when you were driving that Explorer back from Terre Haute."

Tweet gave Delilah a puzzled look. "We were?"

"Oh, that's just Laney talking to hear her head rattle." She narrowed her eyes at me. "She does that sometimes."

"Seats seven," I said, a reminder of what she'd told me about that Explorer.

"We were just yakking while we were driving," he said. "We were just playing." He twisted his mouth around and chewed on his bottom lip. "Least I thought we were."

"Sure, baby, that's what we were doing." Delilah waved her hand at him, like she was batting down any notion that they might have been serious. "We were just shooting the breeze."

He nodded his head in agreement, but I thought he looked spooked.

THEN IT WAS Memorial Day weekend, and Helmets on the Short Bus were playing at the Amvets Pig Roast and Raft Regatta up at Dark Bend, playing at a club called the Boar's Nest. Lester said he wouldn't go.

"Tweet turned me out," he said, "and that's the way it is."

We were on our break at work, sitting in his truck, an old Ford F-150 that used to be red but now was faded to an orange almost the color of rust.

"Well, if you won't go, then I won't, either."

He shrugged. "You can go if you want. I don't mind."

But I could tell he really did mind. I thought of how it made me feel the first time I saw Tweet play that guitar of his. "We'll see," I told Lester, and then it was time to go back to work.

"Oh, Laney, you *have* to go," Delilah said when I told her I probably wouldn't.

We were driving back to the trailer after work, and she stopped the Malibu on the railroad tracks. There was a freight that came through town that time of morning, and I thought about how the crossing arms came down, their lights flashing and their bells clanging.

"Delilah, drive!" I told her. I didn't know how she could bring herself to do such a fool thing after what her mother had done.

"Not until you say you'll go."

"What if the train comes and the arms come down on your car?"

She put the tip of her finger in her mouth and gave me an innocent look. "Gonna leave a mark," she said.

"All right, I'll go."

She took her foot off the brake and drove on over the crossing. "We're going to have fun," she said. "You'll see."

We drove up in the evening just as the sun was setting, casting streaks of orange and purple low in the sky. We zipped by bean- and cornfields that stretched back to tree lines, and everything felt as wide open as the land around us, the plants, barely ankle high, running in neat rows as far as I could see. The wheat fields were turning, going from green to what would soon be that yellow gold I always loved. It was just warm enough to make things nice, but not too hot, and I could tell that Delilah was jazzed. She had on a new pair of Lee jeans and a hot-pink tank. She wore a cowboy hat on her head—"a little special touch," she said as we left the trailer. It was one of those straw hats with the brim curled up at the sides. A long red feather stuck up from the band. "What do you think, Laney?" she asked when she was getting dressed. She put on the pink tank and tucked it into her jeans. "Gretchen Wilson?" One of her favorite singers, a girl from Illinois who wasn't about to let anyone run over her. "Or…" She slapped on that cowboy hat. "Lucinda Williams." Lucinda was my favorite. I loved her sad-old, wise-to-the-world ways, and that voice that told you she'd been hurt every way there was for a woman to be hurt, and still she hoped for love. "I'm working on my image," Delilah said. "I can't decide." She took off the hat. "All jacked up?" Then she put the hat back on. "Or Mister, you and me, we're right in time, and if you ever forget it, I'll roast your ass in a song?" I told her it depended on the message she wanted to send: "Take me." Or "Careful, cowboy. Paybacks are hell."

She nodded. "Both," she said, and then she asked me to grab her purse and hand it to her. I picked it up from the doorknob where it was hanging, and I felt the weight of that Taurus .38. She was ready to go.

Now she turned up the volume on the CD player. Trace Atkins was singing "One Hot Mama." She winked at me. "Just wait till Tweet gets his eyes on me. Laney, I can bet you, he's gonna wanna."

I just looked out the window, watching the twilight come on while we moved deeper into the river bottoms. Pole lights were coming on in farmyards, and I thought about that Lucinda song, "Side of the Road," where the woman tells her man she wants out of the car. She walks out into a field and looks at a farmhouse far away and wonders whether a husband and wife live there and whether they're happy. She wants to know what it's like to be away from her man, to be by herself. I wondered sometimes if that's what I should want, to be separate from Delilah, to know what my life might be like without her, but like the woman in the song, I was scared to find out. So there I was on my way to Dark Bend, where I knew Delilah would want me to stand as witness so she'd have someone to crow to about the night and how wonderful Tweet was and how much they were in love, and my-oh-my, all the drive home.

"Meow," she said, and she curled her fingers into a claw and scraped her nails over my bare arm. "Look out," she said, "I'm on the prowl."

When we walked into the Boar's Nest, Helmets on the Short Bus were finishing their first set. The last licks of that old Creedence song "Fortunate Son." I remembered my daddy singing that song around the house, a song about those who had and those who didn't, and guess which ones went off and fought the wars, he said. Sure as hell weren't the ones with the silver spoons. "It ain't me, it ain't me," Tweet sang into the microphone. "I ain't no fortunate son, no, no, no."

"That's for all you vets who got out of Vietnam," he said as the last chords faded away, and the men in the Boar's Nest gave a shout and raised their glasses high in the air. "We're Helmets on the Short Bus," Tweet said. "We're taking a little break now, but we'll be back before you know it." He lifted his guitar over his head, turned his back to us, and leaned the guitar into its stand on the low pallets covered with plywood that, pushed together, served as a stage.

Out of the corner of my eye, I saw Delilah raise her arm to wave at him. I even heard the little push of air at her lips as she started to say his name. Then she stopped. I heard that catch of breath, and I turned to look at her full on. She still had her arm in the air, but her hand flopped forward, the wave she intended wilting. Little by little, the arm drooped to her side. Then she said, "There she is. There's that tramp."

She was talking about Rose, who was standing by the stage, offering a bottle of Corona to Tweet. He took it by the neck and swung it up to his lips.

"Bitch," Delilah said, and then she was on the move.

I didn't know what to do but to follow, so there I was, 'Lil Sis tagging along, weaving my way through the tables where the men and women were starting to catch the scent of trouble. They were putting down their beers, stopping their gab, elbowing one another in the ribs, and gesturing with their heads toward Delilah, who was on the march.

"Hey, baby," Tweet said to her when they were finally face-to-face. She stepped right up on that stage and snatched the Corona from his hand. She put her mouth around the bottle and took a good long drink. Then without even looking, she handed the bottle back to Rose, who had no choice but to take it.

"Get on out of here," Delilah said to Rose. She still wouldn't look at her, and her voice was husky and low.

"We were just talking," Rose said. "Jesus, Dee, don't get your panties in a twist."

Delilah just kept looking right at Tweet. "What makes you think I'm wearing any?" She put her arms around his neck and kissed him, one of those long, openmouthed kisses usually saved—I'd never had one, but even I knew this—for those alone times in the dark. I was more than a little embarrassed to see it, and yet I couldn't stop myself from watching. Delilah pressed against Tweet, and her hips did a little grind. What must it be like, I wondered, to feel so comfortable with who you were that you could do something like that on a stage at the Boar's Nest with everyone watching and whistling and hooting?

"Jeez, Delilah." Tweet tried to pull away from her, but she held on. "What's people going to think?"

"They're going to think you're lucky," Delilah said, and she ground herself against him again.

Rose was wearing a pair of jeans with glittery gold stars painted on the hip pockets. Her white button-up shirt was tucked neatly into her jeans, and I could tell she'd taken extra-special care with her hair and makeup. Her lips were shiny with gloss, and she'd used mascara and liner. Her long lashes swept up from her eyes.

The air was thick inside the Boar's Nest. It didn't matter that the windows were wide open, and we could hear the river moving outside and the sounds of peepers and tree frogs. Under the lights, and with so many people crowded together, it was hotter than hot. Rose had a few strands of hair stuck to her sweaty neck. That made me feel sorry for her. I can't really explain why, just that it was something about the fact that she'd gone to so much trouble to get herself fancied up and what was she doing but having a little chat with Tweet, and then there was Delilah making a fool of her in front of all those people. Of course, I knew the offer of that Corona was something more selfish than a kindness. It was clear to Delilah and everyone else that Rose intended to make a play for Tweet. A part of me thought, Good for her, good for going after what she wanted. Maybe I secretly wished that something might happen to mess up what Delilah and Tweet had going so she'd be mine again, and mine alone.

She pulled away from him, and she turned to look at Rose for the first time. "Maybe someday," Delilah said, "you'll know how to get a man of your own. In the meantime, stay the hell away from Tweet. I mean it, Rose. I'm not going to say this again. If there's a next time, it'll be the last time. You can count on that."

"I can talk to whoever I want to." Rose lifted the Corona up to Tweet again. "Tell her, Tweet."

I knew how much Delilah needed him after what she went through with Bobby May. She and Tweet were just at the beginning of things, but I knew she was hoping he'd be the one to stick, the good-hearted man she'd been dreaming of all her life.

But there he was reaching for that Corona. As soon as I saw his hand open to take it, I wanted to tell him he was making a mistake, but I didn't know that it would make any difference at all. He took the Corona, and he said in that soft voice of his, "Jeez, Delilah. People are watching."

"You think they're watching now?" Delilah said. "You just wait."

She reached her hand into her purse and brought out that .38. She leveled it at Rose. "I told you to leave him alone."

Some of the people in the crowd saw that gun. I heard a woman scream, a man say, "Jesus Christ."

"Good God, Delilah," Tweet said. "Get some sense."

Rose said, "She's crazy. She's always been that way."

I saw Delilah's finger move the safety off.

"Delilah, listen to me," I said. "It's Laney. You don't want to do this. We need to go."

She looked at me, and I could see in her eyes how afraid she was. She'd gone too far, and maybe she could see how little it would take for her to go the rest of the way.

"Laney," she said, like a plea, and I knew I'd be able to get her out of there. I knew there wouldn't be any more trouble, at least not that night.

She let me take the .38. I put the safety back on. "Come on," I told her. "Let's go."

We made our way through the crowd. I didn't look at anyone, just set my sights on the door and shoved my way through. A man bumped into Delilah, and her hat fell to the floor. I didn't stop to pick it up. We had to go before she changed her mind about doing harm to Rose. That hat was gone.

When we were outside and at the Malibu, I took the .38 and put it in the glove compartment. Then I wrapped my arms around Delilah's waist. She let me, and there we were just holding on. I could smell the cigarette smoke in her hair and the Euphoria cologne on her skin and the salt of her sweat. I let the moment go on and on, afraid to say a single word, afraid of what might happen next.

Then she said, "Oh, Laney. Oh, Jesus God. I'm going to lose him."

I didn't know what to say. Right then, I didn't know how anything would turn out. A couple walked by in the dark, their boots scuffing over the gravel. The woman, either not knowing we could hear her or else not giving a squat, said, "That was Delilah Dade in there. She used to run with that Bobby May. She's got a way of finding trouble."

I wanted to say something to that woman, tell her to mind her own damn business, tell her she didn't know Delilah at all, but before I could open my mouth, Delilah said, "Let it go, Laney. She's right. I haven't had much of anything but trouble all my life."

It was true that she'd had more than her share of rough spots—some of them, like her time with Bobby May, the result of her own poor choices—but that woman and others like her who wanted to stand all high and mighty above Delilah could go to hell for all I cared. They'd heard the stories of how Delilah's father left and then her mother sat in her Impala on those railroad tracks and waited for the train. *You* try finding a way of loving yourself after all that. That's what I wanted to tell all those people.

"Nothing bad's going to happen." I kissed Delilah's hair. "I won't let it."

"You've always stuck by me, Laney."

No one knew—not that woman, not anyone except Rose and me—how it was for Delilah sometimes. No one knew how she couldn't go to sleep at night unless I got into bed and held her in my arms. No one knew how she'd wake up screaming from the bad dreams. I'd tell that woman—even now I want to tell them all—but the truth was she didn't deserve to know any of it. It was all mine and Delilah's, still is, ours alone, this story of how in a snap the world can fall down around you and leave you, for years and years, trying to get back to a place where once upon a time you were happy.

"I've always loved you," I said to her. A chill passed over me, and I shivered. When I think of it now, I wonder if Lester felt it, too, wherever he was that night, the chill of all our lives beginning to change, all because I made a vow. "I'll take care of you," I whispered, holding tight to Delilah. "Forever and always. I promise."

"Do you mean it, Laney?"

"I do."

WE HAD TO WORK the next night, our usual eleven-to-seven shift. "Hoot owl," Delilah called it, or sometimes, "the gravedigger." Bobby May, when he was still around, worked nights at the oil refinery in Phillipsport, and she'd picked up those words from him. That was before everything went to pieces.

Lester was already in the break room, clocking in when we got to the store. Delilah said to him, "Another gravedigger shift." She punched her time card. "Enough to bury me. Enough to bury us all."

It was Lester's job to stock shelves when he wasn't corralling carts from the lot. It was a job meant for a high-school kid and not a man Lester's age. It might have even embarrassed him to have to do work like that, but it kept him in groceries and gave him a place to be.

He lived in an old house he rented out on Highway 130, a simple frame house, the paint peeling from the clapboards. I'd been there a couple of times to watch movies. He loved all the *Harry Potter* ones.

One night he said, "You ever think it might be possible? All this magic?"

I told him about Rose's spell that brought Tweet to Delilah and also him to me. "We were just fooling around," I said, "but look what we got for it. We put that wish out into the world."

He didn't laugh the way I feared he might. He just nodded, a very serious look on his face. "Do you ever wish you were better looking?" he asked me. I told him that was no way to sweet-talk a girl. "Sorry," he said. "I just meant... Well, gee, Laney, I thought maybe you were like me." I told him not to worry about it. I knew exactly what he meant, and the answer was yes. Yes, sometimes—hell, who was I kidding, a lot of times—I wished for things I didn't have. "Some people," he said, "they have whatever they want. Why is that, Laney?" Well, that was a million-dollar question. Find the answer to that one, I told him, and you'd really know something. "Sometimes I wonder what it would be like to know magic spells," he said. "I could have more money. I could look like a movie star. I could make people like me."

When Delilah said what she did that night about the gravedigger, he just started rattling about how he was out driving before he came to work and he went down Whittle Avenue, past the South End, and who should he see coming out the door but Tweet. Lester was shy about it, but he had a little grin on his face, and I got the idea that he was telling Delilah this because he hoped she might put in a word for him and get him back on Tweet's good side, get him back in with the band.

Then Lester said, "At first I thought it was you he had with him. Then I saw I was wrong." I think he knew right away the mistake he'd made. He'd been so excited and he'd said too much. Then he got all flustered. He took off his derby hat and tried to twirl it on his finger, but it spun off and fell to the floor right at Delilah's feet. She gave it a little kick, and Lester had to chase after it. He stooped to pick it up. "I'm sorry," he said. Then he turned and walked out of the break room, and there was Delilah, who had too many hours ahead of her to imagine the worst.

"Ain't that dandy?" she said to me. Already, the tears were starting to come. She dabbed at her eyes with the heel of her palm.

"Maybe it doesn't mean a thing." I handed her a tissue. "You don't know."

"I know enough to be afraid." She blew her nose on the tissue and threw it in the trash. "Hell of a way to start a shift," she said. Then she went out into the store.

I worked checkout twelve that night, right across from the Vision Center. Delilah was on the floor, setting up displays in Women's Wear. I caught a glimpse of her from time to time, and I could tell from the look on her face that she was mulling it over, this news that Tweet was coming out of the South End with another woman. Lester hadn't said who that woman was, and neither Delilah nor I had said the name, Rose, for fear that saying it would make it true.

Then, around two in the morning, when the store had emptied out except for a handful of customers shuffling up and down the aisles—"the Zombies," we always called them—I noticed that Delilah had Lester cornered by the Vision Center. She had him backed against the security grate that slid down in front of the center when it was closed. She poked him in the chest with her finger. A skinny man with glasses too big for his face came to my register, and as I scanned his items, I kept my ears open for what Delilah was saying.

"Who was she, Lester? That girl you saw Tweet with?"

"What girl?"

"Coming out of the South End. Was it Rose?"

"I couldn't tell."

"It was Rose, wasn't it?"

"Really, Delilah, it was dark. I'm not sure."

"Don't lie to me."

"I'm not."

Delilah said, "You know I could make you pay." She was talking big now, but I couldn't help but think of that .38 she carried. "I've got ways. I swear, Lester, don't mess with me."

"I've got to get back to work."

He tried to brush past her, but she grabbed him by his arm and spun him around so violently, his derby hat slipped down over his face, and he had to grab at it to get it straight again.

"You better tell me the truth," she said.

I could see it was a hard thing for him to say. He must have known it was going to get back to Tweet that he'd tattled, and then there wouldn't be a chance in the world that he'd ever hang around with the band again. But there was Delilah, mean as she could be. I could tell she was squeezing his arm so hard it hurt, gouging him with her nails, and finally—maybe just to get her to stop—he said yes. "Yes," he said. "It was Rose."

Delilah's spine stiffened. She held him a moment longer. Then she let him go, and she stomped away. I watched her until she turned down an aisle in Housewares and disappeared from view. My customer was gone, and I was alone.

Lester came over and said, "What's she talking about, Laney?"

I know I should have told the truth, should have told him Delilah was just blowing hot air to try to get back at him because she didn't know what else to do in light of the news that he'd given her. I should have put him at ease, told him it wasn't his fault that he'd seen what he'd seen. The real fault lay with Tweet. It had nothing to do with Lester. I should have made that clear to him, but something held me back. Maybe I liked having this one person in my life who was so taken with me he'd believe anything I said.

So I told him there were as many ways to hurt people as there were to help them. We all had that power and we needed to be careful how we used it.

"Tweet told me to stay away after he took up with Delilah," Lester said. "You don't think that hurt?"

"That's what Delilah was trying to say." I was thinking about Tweet and Rose and what might happen now that Delilah had the facts. "Keep your eyes open. You never know who might be out to get you."

AS SOON AS our shift ended, Delilah said, "C'mon."

We jumped in the Malibu and drove to New Hope. We drove east on Route 50 and made the turn south on the New Hope Road. Delilah didn't say a word the whole way. I'd seen her like this once before, the day she bought that .38 and she said let Bobby May try to come after her with a knife again and see what would happen. I knew enough to keep my mouth shut. Once she had her mind set on something, I couldn't talk her out of it even if I wanted to. I knew she was on her way to New Hope to ask Tweet what was what, and I wasn't sure how I felt about that. Certainly a little sad, because I'd seen what that mess with Bobby May did to her, and I was afraid it was going to happen again with Tweet. A little excited, too, because I knew if everything came apart, she'd turn to me for comfort and, at least for a while, we'd be closer. I know I should be ashamed to admit that, but truth be told, I'm not. I still know the girl I was then—a girl starved for love—and when I think back on it, I can't say I'd have done anything different. I'd have been who I was, having to live through all that I did in order to know the things I do now.

So we drove toward what was waiting. The sun was up, burning off a little ground fog that lingered over the fields. I could make out the dark shapes of crows pecking at the ground. Old trash birds, my mother called them, but to me, there was something about them that was all right. I think it was their calls and the way they were so urgent that plucked something in my heart and made me think of people like Lester and Delilah and Rose and me, people who had things to say if we could just figure out a way to make the world listen.

A murder of crows. That's what a pack of them are called. A shrewdness of apes, a troop of baboons, a wake of buzzards. I've made a little hobby out of knowing such things, now that I've got time. A raft of ducks, a convocation of eagles, a seething of eels. Amazing, all the names we have for animals and who they are when they're together.

The water tower stood tall at the edge of town, black letters painted across the curve of its tank announcing NEW HOPE. Mother always said it was an unfair burden on its citizenry, given the fact that so much had dried up in that place—the grain elevator was gone, as was the post office and the school and the general store, where once upon a time folks could buy everything from hardware to groceries. Most of the people in town were just hanging on—212 of them by the government's last count. A bedroom community to Mt. Gilead, if you wanted to give things a positive spin. A ho-hum, no-chance-in-hell town if you wanted to tell the truth. A nowhere place in southeastern Illinois, laid out in the middle of farmland, a town of retired folks and too many meth addicts and people just waiting for the next thing.

People like Tweet.

He didn't know what was coming that morning. Like any of us, he had no way of seeing what was bearing down on him from the future. It was just an early-summer morning, birds singing in the trees as Delilah pulled the Malibu into Tweet's driveway and shut off the motor.

We sat there awhile. It was a beautiful morning, the air cool the way it is here in early summer before the sun gets full up, and I listened to the birds and watched Tweet's neighbor, Curtis Hambrick, and his grandson, Poke, out in their garden, picking lettuce and sweet peas. They stooped and bent and moved up and down the rows. I could hear the sweet peas make little clicking noises as they fell into the plastic bucket Poke Hambrick carried. Poke's real name was Gerald, but no one except his grandfather called him that.

Poke was the curious sort, always sticking his nose into other people's business. He was living with his grandfather because his mother was a meth addict, and his father—well, it was anyone's guess what happened to him.

"I guess I got to go in there," Delilah said.

"You want me to stay in the car?"

She shook her head. "Nah, I want a witness."

When we got out of the Malibu, Poke straightened up from his picking and gave us a wave. He was at that age, fifteen, where he was eager to grow up, where he thought himself, as his grandfather said from time to time, "too big for his britches." And he was—big for his age, that is. A big boy with belly fat that hung over the waistband of his cutoff blue jeans.

"Laney." He waved his arm back and forth over his head like he was drowning and was desperate for someone to save him. "Hey, Laney. Over here."

Sometimes, when I came to visit my mother, I saw him in the garden grubbing out weeds with a hoe. He'd stop from time to time and lean on the hoe handle and gaze off toward Route 50 where cars sped by, and I knew he was imagining where those cars were going and all the places he himself would go when he got the chance. I knew because I'd done the same thing at that age, still did it from time to time, truth be told.

Now he pushed his glasses up on his nose, those thick-lensed glasses that magnified his eyes so much I sometimes had trouble looking at him, and he waited for me to acknowledge him.

"Hey, Poke," I finally said, and I gave him a wave.

"Go talk to your boyfriend if you want," Delilah said.

It was clear that Poke had a schoolboy crush on me, and she always gave me a hard time about that.

"You're the one with a boyfriend to talk to," I said.

Mr. Hambrick was on his knees in the lettuce patch. He was hard of hearing, but even he could hear Poke's shouts to me. Mr. Hambrick took his straw hat off his head and waved it at me. He was wearing bib overalls over a white T-shirt, and one gallus had slipped off his shoulder.

"Laney, you want some lettuce and sweet peas to carry to your mama?"

"Maybe in a little while, Mr. Hambrick." I had to shout to make myself heard.

He nodded his head, put his straw hat back on, and kept picking.

Then Tweet's front door flew open, and he came out onto the step, barefoot and wearing nothing but a pair of jeans. His bony chest was white and freckled. His dreadlocks stuck out at odd angles from his head. I saw a shadow step back from the screen door behind him.

"Delilah." He came down the steps and walked toward us across the yard. "Baby," he said, and he gave Delilah a hug.

"Who's in there?" She pushed free from him, and I knew she'd seen the shadow, too. "Don't lie to me, Tweet."

He scratched his head. "Baby," he said again.

"It's her, isn't it?"

He stuck his hands in his pockets. He bowed his head.

"There she is," Delilah said, though I didn't think she'd seen a thing. I was watching that screen door, alert for the slightest movement behind it, and I'd noticed nothing. "There's Rose."

He raised his head then, and just for an instant he looked behind him. That was all it took, that glance, to tell Delilah that what she suspected was true—Rose was in that house and probably had been since the time Lester had seen her and Tweet leaving the South End.

Delilah slapped him across the face, and he didn't say a word. What could he say? He was caught.

"Let's go, Laney." She stomped off toward the Malibu, and that was that.

UNTIL EVENING when I said, "I'm going to talk to her."

Delilah was at the bathroom mirror, holding a damp washcloth to her eyes, which were red and puffy from the buckets she'd cried since we'd been back from New Hope. I'd let her. I'd had no choice.

She'd closed the door to her bedroom, and I'd listened to her sobbing. Finally, I couldn't stand it, so I opened the door and I went to her bed. I tried to hold her to me, but she squirmed away. "Just leave me alone," she said. "There's nothing you can do." I didn't like the way she barked at me. I'd promised to take care of her and now she wouldn't let me. I lingered, hoping she'd give in and slip into my arms and let me comfort her. I'd rock her while she cried. I'd tell her everything would be all right. But nothing like that happened. She just stared at me as if somehow she found me to blame for the fact that Rose and Tweet had thrown in together. "I know you've always liked Rose," she said. "I suppose you're happy about all this. If you ask me, Tweet turned to her because you were always hanging around us. Just like a little sister, always in the way."

I told her she was being ridiculous, but she rolled away from me, turning her face to the wall, and I went out into the hallway, closing the door behind me. I left her alone until evening when she came out to get ready for our shift at work, and I told her that tomorrow I was going to have a little chat with Rose.

"Why would you want to talk to that tramp?"

"I want to know what's what. I want you to know it, too. I want you to understand that I didn't have anything to do with Tweet having his eye on her."

Her voice got softer. "I never should have accused you of anything. I was just hurting. I'm sorry."

"It's all right," I said, even though I was still smarting from the way she'd treated me. "But I'm still going to see what I can find out."

"Don't, Laney. Just let it go."

"I can't. I have to know why this happened so you can know it, too."

"Laney . . ."

I should have let that be the last word. I know that now. I'll have years and years to know it. But then I only wanted to prove to Delilah that I loved her. "It's wrong what Rose did. She needs to know that."

Delilah took my hand. She put her face up close to mine. She let me slip my arms around her and press her to me. She whispered in my ear, "Not just know it. She's got to pay."

MOTHER BELIEVED IN the signs: A shooting star meant someone just died. A toad crossing your path meant your sweetheart was nearby. Dream about the moon, and money was coming your way. I grew up with such talk, my mother's girl through and through. She taught me what to watch for, the signs and the portents. So when I borrowed Delilah's Malibu and drove out to New Hope to have a chitty-chat with Miss Rose MacAdow, and I saw a dove settled on the roof of Tweet's house, cooing its mournful sound, I knew there was nothing but ill fortune behind the front door.

Rose, though, was chipper as could be when she answered my knock. It didn't faze her a bit that I was there.

"Hey, Laney," she said. "What's shakin'? You looking for Tweet?"

"It's you I'm wanting to talk to."

She grinned. "Well, it's a good thing, because I'm the only one here. Tweet's in town."

The day had broken clear. It was one of those June mornings with a high blue sky, not even a wisp of a cloud, and dew sparkling on the grass. New Hope was quiet, just the sound of a screen door slapping the frame somewhere up the street. Someone was coming or going, and someone else was getting ready to tar a roof. I could smell the hot sulfur in the air.

I hadn't been to bed after my shift. I'd waited until Delilah was asleep, and then I'd taken the Malibu.

"It's about Tweet," I said to Rose.

"I guess Delilah's going to try to cause trouble." She turned and walked into the house, leaving the door open, so I could follow. "Well, let her try. Tweet's finished with her."

Rose had been fast about staking a claim to the place. It was clear she'd moved in for the long haul. In a few days' time, she'd done the sorts of things only a woman can do to a house. She'd draped a crocheted afghan over one arm of the couch. A candle burned on the coffee table and gave the air a scent of cinnamon. A vase of silk tulips, red and yellow, sat in the center of the dining-room table, on top of a white lace runner.

I took a deep breath. "Cinnamon," I said.

"Woman's touch," said Rose, and she winked at me. She ran her hand over the afghan, and I could see she was satisfied with everything she'd been able to do to turn Tweet's head. I couldn't say I approved, but I had to admit that a warm feeling came over me, much to my surprise. That's how happy she was, how content. So happy I couldn't help but feel it, too, even though I tried to convince myself that I didn't for Delilah's sake.

I thought of the days when Rose lived with us, and I remembered that she always had a way, even when things were good, of making

Delilah feel that she didn't quite measure up. Rose was always giving her tips on how to use makeup and how to dress, as if Delilah didn't know how to look after herself. Even when Rose gave her a compliment—maybe she'd say, "It's really interesting what you've done with your hair"—she did it with the back of her hand. One day, she said, "Delilah, those jeans look good on you. They make your butt seem smaller." It took a while for that one to sink in, for Delilah to understand that Rose had just insulted her. "Where does she get the nerve?" Delilah said to me. "Like she's some catch."

But apparently she was, at least to Tweet.

I asked her straight out how she'd done it, how she'd wrangled him away from Delilah.

Rose gave me a sad smile, the kind that said she understood something I didn't. "Oh, Laney, you think he wasn't looking?"

"He had Delilah," I said.

"Sweetie, can't you see he'd never be able to make a life with her?"

"She loves him."

"Not enough to matter." Rose leaned over and blew out the candle. "She went and embarrassed him that night up at Dark Bend. Kissed him in front of all those people, ground herself against him." Rose shook her head like it was all a shame. "Like she was a whore, Laney. And then she pulled that gun? That was crazy. She's one of those women who try too hard, who go off the deep end. Women like that always get left out in the cold."

I knew I was in over my head. Even though I had Lester, I didn't really know a thing about what it was that brought men and women together and kept them there the rest of their lives. I couldn't let Rose know that, though. I had to stick up for Delilah.

"You stole him," I said.

Rose gave me that sad smile again. She even reached out and touched my face. Her hand was warm and I liked the way it felt against my cheek. It made me remember how, when she used to run with me and Delilah, she always had a way of making me feel like I mattered to her. Whatever her reasons, she liked me. "He found *me,* Laney." She leaned in and kissed me on my forehead. "Guess my spell worked, didn't it? You tell Delilah that."

I COULDN'T. Not for the life of me. I couldn't let Delilah know that Tweet had just turned his back on her, simple as that. He took a hard look that night at Dark Bend, Rose said, and decided to set his sights elsewhere. Was it any wonder, the way Delilah was such a tramp that night? And of course, there was the matter of that .38. *Good God, Laney. She's crazy. Who can blame Tweet for getting away from that mess?*

He said as much himself. As I was leaving the house he now shared with Rose, he pulled his old van into the driveway and called to me. He got out and walked across the grass to where I was standing, and I let him come to me with that long, easy stride of his, the one that always made me feel that no matter how dicey things got, he'd stay cool as could be, and everything would be all right.

"Laney-Girl," he said. It felt good to hear that nickname, like we were old friends who wouldn't stop getting along just because he and Delilah were on the outs. "Did Delilah send you out here?"

I shook my head. "There's more to me than Delilah, you know. I can make my own choices."

He put his hands on top of my shoulders, bent down, and touched his forehead to mine. I breathed in his scent, a smell of sheets left to dry on the line, a clean, fresh scent that made me want to stay close to him forever. "You remember that, Laney. Don't let her run your life."

We were whispering, and I wondered what Rose would think if she looked out the window and saw us. Then I realized she probably wouldn't think a thing because I was Laney Volk—Little Bit. I'd never be a threat to steal another woman's man.

"Is that how you felt with Delilah?" I asked Tweet. "Like she owned you? Like there was no room to be you?"

"You know the story, don't you, Laney-Girl?"

I suppose I did. I didn't know it until he asked me, but once he did, it hit me so hard it nearly made me tear up. It was one of those moments you can't see coming even though it's been waiting for you all along. A moment to take your breath away with how true it is. As soon as Tweet asked me that question, it became clear to me that this was the way I'd started to feel about Delilah, like being in her shadow was making me invisible. I didn't want to say that to Tweet, though—didn't want him to know I was afraid of losing myself—so I didn't say a word. I turned my head to the side and told myself not to cry.

He started talking about the day he and Delilah ran that Mustang to Terre Haute and how they came back in that Ford Explorer and she said she wanted all those kids. "It was like she was mapping everything out," he said, "and it scared me." I started to tell him that she was only making up what she thought he wanted to hear, but just then he took a deep breath, and I let him go on. "With Rose, I can breathe. She takes things as they come. Delilah always made me feel like I was marching to her time."

"So you left her?" I wanted to verify what Rose had told me. "You looked around and you found Rose."

"I'm a grown-up, Laney. We're all grown-ups here."

I TOLD DELILAH THAT. She was waiting for me when I got back to the trailer. She was sitting at the breakfast table, drinking a cup of coffee. "Well?" she said as soon as I stepped through the door, but she didn't look up from her coffee, as if she was afraid to face what might be coming.

My mouth just started running. I told her about the candle and the silk tulips and the lace runner Rose had on the dining table. Delilah let me yak, until finally she put down her coffee cup, looked me straight in the eye, and said, "What are you trying to say?"

I told her we were all grown-ups, and I guess we'd have to face the fact that sometimes people fell out of sorts and found other people to love.

"It's no one's fault," I said. "It just happens."

Her eyes went hard. She pressed her lips together in a tight line. Finally, she said, "Now you've got Lester, you think you're the expert when it comes to matters of the heart? Come on, Laney. What could a kid like you really know?"

It was a hurtful thing to say, and I knew she meant it to be.

"You can't run people's lives, Delilah." The words were out before I could stop them. "And you can't make Tweet love you again. He's gone. He's with Rose."

"Sounds like you're taking her side."

"I'm just saying—"

"You've said too much, Sister." She carried her coffee cup to the sink. She turned her back to me. "You better stop while you're ahead."

But I couldn't. I pressed on. I was always a fool back then. Just couldn't stay away from trouble. Couldn't look far enough down the road to see where I might be heading. I was living on trust, hoping for a sign of where I should go and what I should do.

I said to Delilah, "You'd miss me if I took a notion to leave."

She spun around, a scared look in her eyes. "Go back to your mama, then." She chewed on her lip, and I could tell she was trying to decide whether to say the rest of it. "You're nothing, Laney. Nothing I'd miss."

I felt an ache in my throat, and I knew if I stood there a second longer, I'd start to cry. I didn't want her to see how much she'd hurt me. "We'll see," I said. Then I turned and walked out of that trailer, telling myself it was for good.

From a pay phone at the B&L Liquor Store, I called Lester. "Come get me," I told him, and he said he would.

He took me to his house. He drove the whole way, quiet, like I asked him to. It felt like Delilah and I were at the end, and the thought of it left me all scraped out and empty.

"We're here," he said when he pulled into his driveway, like this was our house and where else would we have been going but home?

"Could I just sit here awhile?" Even though it was hot, the sun full up and warming the inside of Lester's truck, I didn't want to move, didn't want to take the next step down whatever road I was traveling. "Please," I said, and he told me yes.

"I'll sit here with you, Laney." He switched off the ignition and without the engine noise such an awful silence settled down around us. "We'll just sit."

Then a mockingbird started singing somewhere close by, and the air around us was suddenly full of its song, a stream that went from some of the prettiest music you could ever hear to squeaks and barks and chewks, a whole repertoire of what the bird had listened to and was now imitating: other birds, creaky gates, people whistling, machinery—anything was fair game.

"That's a mockingbird," Lester said, and then we just sat there in the sun some more.

Finally, I couldn't stand the silence, and I said, "I don't know where to go."

"We're here now." He reached over and put his hand on mine. "We're right here. You and me."

At that moment, it was the most wonderful feeling in the world to feel his touch and to hear his gentle voice. That gap between his front teeth made him seem younger than he was. That and his pale skin, hardly marked except for a line of three freckles across one cheek. Those freckles were enough to make me want to touch his face, to brush back the hair poking out from under the brim of his derby hat. It was the hat that made him seem like someone who knew things I didn't. Someone who had stepped out of another time. Someone who could make magic happen. I needed to know I was worth caring for, and he gave me that. He looked at me with those blue eyes that struck me as being tinged with a beautiful, hard-earned knowing, and he seemed to be saying that he understood what it was to be at a crossroads, that place where your life could go this way or that, and you wouldn't know until after it was done if you'd chosen the right path.

"Tweet said you were in Iraq." I said it before I could stop myself, and once I did, I wished I could grab the words from the air and stuff them back into my mouth. "I'm sorry, Lester. I know it's none of my business."

"I was in the war." He didn't shy away from what I'd asked. It was like he'd been waiting for someone to ask it, so he'd have a chance to tell the story. "When I got out, my folks said I was someone they didn't know."

He said he'd told them about the things he'd seen. Horrible things. And the things he'd done. Things he'd had to do to stay alive. One thing put him over the edge. One thing he kept trying to forget even if his folks couldn't. He didn't want to tell me because it was too gruesome to tell and he was afraid that like his folks, I'd turn away from him.

"If I tell it," he said, "you'll have it in your head forever, and I don't want that to happen to you."

I laced my fingers through his. "You can say it if you want. Like you said, it's just you and me. We're right here."

A little breeze came up, and all of a sudden the mockingbird was gone and the quiet was back, and I listened to the wind moving through the leaves on the maple in the front yard, a shivery noise that raised goose bumps on my arms and left me feeling like I'd just opened a door to my heart, and Lester was about to step on through.

"It was in Al-Qa'im near the Syrian border of Iraq," he said. "Operation Matador. We were after Al-Qaeda fighters. Intelligence told us they were there."

I knew about Al-Qaeda and Osama bin Laden, and everything that happened after 9/11.

"Warplanes were dropping bombs." Lester wouldn't look at me. He kept looking down at our hands, still laced together. "Then the Chinooks came in and the gunners were firing. Finally, we were sent in on foot to sweep through homes and mosques—any building where we were convinced Al-Qaeda fighters might still be hiding. In one house, there'd been a wedding going on. I saw the lutes and drums and flutes, the bodies of men and women. I saw the headless body of a little boy. I saw things like that, Laney."

I let the seconds go by, feeling inside me such a sadness over what Lester had lived through. He'd been right when he'd been afraid to tell me; now I had it all in my head, and I didn't know what to do with it.

Then he told me something worse.

"Some of the people were still alive." His voice broke then, and I watched him as he gathered himself. He took his hand away from mine and rubbed it over his face, letting it linger at his chin as he stared off through the windshield, going back in his memory, I imagined, to what he was about to tell me. Finally, he eased his hand down to his lap. He bit his bottom lip once. Then he turned to me, and in a rush, as if he couldn't bear to have the words in his mouth any longer, he said the rest of his story. "They were alive, but no one called for the medics. Our sergeant gave the order. 'Put 'em down,' he said, and that's what we did. We put our rifles to their heads. One shot was all it took, and then we moved on."

"Were they Al-Qaeda fighters? You said it was a wedding, right?"

"It was a wedding. They might have been just folks. No one asked. We did what we were told."

"You?"

"Yes, Laney. Me."

That's when he let go of my hand and turned his face away from me. He looked out his window.

I put my hand on his back and rubbed slow, gentle circles. "I'm still here," I told him. "It's going to be all right." And though I said it, I had no idea how to help him. "Let's go inside," I said, and that's what we did.

We were never lovers. I want that known. We were just two people, a man and a woman, who had each other's company at a time when they both needed that. I stayed at Lester's the rest of that day. I slept on his couch. He slept in his bed. Finally, after it was dark, we both got up, and he fried us some hamburgers. We sat at the old chrome-edged breakfast table and ate our burgers and talked a little about nothing that mattered—just the weather and whatnot and what we'd be doing later at work. Then he said, "I never should have told you that stuff about Iraq."

He seemed so miserable, afraid that he'd told me things that would make me turn away from him. I didn't know what to do but trust him with a story of my own. That's how I came to tell him about Delilah and me having a falling-out and why I'd called for him to come and get me.

"She said I was nothing she'd ever miss."

Lester shook his head. "That's a mean thing to say. How can someone be a friend to you and then turn around and say something like that?"

I let the question go unanswered, rather than face what I suspected was the truth. Deep in the heart we were all like that, all mixed up with meanness.

"Lester," I said, "Rose taught me some of her magic." She'd even given me a book on it that told how to cast all sorts of spells, some for love, some for revenge. "Spells," I said to Lester. "Hexes. Things like that."

He put down his burger. He crossed his arms on the table and leaned toward me. His voice was a whisper. "I've always thought if anyone had the gift, it was you."

"Why would you think that?"

"I feel it in your energy."

"You've got that kind of energy, too," I said, and that pleased him.

"I've never tried to cast a spell," he said. "Do you think I could?"

I was just tagging along at this point, letting him go where he wanted—at least that's what I told myself then. "Is the moon full?"

He got up and went to the back door. He opened it and stepped outside, and I heard the night all razzy with insects buzzing and the noise of cars heading up and down Route 130.

"Laney, come out here," he said, and I got up and went outside to where he was standing pointing up at the sky. "The moon," he said, and I looked up and saw it hanging full and bright above us.

He was like a little boy wanting to believe in something so bad, and

I couldn't let him down. "Just say these words," I told him, and I recited a spell I remembered from Rose:

Lady of luck, come out of your hidden course
bless your light upon me as the light of the moon shines above
and in the light of luck I will be blessed, when the moon is next to be full.

He did what I told him, said it all in a whisper, and when he was done, neither of us spoke for a good while. Then he said, "Do you think it'll work?"

"Guess we'll have to wait until the next full moon to see."

"I think it'll work," he said. "Laney, I really think it will."

WHAT DIDN'T WORK was Delilah and me. I had Lester drive me back to the trailer so I could get some clothes and whatnot, and she followed me into what had been my bedroom. She said, "So you moving in with Lester?"

She never said she was sorry, never acted like my leaving made one bit of difference to her.

"What's it matter to you?" I said.

She shrugged her shoulders. "Guess it doesn't." She turned then and walked out of the room.

I changed into my work clothes—khaki pants and navy blue polo shirt—and then packed as much as I could stuff into the old Army duffel of my dad's that I kept around: more khakis and blue polo shirts, underwear, some shorts and T-shirts, flip-flops, the book on hexes and spells Rose gave me. I slung the duffel over my shoulder and went out into the living room.

Delilah was at the kitchen sink washing dishes, a chore I'd always done. She was cleaning a vegetable grater. I said her name, and when I did, she looked up from the grater and she pricked her finger on one of its teeth.

"Damn it, Laney," she said, and then stuck her finger in her mouth.

"Sorry," I said, and I hated myself for saying it. "I'll come back later for the rest."

I stood there awhile, giving her a chance to say something to keep me there, to make it clear that I mattered to her.

She took her finger out of her mouth and looked at the cut. "I need a Band-Aid," she said, and she went down the hall to the bathroom.

I listened to the squeal of the medicine cabinet door, a sound I'd heard time and time again, and I thought of all the things about the trailer that had always annoyed me—that door, the sagging spot in the floor of the living room, the windows that were hard to slide open—things that, no matter how irritating, had been our things, Delilah's and mine, in this place we called home. I waited a few more seconds to give her the chance to come out of the bathroom and say something that would keep me from walking out the door, and when she didn't, I went out to the truck where Lester was waiting.

"Ready?" he said, and when I didn't say a word, he finally put the truck in gear and backed away from the trailer.

When he swung around to head out the driveway, I looked back, and that's when I saw Delilah at the window, watching. It was all I could do to keep myself from telling Lester to stop. I wanted to run back into the trailer and tell her I knew she was sorry for what she'd said to me. I wanted to throw my arms around her and tell her I needed her, but it was too late for that—at least that's what I told myself then; I was on my way.

AFTER WORK, I asked Lester to drive me to New Hope. I went to my mother's house, and I told her I wanted to come home.

"What about Delilah?" Mother stood with her hands on her hips. She was a little woman, like me, legs and arms starved of flesh, but she didn't take guff. She had a strong jaw that she jutted out ahead of her like she was daring someone to take a poke at it. "What's gone on with the two of you? I thought you were like that." She held up her hand and crossed her pointer over her index finger. "Two peas in a pod."

"Nothing, Mother." I dropped my duffel onto the floor. "I just thought you might need some company."

"Bull." She took me by the shoulders and put her face close to mine. "You've had a falling-out. I can see the hurt in your eyes."

I was glad to have it out in the open. I told her yes, it was true, and she wanted to know what it was about. I told her the story of Tweet and Rose. I told her that's where it started, and Delilah thought I was taking sides.

"Well, lonely hearts find lonely hearts," Mother said. Then she gathered me into her arms and held me. Just like that, she forgave me for leaving home, for dropping out of school, for running with someone like Delilah.

"Maybe I should finish school," I said. "I could get my GED, and then maybe college."

She eased back from me and held me with her hands on my shoulders. I could see the light come into her eyes. She kept her voice steady like she didn't dare hope for too much, but it was there, that hope, and I wanted to make sure she kept having it. Who knew? Maybe I could believe in it, too. I could find my way back to the path she'd imagined for me all along. I could sing.

"We can make that happen," she said. "If you're sure that's what you want."

"It is," I told her.

It felt so good to be home, to have my mother touch me, to breathe in the scents I'd always known as hers: the rose of her Avon Sweet Honesty perfume and the woodsy smell that lingered on her clothes from her cedar-lined closet. I wanted to sleep in my bed under the slanted second-story ceiling. I wanted the window open so I could feel the night breeze and smell the honeysuckle and the fresh-cut hay curing in the fields around New Hope. I wouldn't have to smell the stink of the poultry house in Bird Town. Delilah could sleep there and make whatever life she was going to make without me.

"So it's all right for me to come back?" I asked Mother.

"Yes, baby, it's finer than frog hair in March." She looked out through the screen door. "Who's that in the truck that brought you?"

"That's Lester. He works with me."

"Are you two sweethearts?"

"We see each other now and then."

She nodded. "I'll put fresh sheets on your bed, while you tell him good-bye."

I went out to the truck and I thanked Lester for taking care of me when I needed him to.

"I'll do whatever I can for you. Really, Laney. I mean it. Whatever you need."

"I'm all right now."

When he backed out onto the street, I waved at him and he gave me a smile. Then he headed out to the highway and I stood there, missing him. I faced the truth—I was gone from Delilah. I was back in New Hope, and I'd given Mother reason to believe I could make something of my life. I could be the person she'd always had faith I was—a good-hearted girl with a singing voice the likes of which no one would be apt to forget. All I needed to do was to make friends with that girl again, to ask her to forgive me for running off and leaving her behind. I needed to get away from that other life, the one that put me in places like the Boar's Nest in Dark Bend with a woman like Delilah, who could make a scene by pulling a .38 and waving it about. I hadn't known it then, but despite how much I wanted to take care of her, I'd been too close to trouble, about to lose myself forever. Things would be different, I told myself, now that I was home.

But Rose was just up the street. That morning in June, I didn't know that in the days to follow—all through the autumn and winter and into the next spring—I'd find myself caught between her and Delilah, unable to determine what was true, even the stories I'd tell myself. Stories I still think on, wondering how in the world they could ever be real. Stories I'd change if I could.

MISS BABY

Pablo moved in with Emma, imagining that if the police or the Rangers or Slam Dent came for him, the house next door to mine would be so obvious they'd overlook it. That's what we were betting on.

"I'm tired of running," Pablo said. "Miss Emma, what do you say?"

We were in my house, and Pablo was resting on the couch, his arm in a proper sling now that Carolyn and Donnie had picked one up at the medical supply store.

Emma stooped over to look at the cuts and bruises on Pablo's face. She reached out a trembling hand and almost touched him before she stopped herself and pulled back her hand. "Mercy, God," she said. "Hadn't no one ought to do a body like that. I don't care how much call there is."

"World's a rough place, Miss Emma," Pablo said. "No one has to explain meanness. It just is what it is."

"You don't have to tell me that, Pablo Omar Maximillian Ruiz." Emma stamped her little foot. "You think anyone can live as many years as I have and not know that?"

"I don't want to trouble you, Miss Emma, but I swear I don't know what else to do but squirrel up at your house."

"A fugitive," she said. "Lord-a-mighty. I must be out of my head."

I suspected that, secretly, it pleased her. A man to take care of. A little danger to boot. Her husband, the late Mr. Hart, was an employee of Jack Ruby, the man who shot JFK's assassin, Lee Harvey Oswald. Mr. Hart played saxophone in the five-piece bump-and-grind band at the Carousel Club, Ruby's burlesque joint on Commerce Street in Dallas, and for years after Ruby killed Oswald, the FBI kept an eye on Emma and the Mister in case they knew anything about the plot to kill the president. There was talk, of course, that the Mafia was involved and that when Ruby killed Oswald, he was making sure none of the story came out. To Emma, it was business as usual. The late Mister had a history of shady dealings—mysterious phone calls in the middle of the night, men knocking on the door and asking for him, sudden money that took Emma out on the town to all the best spots—so a little attention from the FBI was nothing. In fact, she told me, it was something that put a little spice on the blah-blah-blah. Having Pablo hiding out in her house would be, I suspected, like old times.

So the deal was done, but still there was the issue of the money, and like I said, we had no answers for that.

"Can't get blood from a turnip," Emma said.

"Unless I'm the turnip," said Pablo. "Then there's plenty to squeeze."

This all took place on a Monday. On Thursday evening, the police came. It was the same officer who'd come the night I'd called to tell the story of Carolyn and Slam. The bug-eyed man with the red mustache and, hidden beneath his shirt, the heart tattoo I'd given him. It was just me and Donnie in my house, having our supper and trying to come up with some way to help Pablo, who was tucked away in Emma Hart's spare bedroom.

"Miss Baby," the police officer said, "we've heard some talk about someone whupping up on a man down on Fry Street. Broad daylight. A Mexican man. Any reason for me to think it might be someone other than Pablo? Slam Dent finally find him, did he?"

I sat back down at the table and picked up a butter knife. "Maybe you should ask Slam Dent."

"Well, I would if I knew where he was."

I spread a little butter on a piece of bread and then laid it on my plate. "Sounds like you just can't keep track of folks."

"People disappear," Donnie said.

"That's right," said the officer, "but they always show up, now, don't they?" He shifted his weight, and the leather of his gun holster creaked. "Mind if I take a look around?"

The portable TV on the counter was tuned to CNN with the volume down low. I could see footage of the war in Iraq: soldiers in camouflage fatigues, rifles drawn as they broke down the door to a squat stone house. What else could I say to the officer but "Go ahead. You won't find Pablo."

I imagined Emma had already seen the patrol car parked along Scripture, had maybe even watched the officer come up to my door. I felt sure she was right now keeping an eye on things, ready to send Pablo out the back if for some reason the officer decided to pay her a visit. We'd cleared out all of Pablo's things, except for the clothes in my bedroom closet, the ones Donnie wore as his own, so I knew the officer wouldn't find anything different than what was there the night he came about Carolyn.

"You ever do anything to Slam Dent from when I called you before?" I put the question to the officer as he came out of the spare bedroom and started toward mine. "About Carolyn? Or can a man get away with holding a gun to a woman's head and making her take off her clothes?"

"Now, Miss Baby, you know there's laws against such things."

"So you did something?"

"Soon as we can find him, you can bet we will."

The officer slipped into my bedroom, and I whispered to Donnie, "If you ask me, they don't want to arrest Slam. They'd rather get on his trail and let him lead them to Pablo."

That's the way it would work, I decided, if the string played itself out too long. Either Slam would be back for Pablo, and he'd finish what he started when he beat him, or else the police would let the hunter take them to the prey. Maybe it would be better if I just turned Pablo in. He'd do time, no doubt about that, but at least he wouldn't end up dead.

I thought about doing it. I really did. I thought about telling that officer exactly where Pablo was.

Then Donnie said, *"Hay mas tiempo que vida,"* and I went dumb. It was something *mi abuelita* used to say whenever I got in a hurry. *"Bebe,"* she'd say, "slow down. There's more time than life."

Hearing Donnie say that gave me the shivers. "I didn't know you could speak Spanish."

He shrugged his shoulders. "It's just something I heard once."

The officer came back into the kitchen then, and my heart leapt because I saw that he had my wallet—he'd found it in my purse and taken it just like that—and he had the Illinois driver's license, the one I'd cut Lester Stipp's name and address from, so now all it showed was his picture and his vital information.

"You've got no right." I got to my feet so fast the kitchen chair fell sideways to the floor. I grabbed for that driver's license, but the police officer jerked back his hand and held it over his head so I couldn't reach it. "You went into my purse," I said. "You've got no legal right to do that."

"Now, Miss Baby, you said I could take a look around." His voice was all singsong like he was talking to a little girl. He tossed my wallet onto the table. "Awful interesting what you can find if you just look hard enough. Now, why would you have this Illinois driver's license in your purse, and who cut the name and address out of it and why?"

Donnie took his wallet out of his hip pocket and opened it. He pulled out the cash and the four-leaf clover laminated in plastic. Then he put them back and folded up the wallet and laid it on the table. He said to me, "Baby?" I knew that, like the police officer, he was waiting for me to explain.

"I had to make a Xerox copy." I talked fast, letting the lie unravel before I could think too much about it. "A copy to carry to the bank so we could open an account. We must have forgot I still had it in my purse."

The officer slapped the license against his palm. "Someone's taken a pair of scissors to this. It's illegal to deface a driver's license, you know."

"Yes," I said, as if I was just noting a fact that didn't mean much at all. "I know that."

The officer waited for me to say more, and when I didn't—when I couldn't find any believable explanation at all—he said to Donnie, "Exactly who are you, Mister?"

Donnie didn't flinch. "I'm Donnie," he said. "Donnie True." Then he went on, only now in a voice that stunned me—hard-edged and straight to the point as it was. "I chopped up that plate. I had my reasons. They don't have anything to do with what you're looking for here."

The officer came over to where Donnie was sitting. He put his hands on the table and leaned in close. "I'm going to take this license, and I'm going to find out who you really are. Once I know that, I'm going to figure out what it is you're ashamed of."

"I didn't say I was ashamed of anything."

"A man cuts out his name and where he comes from?" The officer drew himself up, pushing out his chest. "Mister, that's a man who's trying to hide."

Donnie kept his voice even. "You can't take that license. Baby's right. You've got no legal call."

The officer laughed. He tossed the license onto the table. "Keep it," he said. "I've got everything I need."

Then he was out the door, leaving us to wonder what he meant, leaving Donnie to say to me, "All right, Baby. How come you did it?"

I tried to explain the whole thing. How I found him on the street, and he looked so lost I just claimed him. "Remember?" I said, and he snapped at me. "Of course I remember." I kept talking, telling him about finding his wallet and taking out his driver's license and cutting out his name and address, not wanting him to see them and remember who he was and where he came from, not wanting him to go back home and leave me alone.

Donnie took it all in. Then he said, "So who am I, really?"

"You're Lester Stipp."

"From Illinois?"

"Mt. Gilead. Do you know that place?"

He thought for a good long while. When he looked up, I could see the pain in his eyes. "Yes, I know it."

"And you want to go back there?"

He shook his head. "I wouldn't say that. No. Not really...I don't know."

"Is that why you keep lying to save me? To save us? Do you remember more than you let on?"

"More than I wish I did," he said, and then Emma came through the door.

She was out of breath, and she was waving her hands in the air. "Miss Baby, Pablo needs you. He says you got to go to Deep Ellum. He says you got to go right now."

I WAS SUPPOSED to go to Club Dada, and there I was to meet up with one of Pablo's *hombres,* a man named Amos. He'd have on a panama hat, Pablo told me, a gold cross dangling from his left ear. He'd find me in Club Dada, after the band came on. "Amos," Pablo said. "Remember that." He'd come up and say, "You must be from out of town." That was the sign that I was to follow him. "You go," Pablo said. "You do whatever he tells you to do. He'll take you to where the money is. He's my only chance."

Amos had the money that would save Pablo from Slam Dent, but I knew it wouldn't come free. "What's it going to cost?" I asked.

"One thing at a time," Pablo said. "You let me worry about that. Now go."

So we did, Donnie and I. He was still Donnie to me. I couldn't think of him as Lester because when I did that, I had to face the possibility that I'd end up losing him. We drove down 35E, through the metroplex sprawl—Lewisville and Carrollton and Farmers Branch—toward the lights of Dallas, toward the Bank of America Tower outlined in bright green argon lighting, and the white diamond argyle pattern along the length of Renaissance Tower, and the dandelion ball flashing on top of Reunion Tower.

I was afraid to ask him what he remembered about Illinois and who and what he'd left there, but finally I couldn't stand the silence anymore, and I said, "Why'd you leave where you're from? Why'd you buy a one-way bus ticket to Texas?"

It took him a long time to answer. He kept fiddling with the glove compartment, unlatching the door and then closing it again, over and over, two, three, four times. Then he said, "I was in the war over in Iraq. I saw some things there, did some things, things that are hard to think about now...."

I interrupted him. I could tell he was having a hard time, and as much as I wanted to know the truth, I wanted to save him from whatever misery telling it would bring him. "You don't have to tell me..."

This time he was the one who wouldn't let *me* go on. "No, I want to. I owe that to you. It was after the war that I started having spells. Sometimes I'd just pick up and go. Sometimes I'd know right away what I'd done, and sometimes, like this time, it'd take a while. The doctors told me those spells were amnesia. Fugues, they called them. Dissociative fugues."

"I'm trying to understand," I said.

"Things get hard for me." He shrugged his shoulders. "I guess I just run and I don't even know that's what I'm doing."

I knew then he'd run from something hard back in Illinois, something he wasn't ready to tell me.

"Are you going back?" I asked.

"Right now I'm with you." He reached over and took my hand. He raised it to his lips and kissed it. "Right now that's all I'm thinking."

For the time being, I let that be enough. We crossed over the LBJ

Freeway and took the Woodall Rogers to the Pearl Street exit, and then we were in Deep Ellum. Music thumped from the clubs. The night was on the warm side, even for December in North Texas, and the club doors were open. I could see the bar lights inside and the strobes from the stages. I kept my focus on this man, Amos, we were to meet, and the money he would give us to save Pablo. I didn't know what sort of deal Pablo had struck. I just wanted that money.

We walked past The Bone, and I thought of the story I'd told Donnie about how one night we left there and a man hit him with his fist, and that was the start of his amnesia. Something told me we were beyond the power of stories now. There wasn't anything else I could say to keep Donnie from remembering Mt. Gilead in Illinois and whatever was there he wished he didn't recall.

The clubs and bars and restaurants were in squat buildings that used to be warehouses. Now they were painted bright colors—splashes of pink and blue and green and red. Some of them had murals on the exterior walls. My favorite was "Oddities of Our World" on the side of the Prophet Bar. It was a series of drawings—they looked like pencil drawings, all grays and whites—featuring freaks like Fat Ted, Anaconda, and Zen Man. Some nights before Donnie came, I dreamed that I was on that wall: Lonesome Girl.

He stopped in front of a sign that said HELP US HELP YOU TO BE SAFE AND SOUND IN DEEP ELLUM.

"I hope you know what you're doing," he said.

"You didn't have to come with me." I was testing him, looking for some sign that he'd stay and not go to Illinois. "I'm used to doing things by myself."

"It's not like that." We stood on the sidewalk in front of Club Dada, the grotesque faces that lined its facade looking down on us. Faces with noses elongated, lips stretched, eyes bulging, mouths twisted. "It's not what you're thinking. The reason I don't want to go back." He took my hand. "It's you, Baby. How could I leave you?"

He squeezed my hand, and I felt my heart go, just like it had that first night when I found him. "You and me?" I said.

"You and me, Baby."

Then a crowd of frat boys from SMU went brushing by us with their honeys, their blond sorority babes, and Donnie and I let ourselves get swept along into the club.

The band was already playing. Four rockers who called themselves Watershed. Three guitars and drums. A little on the grungy side: sneakers and jeans and T-shirts. The bass player wore one of those tight-fitting watch caps, and he had a voice that lifted high above the music and rang like a bell, clear and lasting, and went right to my heart when he sang about love gone wrong. "Here we are, in the same dive bar," he sang, and I swore he looked right at me, and I thought, *Exactly.*

Donnie held my arm like he was afraid I'd slip off into the crowd and disappear. I loved the feel of his hand, the way he clung to me. I told myself everything was going to be all right. He wouldn't go back to Illinois. He'd stay with me, and our life together would be the one I'd always dreamed of. We'd get the money we needed to get Pablo out of trouble with Slam Dent, and we'd let everything else run its course.

I kept looking around the club for a man in a panama hat, a man with a gold cross hanging from his ear, but all I saw were the college kids, shaking in front of one another on the dance floor, hopped up on booze and hormones and whatever drugs they took to make them believe they were invincible and this was the most wonderful night that could ever be.

Watershed played a song aimed right at those kids, a song about wearing all the latest clothes and seeing all the coolest shows, and they went wild, dancing hard to the driving beat, lifting their arms over their heads and clapping their hands. They sang along: "My steel toes start kickin'. My new tattoo just ain't stickin'. You've got to break the skin. Take the needle just stick it in."

Tattoo ink lives in scar tissue. That's what keeps it permanent. The needles pierce the top layer of skin, and then the layer beneath it. As deep as that. Over the years that follow, the ink migrates even deeper, which affects the clarity and integrity of the tattoo, but it's still there. It's not going anywhere. I put my arms around Donnie's waist, stood behind him, hugging him like that, wishing that what we had would last forever. Even if it got roughed up or smeared or faded, it'd still be ours. We'd feel it inside. Nothing would ever be able to wash it off, cut it out, burn it away.

"This band," Donnie said, but the music was so loud I couldn't hear the rest. Something about Cheap Trick, that old band from the seventies and eighties. Something about a winter night. Something I didn't think I wanted to hear because I suspected it was something from his old life, something calling to him.

"Keep your eye out for that man," I said, and he quit talking.

I squeezed him more tightly, and that's when I felt a stir of air behind me, and I heard a man's deep voice say, "*Chica,* you must be from out of town."

I turned around and there he was, Amos, the man we'd come to find. He turned and started making his way toward the door. I took a deep breath. I grabbed Donnie's hand, and I did what Pablo had told me to do. I followed.

On the street, Donnie and I walked a few feet behind Amos. He was a tall man with long legs, and he moved quickly down the sidewalk, not even glancing back to make sure we were following. He was tall and slender, his arms swinging, the gold cross earring jouncing from his ear beneath the brim of his panama hat. We were almost to The Bone. He turned down an alley, and I followed.

Then I realized Donnie wasn't with me. I turned around and saw him still standing on the sidewalk.

"Come on," I said. "Hurry."

He wouldn't move, so I went back and grabbed his hand.

"This is how it happened, isn't it?" he said. "That man who hit me.

He was in this alley. I wouldn't give him any money, and that's when he hit me."

I had to say it. "You know that didn't really happen, don't you? You know I made it up."

"It feels real to me. Everything you've told me. It feels like mine."

He was afraid to follow Amos down that alley. That's the thing that was true. Donnie was afraid, and because he was afraid, I was, too.

Then a black Chevy Suburban came creeping down the alley. The headlights swept over Amos. He lifted his arm to shield his face from the headlights' glare. Then he turned and ran toward us, ran out of the alley and sprinted down the street. The Suburban sped up. I pulled Donnie out of its way as it roared past us. The driver was Slam Dent.

A block down the street, Amos disappeared into another alley, and the Suburban followed. I listened to the angry growl of its engine, and I felt the whole world start to fall away from me. What would happen with Donnie and me? What would Pablo say when we came back without the money?

All around me, there was the sound of music and people laughing, but for me the night was now filled with everything that wouldn't happen, and I knew, with a certainty that punched me in the heart and took my breath away, what my *mami* must have felt when she was out on the town and the hours were growing small, and her prospects for love were dim. She must have felt her hope go with a drop so sudden it nearly brought her to her knees, pressed down, as she was, with the knowledge that the only thing real was the life she'd have to go back to, the one she'd left just a few hours before, believing that everything would finally change in a way that would make her happy and blessed forever.

LANEY

So there it was, the summer of 2008, and I was back in New Hope, back in the house I'd grown up in, the two-story clapboard house my mother and daddy bought when they were just starting out. He hired on at AMF Wheel Goods, where he painted bicycles and tricycles and brought me home one of each as I got older. He always smelled of the paint and said, toward the end of his sickness, that it was all he could taste. The fumes got down into his lungs and obstructed his airways. It was finally pneumonia that killed him. Mother kept working as a secretary in the Admissions Office at the community college in Mt. Gilead, and she was still there that summer when I came to live with her.

Each morning, she was getting ready for work when I was coming home from my shift at Walmart. I gave her back the keys to her Corolla, so she could take off.

"We're like a hoot owl and an early bird," she said once. "Who's going to get the worm, Missy, you or me?"

She always looked sharp in her skirts and slacks and her bright blouses. She had her hair cut short in a sassy style that looked cute. She favored costume jewelry and a lot of it, always in silver: bracelets lined up her forearms, drop-pendant necklaces, hoop earrings, even rings for her thumbs and, when she wore little strappy sandals, her toes. Miss Bling-Bling, I called her, and she said, "Just a little sparkle to make the old dame feel pretty."

When she was gone to work, I sat at the kitchen table and ate a bowl of Cocoa Puffs, and maybe some toast, or if she'd left half a grapefruit in the fridge, I'd eat that, too. She'd brought me a brochure about the GED program at the community college, and I looked at it—all those brightly colored pictures of students in classrooms, all those testimonials—*Now that I have my GED, there's no stopping me!* I'd look at that brochure and tell myself, *All right, Missy, today's the day you call that office and get back on track.* But I was scared and sleepy from work, and sooner or later I'd crawl into bed and by the time I woke up it was too late to make that call.

A cornfield stretched between our house and Curtis Hambrick's, and some mornings, before the corn got too high, I'd see Poke out mowing the grass. The Hambrick place was, like ours, a two-story clapboard with a wraparound porch. It was next to Rose and Tweet's, those two houses the only ones at the edge of New Hope. As the corn grew that summer, a little more of the Hambrick house disappeared until finally it was September and all I could see, when I ate my breakfast, was the peak of the roof and the old-time lightning rods needling up toward the sky. I couldn't see a thing of Rose and Tweet's shotgun house on the other side. I still hadn't made that call about classes for my GED.

Some mornings, Poke came to visit me. He'd wait until Mother left in the Corolla, and then in a little while, I'd see his face at the kitchen window.

"Laney? You there?" he'd say, and I'd let him in.

While I ate my cereal, he crossed his arms on the table and put his chin on top of them. His glasses lifted up toward his forehead a little. He liked to tell me everything he knew about the folks who lived in New Hope. He knew, he said, because he listened. He knew because he kept his eyes on things.

He claimed he peeked in people's windows at night. At first I didn't put much stock in that. Where would he get the nerve? I imagined he made up his stories as a way of trying to impress me, and I didn't stop him. What was the harm? When he talked, his voice was soft and shy—

such a surprise for a big rough-looking boy like him—and I didn't mind listening to it, didn't mind the gossip he told, looked forward to it even if I thought it was all a lie. He was company those days I was trying to get used to not having Delilah in my life, and I didn't really care what was on the up-and-up as long as he kept talking. Sometimes I even told myself there might be some truth in his stories just for the satisfaction it gave me to think on the lives of people who were surely talking about me and how I'd dropped out of school and moved in with some trashy woman in Mt. Gilead only to come back home to Mother with my tail between my legs.

Jess Raymond, Poke claimed, sometimes came outside in the middle of the night and sat inside his car crying. "Do you know why?" Poke asked, and I said I didn't. "Because his wife doesn't love him. That's why. She loves Mr. Goad, who drives the mail truck."

Poke told stories about the old-maid schoolteacher, Ida Henline, who sometimes took a wedding dress from the back of her closet, a dress she'd once pinned her hope to, and held it in front of her and turned this way and that, looking at herself in her dresser mirror before "what might have been" became too much for her and she put the dress back in the closet and closed the door.

"She was my third-grade teacher," I said.

"I'm sure that's a great comfort to her," Poke said, and I dug my knuckle into his neck until he flinched.

"You can be mean, Laney."

"You've got no idea, Little Man."

He squinted, sizing me up, and I could see he was trying to decide what to do in the face of this anger that could rise up in me from time to time. The truth was I didn't very much like myself those days. Despite what I'd promised Mother about going back to school, I felt all at loose ends. "Laney, here it is autumn already," she said to me that morning. "You know you can get into those classes anytime." I told her I knew it. I told her maybe I'd call after breakfast, but I knew I wouldn't. Sometimes

I sang for myself when I was alone in the house. I sang those songs from *The Music Man,* and even though I still had my voice, it made me so sad to think about all I'd walked away from when I'd dropped out of school and gone to live with Delilah, that I couldn't bring myself to take that first step to getting back to where I needed to be.

"Don't take it out on me 'cause you lost your girlfriend," Poke said.

I gave him the stink eye. "How do you know about that?"

"Rose and Tweet. I heard them talking."

He went back to his stories. The preacher, Luther Gibson, was carrying on a pen-pal correspondence with a woman in Russia, and Rayanne Fines, the State Farm insurance agent, belonged to an organization called The Mutual UFO Network that documented extraterrestrials.

"You wouldn't even want to know the list of crankers," Poke said, and went on to name everyone in New Hope who was tweaked on meth.

"What'd they say?" I interrupted him. "Rose and Tweet."

I could see he didn't want to tell me. "Not much." His voice got extra soft, and I felt the hurt it gave him to say what he was about to say. "Tweet said you'd never had to do for yourself. Rose said she felt sorry for you."

I DIDN'T WANT Rose MacAdow feeling any kind of sorry for me, so later that morning, I took a walk up the street to pay her a call.

She had the front door open, and when I knocked on the screen door, her voice came from somewhere back in the house. "Laney, come on in."

I stepped inside and saw her at the dining table. She had a portable sewing machine set up there, and she was working on a swath of blue muslin. Her hair was swept up and clipped at her temples with butterfly barrettes, but a couple of strands had worked free and were stuck to each side of her face. She stopped the sewing machine and tucked those strands behind her ears.

"Hot," she said, and she had to raise her voice on account of a box fan was running and making noise. "Too hot for any kind of comfort."

It was one of those September days that was muggy and still, but the wind was starting to stir. I'd seen the storm clouds gathering in the west.

"I hear you and Tweet have got opinions about me." I said it straight-out, and I could tell it caught her by surprise. She gave me a glance, then got extra busy with undoing and redoing her hair.

"I'm really sweating," she said, and I asked her if it was true, what Poke had told me.

She said, "That boy gives me the creeps."

"He told me you said you felt sorry for me."

She finished with her hair and put her foot back to the pedal of the sewing machine. The needle whirred. "You can't trust him, Laney." She lifted her foot, and the needle stopped. She looked right at me. "He looks in people's windows, you know."

Just then, the front door creaked on its hinges, a tickle of wind nudging it, and Rose jerked her head toward the noise. I'd remember that look later. I still can't get it out of my head, that scared look just before the wind blew the door shut, and she put her hand flat against her chest and said, "Lord, God-a-mercy."

"It's just the wind," I said, but that didn't calm her much.

She had to push her chair away from the sewing machine. Her fingers were trembling. "I'm all a mess," she said. She had a glass of tea on the table. She tried to pick it up to take a drink, but her hands were shaking too much, and, finally, she set it back down and said, "Jesus, Laney."

As much as I'd been set on getting after her about what Poke had heard her say, I lost all my steam when I saw the state she was in. She was so spooked, all from a gust of wind, and something about that spooked me, too, like I'd carried the fright inside with me. I couldn't help myself from going to her. I rubbed her arm. "Rose, what's wrong?" I asked her.

"I'm going to have a baby. Tweet and me." She grabbed on to my hand and squeezed so hard I felt it in my heart. "Oh, Laney, I'm so scared."

I won't deny I felt a momentary satisfaction, because I thought, Well, now, there you go, Delilah Dade. You won't have a chance in hell of getting Tweet back now, despite what you might want to believe.

"How far along are you, Rose?"

"Just barely am. I'm due in May."

Her voice shook a little, and I could tell she was scared. I felt how much she needed someone to convince her that everything would be all right. I couldn't bring myself to make a call to the community college about those GED classes, but here was something I *could* do—be a friend to Rose.

"Is it true?" I asked her. "What Poke said. Do you feel sorry for me?"

"Oh, baby." She threw her arms around my neck and held on. "I've always had a soft spot for you."

"He's a lonely kid," I said about Poke. I suppose, give or take a smidge, that was exactly how I felt about myself. Now here was Rose. She was just right up the road, and she needed me. I guess that explains as well as anything why I forgave her for saying she felt sorry for me, why I grabbed on to her as my new sister, the one I had now that Delilah and I were done. Both Rose and my lives were changing, and we were afraid. I thanked my lucky stars that we had each other. I hope that she did, too.

I WENT TO HER and Tweet's house all through the autumn. That was pretty much my life. Work and Rose, and, sure, sometimes I hung out with Lester. He never went with me to Tweet's on account of that business with Helmets on the Short Bus.

"He made it clear he didn't want me around," Lester said, and I could see he was still hurt by Tweet claiming he was stealing from the band. I didn't have the heart to tell him that Tweet had admitted that was a lie. I couldn't tell Lester that the truth was Tweet just didn't want him around. "It's okay that you go there," Lester said. His heart was always sweeter than I deserved. "I know you and Rose are friends, and I wouldn't want to take that away from you."

So there was Rose, and some days Poke found me so he could gab. Mother took me out for supper now and then and sometimes we drove over to Vincennes and did some shopping, and every once in a while, we had supper at the Executive Inn and then ducked into the lounge to watch people sing karaoke. "You should get up there," Mother always said. "Lord, Laney, you could sing rings around all those drips."

I usually said I didn't feel like it, when, really, I was itching to give it a try. What kept me from grabbing that microphone? Somewhere deep inside, I was afraid that singing in front of my mother, even though I knew it would please her, would feel like a confession. I couldn't bear the thought of looking out at her in that audience, knowing how I'd disappointed her, how I was still disappointing her because I couldn't bring myself to take that first step with getting my GED. *Now you're all wrapped up with Rose,* she'd told me. *Honestly, Laney. Do you even want to make something of yourself?*

One night, I screwed up my nerve and did it. I got up onstage, and I chose my song—"A Song for You" by the Carpenters. It was their song, hers and Daddy's. From time to time, as if she'd never done it hundreds of times before, she told me the story of how she had an album with that song on it when she and Daddy started dating, and how one night in her room, she put it on her record player and she held his hand and sang it to him. When she told me the story, she always sang a little of the song. Then she said the same thing she always said—*That was* our *song, Laney. That was our song all our lives.* It was the song my mother put on the CD player in the hospital room, the night my father died. I thought of that when I sang it that night at the Executive Inn.

I sang that song with all the love in my heart, and when I came down from the stage, people were clapping and cheering, and my mother was there to wrap me up in her arms. "Thank you," she said. "Oh, Laney, thank you so much."

Then on the drive home we made fun of the other people we'd seen try to sing that night, and we giggled like kids until finally my mother said, "We're bad, Laney," and I told her, nah, we were just honest, and that started her giggling again.

She'd been so lonely since Daddy died. She reached over and took my hand. "You have a wonderful talent," she said. "Why can't you claim it? Don't you want to?"

"I'm hoping I can someday," I told her. "It just seems strange to me now. That's all."

"Strange?"

"Like I don't deserve it," I said. "Like it was meant for someone else."

We rode along in silence for a while. "I just want you to be happy," she finally said, and I told her not to worry, I would be.

That's what I felt when I was with Rose and Tweet—happy. I liked to listen to the sweet things they said to each other. Rose called him her Tweety Bird; he called her his Cutie Patootie. He had a clarinet and a saxophone, and sometimes he'd pick one up and play something jazzy that would get Rose and me dancing. Other times, he'd get bluesy and we'd sit there listening, bobbing our heads, letting the time tick by and with no concern at all about anything.

One night, Tweet got me to sing. "C'mon, Laney-Girl," he said. "Just like you did that night at the South End."

"Oh, I wouldn't know what song to do."

Since that night of karaoke at the Executive Inn, I'd been thinking about what singing meant to me. Those nights onstage in *The Music Man,* I'd let the songs lift me away from my real life. It was the same thing now. Whenever I sang, I got inside the notes and let them carry me away like they were bubbles. When that last note faded away, and the music stopped, and I had to come back to who I really was, I could barely stand it. I suppose the tragedy of my life was the fact that I was afraid of how much I needed to be someone else.

But that night at Rose and Tweet's, I felt so cozy. So when Rose said I should sing whatever was in my head—"You know, those earworms," she said—I just started in with a song that, for whatever reason, I'd been hearing all day.

It was an old song from a CD Mother had played the night before—the Whitney Houston version of Dolly Parton's "I Will Always Love You." A song that let my voice get big and then tender in all the right places.

Tweet picked up his sax and did a few licks, but for the most part it was just me, my voice soaring and then coming back. I closed my eyes, and then, finally, it happened. I went away from myself. I was all breath and voice. I was a shiver up your spine, a lump in your throat, a reminder of everything, no matter how scruffed up your life might be, that you could still feel.

When the last note faded away, I kept my eyes closed, trying to hold on to who I was inside that song as long as I could. I heard my voice, the last tones of it, still ringing in the air, growing fainter and fainter until finally it was gone, and I had no choice but to open my eyes and come back to the here and now.

Rose's eyes were all soft and wet, and there was a blush on her cheeks. She was looking at me like I'd just handed her life back to her, like I'd given her something she'd never know how to thank me for.

"Oh, Laney," she said.

Tweet gave a low, admiring whistle. "Jesus, girl," he said. "That voice. You should come sing with Helmets on the Short Bus."

I shook my head. "I couldn't. Really, thank you, but no."

"Laney, don't be shy." He was grinning. "You should be going places."

But in truth, I wasn't. I wasn't going anywhere at all. I was stuck in New Hope.

* * *

SOME MORNINGS, when I came home from work, Tweet would be up, messing around with his clarinet or saxophone. I'd hear the music as I drove by. On Fridays, after I had some breakfast, I went over to Mr. Hambrick's. He'd started paying me a little money to clean his house once a week.

One morning, he was sitting on his front porch. The air was still, and we could hear the clarinet music coming from Rose and Tweet's.

"That's 'Jumpin' at the Woodside,' " Mr. Hambrick said. "Count Basie. I saw him play the Lakeview once."

As hard as it was to believe, there'd been a resort hotel west of town before the state bought up the land and turned it into a nature preserve and park. People came from Chicago and St. Louis and Indianapolis and Memphis, even farther south, riding up on the train, *The City of New Orleans,* to spend a week or more relaxing at the hotel. Mr. Hambrick had photographs inside his house, framed and hanging on the wall. I dusted them each Friday and stood awhile admiring the grand hotel with its sprawling verandas and the manicured lawns stretching down to the lake. I studied photos of guests navigating that lake on paddleboats and photos of folks dressed to the nines for dinner in the ballroom and then dancing later to the likes of Count Basie and his orchestra, who, as Mr. Hambrick pointed out, had traveled to the heart of the country to play the Lakeview.

Some evenings before work, I went riding with Lester. He came to Mother's house, and we sat around awhile with her, and she told us stories about how she first took notice of Daddy at a basketball game in Mt. Gilead. The regional finals back in 1987. "We couldn't take our eyes off each other," she said. "I thought I'd die if he didn't ask me out."

All my life, whenever I'd risked my heart, I'd had it stomped. Once in high school, I worked up my nerve and wrote a boy a love letter. "I love you," I said. "I dream about you at night." The boy tacked it on a bulletin board in the hallway for everyone to read. The rest of the time I was in school, my phone would ring, and when I answered it, a voice would say, "Oh, Laney, I dream about you at night." Or someone would call it out when I was at my locker or in the cafeteria. Just minding my own business, but I couldn't escape that joke, the one I'd made for myself because I'd been so starry-eyed I'd actually told a boy how much he meant to me.

Anyway, Mother would recollect those tales of love and finally I'd say to Lester, "Come on. Let's go for a ride."

We'd jump in his truck and head out into the country, just riding along, enjoying the night air, and more often than not, we'd end up out at Lakeview, where he'd park at the end of Veterans' Point. We'd watch the ducks on the water, and after dark there'd sometimes be night fishermen on johnboats, the lights of their lanterns passing by, and we'd hear faint voices for a time, and then they'd be gone. It was nice being together. I wasn't yet thinking about loving him. Not until what happened that night.

Across the road at the campgrounds, people were laughing and a radio was playing. Then we heard a woman crying, not a wailing cry, just a low boo-hooing that kept going on and on as if that woman would never get to the bottom of her broken heart. After a while, it seemed like that noise didn't belong to a person at all, but was the sound of a grief that stretched beyond the grave.

"That gives me the spooks," I said.

"Let's walk down to the lake," said Lester. "Maybe we won't be able to hear her down there."

We walked together to the end of the point and then down a path through the pine trees to the water's edge. We stood in the dark, and though the woman's crying was more distant now, we could still hear it. Lester said, "I wish she'd stop. I don't like hearing anyone cry like that."

I wondered if he was thinking about that wedding party in Iraq and what happened to the spirits of the dead. I wondered if he heard them sometimes, if he dreamed about them, if they haunted him in the night.

Just then, a johnboat passed close to the shore, and the glow of its lantern fell across our feet. Something sparkled on the ground. Then the boat was gone, and we were in the dark.

"Did you see that?" Lester asked, and I told him I did. "Something shiny," he said, and then he crouched down. I heard him running his hand over the grass. "Got it," he said. "Laney, it's a ring. It's a woman's gold wedding band."

We went back to the truck, and there, with the dome light on, he showed me the ring. "You said I'd have luck." He pointed out the window at the moon over the lake. "Remember, Laney? When the moon was full? You cast that spell."

I laughed. "If you were really lucky, you'd have found a pile of cash."

"Laney, I'm already lucky. I'm here with you."

It was a sweet thing to say. I told him to turn out that dome light in case anyone was watching us. Then I leaned over and kissed him on the cheek.

"You're a good man, Lester."

That was enough to break him, and I thought later how it must have been the thing he wanted to hear someone say most of all. He'd done what he'd done in Iraq, and he'd come back, and someone like me could still think well of him.

"Laney, if I'm really lucky—if *we're* really lucky—well, just give me your hand."

The ring slid onto my finger, a perfect fit. Just like that, the woman stopped crying, and the night settled in around us with the sounds of the water lapping at the shore, and crickets singing, and I said to Lester, "We should take out an ad in the paper so whoever lost this ring can have it back."

"Maybe someone threw it there," he said. "Maybe that woman who was crying."

"Should we try to find her?"

"No, if she threw it away, she had a reason, and besides, she's quiet now."

"Maybe it wasn't even hers."

"If you ask me, we found it for a reason." We were making stories, the ones we wanted to believe. "Keep it, Laney. Finders, keepers."

"You know the rest of it. Losers, weepers."

"She's not crying anymore. Everything's fine."

I couldn't keep that ring and have a clear conscience, so I put an ad in the *Daily Mail*'s "Lost and Found" and even called it into the *Swap Shop* program on the radio where folks had things for sale, or things they wanted to buy, or things they'd misplaced or come across, and it wasn't long before I had a call. Libby Raymond, Jess Raymond's wife, the one Poke said was keeping time with Bernard Goad.

"Lands, I thought I'd seen the last of that ring," she told me when she came to claim it. She was a slight woman with nervous hands that were always skittering through the air as she talked, or touching her face, or pushing up her glasses, or combing through her hair. "Jess and I were fishing off the point, and I took it off so I wouldn't get it slimed up with bait, and, well, Laney, I've just been out of my head ever since."

I couldn't help but wonder whether she'd tossed it down some night when she'd been in Bernard Goad's arms, and now she'd had a change of heart.

That's what I told Lester when I gave him the news.

"I hope you're not mad that I gave it back to her."

"No, Laney. It did what it was meant to do. It got us to say what we think of each other. It was the lucky gift you conjured up for me."

ONE NIGHT, WHEN we didn't have to work, Lester and I went into the South End to have a drink.

Delilah was there. She sat by herself at a table in the corner. She wouldn't even look my way. She finished her drink, got up, and headed toward the door, wobbling a little. She bumped into a chair and almost fell. I couldn't stand to see that. No matter the trouble between us, I still cared about her and didn't want to see her hurting. I went over and put my arm around her waist.

I asked her if she was okay. "You need any help?"

"Honey, I'm fine," she said in a little voice that held just a smidge of embarrassment. "I really am," she said, and then she walked on to the door.

I thought about going after her, but I didn't.

That night, I couldn't get her out of my head, wondering, as I was, what life was like for her now that I wasn't there to be a part of it, now that I was starting to make a life of my own. I wondered how she was getting on with her rent now that it was only her there to pay it. I still saw her at work, but we never had much to say, and it started to feel like we'd never really been close as sisters, never told each other the most secret things in our hearts. I told myself she was just a woman I worked with, just someone who didn't matter to me at all.

Then one morning in October, I saw her leave the store and get into a black Camaro. A man was behind the wheel. He pulled her close and kissed her. Then he turned toward the store, ran a hand through his shaggy blond hair, and I could see it was Bobby May. I hadn't known he was back in town, and I got a sick feeling in my stomach to think that Delilah had picked back up with him. He'd been no good for her the first time, and now there they were, and I couldn't get comfortable with that fact.

Lester came up beside me. "Watching anything interesting?"

"Delilah," I said. "I think she's headed for trouble."

ROSE SAID IT WASN'T any of her concern what Delilah did with Bobby May, and she didn't see why it should be any of mine. "She turned you out, Laney. If you ask me, she can make her own road."

It was close to Halloween, and we were on the porch at Rose's house, carving jack-o'-lanterns. We sat on the porch floor, the pumpkins on newspapers between us, knives at the ready. It was one of those Indian summer days, the kind we get in Illinois in late October when the first cold snap has come and gone and the days have warmed and for a while you can almost believe that winter won't ever set in for good. The sun was out, and there was just a little breeze stirring the tree branches. All those yellow and orange and red leaves, some of them letting go and drifting to the ground. The sun was warm on my face. A set of wind chimes over at Mr. Hambrick's was making a merry little song, and if not for the fact that Rose had just made me feel like a fool for worrying over Delilah, that moment would have been just fine.

"Don't you ever feel sorry for her?" I pressed the tip of my knife into the pumpkin rind. "She's all alone."

Rose gave a little laugh. "Nah, sweetie. She's got Bobby May."

It was clear Rose knew she was being a smart-ass, and even though I understood that she'd sharpened her tongue on all the bitter seeds she'd chewed with Delilah over Tweet, I couldn't bring myself to forgive it. The truth was Rose could have had a happier life if she'd only been able to spit out that bitterness. I suppose I could have, too, if I hadn't let myself get caught up in this feud between her and Delilah. I could have given myself more fully to the love I was feeling for Lester. Rose, even though she was scared about how she and Tweet were going to care for their baby, could have better enjoyed their days together. I won't speak for Delilah. I think in the end she was all eaten up with jealousy, but frightened, too—scared of a lonely life—and even now, though I sometimes feel sorry for her, I can't imagine any way things could have been different. She was dead set on making someone pay for everything she'd lost—her father, her mother, and now Tweet. I wish I'd seen that then, but I didn't. I only thought that maybe, just maybe, something would happen that would bring us all back together—Delilah and Rose and me—and barring that, at least maybe we could each forget the hurt that the whole business with Tweet had caused, and then we'd go on with our lives. We'd make them happy lives, the ones we'd always longed to have. I truly think it could have been so simple for Rose and me if only we'd been able to forget about Delilah. I couldn't, though, and I knew Rose couldn't, either.

"You can be evil," I told her.

"Aw, Laney. Don't be like that."

Tweet came out onto the porch carrying his guitar case. He was getting ready to leave for a string of gigs in Kentucky.

Rose said to him, "I'm going to miss you, baby."

He went down the steps. He was wearing flip-flops, and the tendons stood up on the tops of his feet as he slapped them over the cement.

"I'll miss you, too," he said, but his voice was all flat. He went on out to his van, and with no word or wave of good-bye, he started the engine and drove away.

The problem was, as it always was with Rose and Tweet, money. After he was gone, she told me how he played his gigs, throwing in an old-timers' class reunion now and then, a supper club over in Vincennes, a wedding reception here and there, and he made what little he could from jockeying cars.

Rose was still sitting with old folks from time to time, so their kin could take off for a while and run to town or have a night out or just take a breath after all that caretaking. The work wasn't regular, and she didn't bring in much, but with what Tweet was making it was enough to keep them square. But a baby—that was a whole different ball game. With a baby, Rose explained, he'd probably have to get a real job, maybe hire on at the poultry house in Mt. Gilead or the Kex Tire Repairs factory. Put in his time, seven to three-thirty, gutting chickens or making tire patches and plugs. Same old same old, day after day, just to put the bread on the table, and what would happen to his music then?

"He's going to have to be a man about it," Rose said. "We're not kids.

It's time we thought about the future. Don't tell him I told you all this. He'd pitch a fit if he knew."

I couldn't help but think about Delilah then and what happened when she tried to play house with Bobby May before.

"Looks like you've got everything right where you want it," I said to Rose. "Got the man you wanted and a baby on the way to make sure he stays."

It was an accusing thing to say, and the words surprised me. I would have taken them back and stuffed them into my mouth if I could have.

Her face turned hard. "Tweet's no dummy. He knew a good thing when he saw it." She laid her knife down on the newspaper. "Honestly, Laney," she said, like I was a little girl who didn't have a brain in my head. I could tell she thought I wasn't made for anything hard, that I'd always be Laney, as flimsy as my name.

"Delilah's hurting," I said, "and who knows what kind of stupid thing she'll do with Bobby May? It might not matter to you, but it does to me."

I shoved my knife into the top of my pumpkin and let it stick there. Then I got up and walked away from Rose.

"Laney, come back," she called after me, but I kept walking.

IT DIDN'T TAKE LONG for things to go to hell between Delilah and Bobby. One night in the break room at work, I caught her peering into the mirror, touching a finger gingerly to a bruise on her cheekbone before covering it over with foundation.

"He did that, didn't he?"

"It's none of your concern, Laney."

"Delilah, I—"

She cut me off. "Forget it." She gave me such a hateful look, I almost turned around and went back out onto the floor.

Then I said, "I've still got some things at your trailer. I thought I'd come by for them."

"Sure," she said with a smirk. "Come by. We'll shoot the breeze. It'll be like old times."

I could see I wasn't welcome, but the next day I drove over there in Mother's Corolla. I had Lester come with his truck on account of I had a cedar chest at Delilah's trailer I needed him to carry to New Hope. I made it to the trailer park first, but Lester was pulling in behind me as I got out of the car.

The door to the trailer was standing wide open, and I thought that was odd, given that it was now November, and the day was cold and gray with little specks of rain in the air. It was the kind of day when the clouds and the damp seemed to trap in the stink from the poultry factory. The kind of day no one would have a door open unless they were in the midst of some sort of trouble that'd taken them by surprise.

Bobby May came out of the trailer, toting a cardboard box. He didn't have on a shirt, but he didn't seem to care. He came out into the cold, that box hugged to his bare chest. He carried it to the big common Dumpster across the parking space in front of Delilah's trailer, hefted it up, and tossed it inside.

Delilah wasn't far behind him. She had Mama's Little Helper with her, that .38 Special. She came up behind Bobby and pressed that pistol to the base of his skull. She told him to get his sorry ass out of there. "Just get in your car and go," she said.

He put his hands up above his head. "I don't even have on a shirt. Jesus, Dee."

"Now," she said. Her hair was all undone and wild about her face. Her blue polo shirt from work was torn across her breast and I could see the white of her bra. She didn't care. She had business to take care of. "Move," she said, and she put more pressure on that .38 until Bobby started walking across the lot to his Camaro.

"You're some bitch," he said. "You know that?"

I was moving before I'd even thought about what I'd do. I jerked open the door to that Camaro and I said, "Get out of here before I call the cops, you asshole."

He stopped walking. He looked at me, and I remembered that look from the first time he and Delilah were together. That tight-jawed look he always had just before he exploded. He let his arms drop to his side. Then he lifted the right one and pointed a finger at me. "Don't talk big, Laney, unless you can back it up. Little, know-nothing girl like you."

Delilah took the .38 away from his head, and for just an instant I was afraid she might shoot him. I looked at Lester, who had started to move toward Bobby, and when I looked back to Delilah, I saw her with her arm raised. She was holding the .38 by its barrel, and she brought her arm down with a grunt. She clubbed Bobby on the back of his head with the butt end, and he went down to his knees.

"Oh, Lord," said Lester. "You've killed him."

"Nah," said Delilah. "Takes more than that to kill a snake."

Indeed, Bobby was just stunned. He got to his feet, his hand touching the place on the back of his head where Delilah had hit him, and he stumbled to the Camaro and got inside. I slammed the door shut. He shook his head, trying to get back what little sense he had. Then he started up the car and drove away.

Delilah was crying. She was screaming after him. "You bastard. Don't come back, you miserable bastard."

"What in the world?" I said.

"Oh, Laney." She bent at the waist, and I thought she'd go down. I put my arms around her and pulled her up. "He's thrown it all away." The "it" turned out to be mementos from her childhood: schoolbooks, storybooks, snapshots—most of them of her taken at birthday parties, Christmas, school. Things like that. She'd saved them as she'd moved from foster home to foster home, and there were even things that her mother had left for her before she'd put her Impala on those railroad tracks. "Everything that was me when I was a kid," she said. "My baby book, locks of hair from my first cut, things I'll never be able to replace. He pitched it in the Dumpster. That was the last box."

"Don't worry," I said. "We'll get it all back."

She couldn't stop crying. "It's down in there on the bottom. It's too far to reach."

"It's no problem for me, Sis. It'll be easy-breezy."

All it took was for Lester to give me a boost. He took me by the waist and lifted me up until I could sit on the rim of that Dumpster. Then I jumped in, and from there it didn't take much to retrieve the boxes, to gather up the few things that had fallen out, and to lift them up to Lester. I did all that for Delilah because she needed me to do it, because somehow circumstances had brought me there at just the right time.

We carried the boxes back into the trailer and shut that door so the cold would stay out, and I never said a word about how stupid it'd been for Delilah to take back up with Bobby May.

"Laney," she said, smiling at me through her tears, and I told her everything was fine now. She didn't need to say another word.

I shouldn't have been so forgiving. I let her back into my life, and though I didn't know it then, I started down my final road toward trouble—a trouble so big I'd never be able to make it right.

IT WAS JUST about Christmas when the headaches started. Horrible, raging headaches that left me dizzy and sick to my stomach.

Migraines, the doctor told me.

"Why, I've never had a migraine headache in my life," I said.

The doctor ran tests. Everything came back clean. Migraines, he told me again and gave me a list of foods to avoid and relaxation exercises I should do to keep my stress level at a minimum. If I got worse, he could prescribe a medicine, but first things first. Why take the medicine if I could manage the migraines myself?

"Well, it seems odd to me," Delilah said. We were at the Town Talk restaurant one morning after our shift, having breakfast, and I was telling her about the headaches. It was Saturday, so Mother wouldn't need the Corolla to go to work, and I could enjoy this time with Delilah. "Why in the world would you start having them now? All of a sudden when you've never had them before?"

"The doctors don't know."

"Doctors," Delilah said with a smirk. "They don't know shit."

It was cozy in the Town Talk. Outside, the streetlights were still on, and snow was coming down, whitening the pine flocking and the glittery stars and candles and bells on the poles. Snow was piling up on the sidewalk, sticking to the pickup trucks parked at the meters. Men came into the restaurant shaking snow off their feed caps before hanging them on the peg hooks by the door. The griddle sizzled with eggs and pancakes and sausage and bacon. The coffeepots steamed, and the men called out to one another. "Cold enough for you?" "Hell, yes. Colder than a well-digger's ass." They brought in the smell of the cold and the snow on their insulated coveralls. They sat on the swivel stools at the counter and wrapped their big hands around coffee mugs. Delilah and I sat in a booth along the wall. The high back of the red vinyl rolled up above my head. I closed my eyes, worn out after my shift.

"I'm beat," I said. "I'm a drum just beat to death."

Still I liked being there in the Town Talk, in the midst of all the chatter. Being there with Delilah, who was buying my breakfast. Just being with people on a snowy morning.

She said, "Rose used to have those dolls, remember? Those poppet dolls?"

I gripped the edge of the Formica-top table with both hands. The metal edge dug into my thumbs. "She still makes them from time to time."

"Remember what she did with that one she made of Mr. Mank?"

She'd tossed it into the creek, sent him out of her life, but not quite in the way she expected.

I nodded.

"Makes me wonder if she's made one of you." Delilah leaned toward me and tapped her finger on the tabletop. "Bet she doesn't like it that you've taken back up with me."

It was true that Rose, once she knew that Delilah and I were starting to pal around again, said, *That doesn't make any sense, Laney. Not after how she treated you. That's like a beat dog going back for more. Aren't you any smarter than that?* It was enough to keep me uncomfortable around Rose. I stopped going down to see her as much, and then I finally stopped going at all.

The men at the counter burst out in guffaws over a joke one of them had told, and I felt their booming laughter in my head. I massaged my temples, the way the doctor had taught me. I closed my eyes and started counting to a hundred.

"Do you get my drift?" Delilah asked me, but I didn't want to think about Rose and what Delilah was suggesting, that she'd deliberately try to hurt me. "All I'm saying, Laney, is you better be careful. Lord knows what she'll do to you next."

A MISERABLE HEAD COLD—that was the next thing. It started coming on that evening at work, and by the weekend it'd gone down into my chest.

Bronchitis, the doctor told me come Monday. He gave me a prescription and said to drink plenty of fluids and get lots of rest. I slept all day and then dragged myself into work.

"You're white as a sheet," Delilah said when she saw me in the break room.

"Bronchitis." I took my pill bottle out of my purse and shook it. "I've got an antibiotic."

She just raised her eyebrows and gave me a questioning look, as if to say, *You think that's all it is?*

Well, anyone could get a cold—you couldn't very well point a finger at Rose for that—but then I got a rash under my arms ("Miliaria," the doctor said. "Prickly heat"), and that was odd because it was the dead of winter, and as the doctor explained, folks usually got prickly heat in the summer, when the days were hot and humid and the sweat ducts got clogged with dead skin cells or bacteria. "Prickly heat in winter," he said. "I'm not sure what to make of that."

Delilah was. "She's put a hex on you, Laney. That's my guess. You walked away from her, and now she's going to make sure you come to no good."

"Isn't that a little extreme?"

"Is it?" said Delilah. "I guess we'll see."

I wasn't ready to believe it, not for a second. I chalked up Delilah's suspicion to the fact that she had it in for Rose. Nothing more than that.

Then Poke paid me a visit on Christmas Day, and he told me what he'd seen.

It was the night before, he said. Christmas Eve. After his grandfather went to sleep, he slipped out of the house and took a little tour of the town. Things were quiet at the Raymond house. Jess and Libby were drinking eggnog and watching that old movie, *It's a Wonderful Life,* on television. They were sitting on the couch, and once Libby even put her hand on Jess's, a tender gesture that gave Poke hope they'd call to mind the people they were when they first fell in love. "When you love someone, it should be forever, don't you think?" And I told him yes, I'd always thought it should, but sometimes the world has other plans.

The lights were out at Bernard Goad's, and Poke chose to take this as a sign that he'd gone to bed early, unable to stand the misery of the fact that Libby Raymond was with her husband and not him on Christmas Eve. "I couldn't work up much sorry for him," Poke said. "After all, we usually get what we deserve, or at least that's my opinion on the subject."

I almost asked him what he deserved for peeking into people's windows, but it was Christmas, and he had a little box with him that he'd obviously wrapped himself. I could only assume it was a gift for me, and I was so ashamed that I didn't have anything for him that I couldn't bring myself to say anything that might sound accusing. Besides, maybe what he deserved for all that peeking was everyone's thanks. His vigilance was trying to keep us all on the straight and narrow.

He sat on my bed, the little box in his hands. The wrapping paper was silver, and too loose. The taped ends pooched out and sagged. He'd stuck one of those fake bows on top, the kind with an adhesive backing. A green bow that kept coming loose, so he had to mash it back down with the heel of his hand. Each time he did, the bow flattened out a little more.

Ida Henline was outside when he stopped by her house. She was in the yard looking up at the night sky. "They say on Christmas Eve," she said to Poke, "you can sometimes see clear through the sky into heaven."

The fact that Miss Henline had caught him out and about and spoken to him gave him the whim-whams, but he went away eager to believe in what she'd said because it was a lovely thought. "Who would you want to see," he asked me, "if you could get a window to the afterlife?"

I didn't really know. Daddy, of course, but that was the easy answer. I walked over to the window and looked outside. A flock of starlings had gathered in Mr. Hambrick's yard and were pecking at the ground. Snow was starting to fall. I remembered, I told Poke, a girl in my eighth-grade class who'd died over the summer between junior high and high school. She was alone one day at Lakeview, and she decided to go swimming in the lake even though there were signs that said it wasn't allowed. She dove off a pier into shallow water, hit her head on the bottom, broke her neck, and drowned before anyone even knew it'd happened. Her father found her flip-flops on the pier, and that's how he knew where the police frogmen should look.

That girl—her name was Tess. She was heavyset with a badly acned face, and whenever I looked across the room and saw her hunched over her desk, trying to make herself as small as she could, I knew she was just as miserable as I was. When she died, I felt my heart break, and even though I'd never been friends with her—barely a word had passed between us—there'd always been something comforting about the fact that she was there. When she died, I felt even more alone.

"Tess Raymond," Poke said, and I was surprised to see how much he really knew about the folks who lived in New Hope. "Mr. and Mrs. Raymond's girl." He nodded. "That's where their trouble started."

Sometimes, like now, he could bring an ache to my throat, and even though he was a peeping Tom, it was clear that what he really wanted was to watch over people.

"Yes, Tess Raymond." I turned away from the window. "That's who I'd want to see. I'd want to make sure she's happy."

"She is," Poke said in a very calm voice. "Anyone who goes to heaven is happy."

Rayanne Fines was watching one of her UFO videos. She kept rewinding it and playing it again. She was sitting on the floor right in front of the television, and she was tracing her finger over the screen, following what appeared to be a streak of light. "I'm undecided on this issue myself," Poke said, "but I intend to stay open to the possibility."

The Reverend Gibson was wrapping a Christmas present, and Poke assumed it was for his pen pal in Russia. "That's a good thing," Poke said. "People hadn't ought to feel alone." He mashed down the green bow again. "Especially people like us."

"Us?"

"You know. The shiver spooks. The ones close to coming apart, only no one sees that until it's too late."

I felt a draft of cold air on my neck. Goose bumps came up on my arms. Poke had it just right. Yes, that was what we were—Poke and Rose and Tweet and Delilah and Lester and me, and so many others. A clan of shiver spooks.

"You've pegged us," I told Poke.

He shrugged his shoulders. "I don't take any pride in the fact."

Then he told me about Rose. It was after he left the Reverend Gibson's. He saw a light on at Rose and Tweet's, and he decided he'd stop by just to see what was what. She was in the kitchen.

"She had a doll. A skinny little doll with black yarn for a mess of curls, and she was sticking straight pins into its head." He looked at me for a good while, making sure I got what he was telling me. "That doll looked like it was meant to be you, Laney, and you've been having those headaches."

Seeing Rose sticking those pins into that doll was enough, he said, to scare the stuffing out of him, so he went right home and made sure all the doors were locked. Then he sat in the dark, thinking that what he'd seen was something no good. Rose seemed upset, like she was angry, and he could only assume she was mad at me.

"I don't know what's up with the two of you," he said, "but I know you haven't been over there in a long time. So I got this idea. Here."

He reached out the little silvery box and waited for me to take it.

"Oh, Poke." I withered from shame. "I didn't get anything for you."

He sloughed off any disappointment he was feeling. "I'm used to not getting much. This is just something you might need." I undid the wrapping and opened the box. Inside was a rabbit's foot key chain, worn and yellowed. "It's nothing I bought or anything," he said. "You know. I just had it, and I thought better you have it than me."

I rubbed my finger over the fur. I was trying to find the words to thank him, but I was afraid I couldn't talk right then without crying. My throat was filling up with all I felt on account of he'd made this tender gesture. He was concerned about me, and he'd given me what he could, what he'd had on hand, a lucky charm to protect me.

"Come over here," I finally said.

He got up from the bed and went to where I was standing. I wrapped my arms around his shoulders and hugged him to me, hoping that would tell him what I couldn't say, that I was grateful.

"Hey, now," he said, and he tried to squirm away from me, but I could tell he wasn't trying too hard. "Aw, crap," he said, but I knew he didn't mean it. I could feel it in the way he sank into me, how much he wanted to be held. I could tell this holding, two shiver spooks hanging on, was the best thing he could have asked if he'd been able to tell me what he wanted for a gift.

"Look," he said. "Here comes Tweet."

I had my back to the window, but Poke could see out it as he looked over my shoulder.

I let go of him and went to the window. Tweet was coming down the sidewalk, past Mr. Hambrick's house. It was spitting snow. The sky was that gloomy color of lead, and the branches of the blue spruce in Mr. Hambrick's front yard were shaking in the wind. The flock of starlings lifted up into the sky, chattering as they wheeled off to the south. Mr. Hambrick was sprinkling some salt on his front steps. He waved at Tweet, and Tweet waved back. He was wearing a pea coat and one of those long scarves with a pattern of piano keys on it. He took one end of the scarf and tossed it over his shoulder. Even from my distance, I could see his face was red from the cold.

Somehow I knew that he was coming to see me. Mother was downstairs listening to Christmas music. I thought about telling her not to answer the door, but she'd say not to be such a silly goose. It was Christmas and here was someone else coming to see us.

So I checked myself in my dresser mirror—oh, what was the use?—and when the doorbell rang, I told Poke to wait right where he was, and I went downstairs to see what Tweet wanted.

The thing was, he told me after he chatted a bit with Mother and then she left us alone, Rose was wondering why I hadn't been down to see them in so long. He stood just inside the front door, snowflakes melting on his eyelashes. He smelled like his clarinet reeds, those strips of cane he soaked in water—that clean, woody smell—and I found myself, as I always did, wanting to lean my head against his chest, imagining that's where he kept it, whatever it was that gave me such a calm feeling when I was with him. I guessed he kept it right there close to his heart.

"I thought we were all friends," he said. "How come you stopped coming around?"

I wanted the earth to give way beneath me, just open up and swallow me whole so I wouldn't have to stand there, ashamed. It was a busy time, I said. I had trouble looking at him as I explained myself. The Christmas season left me on the run at work. I was worn out most of the time, and I'd been having those headaches. "Work and sleep," I said. "That's about all I've had time for."

Tweet reached out and laid one of those beautiful hands on my shoulder. "Laney." His voice was soft now and patient. "I want to explain something to you about me and Delilah."

I couldn't imagine where this was going, but I wished he hadn't mentioned Delilah's name, calling attention to the hurt between them.

"You don't have to tell me anything."

"No," he said. "I want to." He took a breath and let it out. "Sometimes you think you're right where you need to be in your life, and then just like in a good piece of jazz, a little variation comes onto the scene. Dig? And you follow it just to see what's possible. That's what happened to me and Delilah when Rose came along. I saw a new way of being. I didn't want to hurt Delilah, but I had to follow what my heart was hearing. Simple as that, Laney." He took his hand off my shoulder, and I missed having it there. "Listen to your heart," he said. He stepped out onto the porch. Then he winked at me. "Come down and see us soon. Rose doesn't want you to be lonely."

It hurt to hear him say that, to know that he and Rose had talked about me, had said, *Poor Laney, not a friend in the world.*

"I'm not lonely," I said, but he was too far down the sidewalk and the wind was too loud and my voice was too soft, so I knew he didn't hear me. "I've got Delilah," I said to no one. Then I closed the door and went back upstairs.

My bedroom window was open, and the screen was leaning against the wall. It was a short drop down to the porch roof and another few feet to the ground. I looked around for Poke, but he was gone.

THE NEWS THAT ROSE had done what she had with that doll shook me, and though I tried telling myself it didn't mean a thing, the longer the migraines went on, the more inclined I was to wonder if what Delilah said was true—oh, it seems silly now—that Rose had put a hex on me.

One night after New Year's, Lester drove me down to Evansville to see a concert. We ate supper first at a Greek restaurant, and he ordered for me and explained what the hummus was and the falafel and the tabouleh. He did it patiently and without making me feel stupid.

Snow slanted down through the lights of the parking lot. We sat in a booth by the window, and I felt the cold from the glass. I told him about the headaches and what Delilah had said. I told him Poke had seen Rose sticking pins into that poppet doll.

"You don't think it's possible, do you?" I said.

He was very serious about it all. "I've seen all kinds of strange things, Laney."

I watched the snow and waited for him to tell me more, but I suppose his story of the wedding party in Iraq was all the story I needed.

"Are you dangerous?" I laughed a little when I said it so he'd know I was teasing.

He looked straight at me, and he kept quiet just long enough to worry me. "Yes," he told me, his voice low and steady. "I'm a very dangerous man."

Right away, I was sorry I'd said it. It was a stupid thing to say, even in jest. I hadn't meant to remind him of what he'd lived through in Iraq.

We drove down the Lloyd Expressway to Roberts Stadium to see

Cheap Trick. "Classic power rock," Lester called their music. I knew who they were. In fact, it was why I'd wanted to come. Daddy had told the story over and over of how, when he was nineteen—this was back in 1975—he saw them play on a hay wagon on the Mt. Gilead courthouse square for the centennial celebration. "Cheap Trick," he always said with a shake of his head that told me he was still amazed. "They were just these kids on a hay wagon. Right before they hit it big." Now they were nothing. Just a band on the backward side of success. Just these men as old as Daddy would have been, playing shows in cowtowns like Evansville. The opening act was a band called Watershed and they were no one I'd ever heard of.

It was nice there at the concert, and at the end, when Cheap Trick sang a song about the fire that burns long after the love is gone, and couples were hugging and swaying together, Lester put his arm around my waist, and I let him.

Later, when we were at his house, he had trouble with the lock. "Here, let me," I said, and without a protest, he stepped back so I could turn the key.

It was, I decided then and there as the door pushed open and I felt the heat inside the house, one of the best moments of my life. I'd said, *Here, let me,* and he hadn't been flustered at all. I'd taken the key, and he hadn't said a word—had acted glad, really, as if we'd loved each other for years and had come to rely on such favors.

When I think back on it now, it's hard for me to say if I really loved him or whether I'd just gotten tired of not having anyone to love, and there he was, a sweet man, who loved me first.

THE MIGRAINES CAME and went. One afternoon, I was at Lester's house, watching a DVD, the Marx Brothers in *A Day at the Races,* and the edges of my vision blurred, and I felt the first stabs of pain in my temples. It was one of those winter days that break clear after a stretch of clouds and snow, and the sunlight slanting through the window was too much for me. I was sitting on the couch with Lester, and before I could catch myself, I slumped over against him, and he asked me what was wrong.

"Headache," I said. "Could you maybe close the blinds?"

The noise from the movie was too much for me. The Marx Brothers were involved in some sort of hide-and-seek game. Doors were slamming, and people were stomping through a room.

Lester closed the blinds. "Do you want some Tylenol?" He turned down the sound on the television. "Laney?"

I was trying to count. I was doing my best to take deep breaths. But the room was spinning, and I felt the nausea rise into my throat. I tried to make it to the bathroom, but I couldn't, and I was sick all over the linoleum floor.

Lester said, "Oh, Laney," his voice all sweet and tender. He helped me into the bathroom, and he wet a washcloth and he cleaned my face. He gave me another damp cloth, and then he said, "I'll be right outside. Just call if you need me."

I ran water from the faucet and caught a little in my mouth and swished it around and spit it out. I dried my face on one of Lester's towels. The pain behind my eyes was still there, and I felt so tired.

He tapped on the door. "Laney, are you all right?" He sounded so worried, so I opened the door and stepped outside.

He'd cleaned the floor, and there was a smell of lilac air freshener, the only reminder that I'd been sick. He'd taken care of everything, and not a word of complaint.

"I'm so tired," I said, and he put his arm around my waist and led me to the couch and helped me lie down.

"You can sleep if you want. I'll turn off the TV."

"Leave it on," I said. "Just turned down low the way it is right now."

In the movie, Harpo was playing. I closed my eyes and listened to that harp music. Lester covered me with a blanket, and he sat down on the floor by the couch, and he held my hand. I drifted off to sleep, but before I did I heard Lester chuckling softly, and I thought it was the most wonderful sound, one I could get used to hearing the rest of my life.

"POOR LANEY." When I woke, it was dark, but Lester hadn't turned on any lights. At some point while I'd slept, he'd switched off the television and come back to sit by me. I reached out and touched his arm. "Do you feel better?" he asked, and I said I thought I did.

"I want you to go with me," he said.

"Where?"

"To see Rose. If she did this to you, then she can make it stop."

I shook my head. "You don't want to see Tweet." I was afraid there might be an ugly scene between him and Lester over the fact that Tweet had told him to stay away from the band. "I know you've got your history with him."

"I want to help you, Laney. That's all that matters."

So that's how I came to be back at Rose and Tweet's. I told the police officers this without confessing everything there was to reveal. I still hoped I wouldn't have to say it all.

Rose let us in the house and then just turned and walked over to the couch, where she eased herself down, her hand bracing her lower back. My heart twisted. I'd never seen her look so tired, her face slack, dark circles under her eyes. And there was Tweet, monkeying around with his clarinet, his eyes closed, so far inside the tune he was playing—"Moonglow," Lester would tell me later—that there might as well not have been anyone else inside that house. Tweet didn't even seem to mind that Lester was there, as if he'd forgotten all about accusing him of stealing from the band and telling him to stay away.

"Rose," I said, and I didn't even try to hide how much it stunned me to see her looking the way she did. She settled a cushion behind her back and then rested her hands on her stomach, which was swollen now. "Rose MacAdow," I said.

"Well, at least you remember my name." She glared at me. "Long time, no see. You've been a ghost, Laney."

"Work," I said. "You know. Busy."

"Sure, I know." Rose lifted an arm and flicked her hand at Lester. "What's shaking with you two these days?"

"Laney's been having migraines," Lester said. "Horrible headaches, Rose. You know?"

I knew he was fishing, hoping Rose would give herself away, some little sign that said, yes, she stuck those pins into that doll, yes, she was the one causing my headaches.

"Rose, did you put a hex on me?" I blurted it out. I stood there with my hands balled up into fists, and I said what was on my mind. "You made a poppet doll for me, didn't you? You stuck pins in it and said a spell and gave me those migraines."

Tweet stopped playing his clarinet, and it was suddenly so quiet I could hear Rose breathing through her mouth.

"Why, Laney," she said, "do you really think I'd do that?"

"I do think that. In fact, I know it."

"Maybe you're just imagining things. Maybe you're—"

She started to go on, but I stopped her. "Poke saw you. He told me everything." I let it sink in, the fact that she couldn't escape the truth. I saw her grimace. I took no pleasure from her discomfort. In fact, it made me sad. I said, "Why'd you do it, Rose? I thought we were friends."

"You went back to being friends with Delilah," she said.

"She was in trouble with Bobby May. I told you that."

"You tossed me away like an old shoe."

"Was that any call to try to hurt me?"

She was reaching her hand out to me, like she was trying to push herself up from the couch but couldn't. "Do you really think I can cast spells?" Somehow I knew that if I took her hand I'd be answering the question. Only I didn't know whether I'd be answering yes or no, or what the right answer should be. Her fingers were trembling, and I listened to her breathing. "Do you, Laney?"

I couldn't bring myself to leave her hand hanging there in the air between us. I took it, and I let her pull me down onto the couch beside her. "Are you all right, Rose?"

"Laney, Laney." She held my face in her hands, and then she kissed me on each temple. "I'm so sorry," she said.

Later, I'd wonder whether she only meant she was sorry that circumstances were such that she had to give me those headaches. At the time, though, I heard what I wanted to, that Rose loved me, that she'd stop causing me misery, that the two of us would be friends again.

And just like that, the migraines stopped. "What do you think about that?" I asked Delilah a few days later.

"Think?" said Delilah. "What do I think?" She tilted her head back and stuck out her chin. "You'll see, Laney. That woman's trouble."

"I think everything's going to be all right," I said. "Really, I do."

More than anything, at least for a time, I wanted us all to have peaceful, easy lives. When we were at our best, I could see the people we could be—people like my mother and Poke and Lester, who all knew what it was to love someone. I'll have the rest of my life to think how close we were to being those kind of people forever—how near we were to being good and faithful and kind.

SO I WAS FRIENDS with Rose again. I drove her to her doctor appointments, and sometimes we'd go through the thrift stores, shopping for baby clothes. For a few weeks, this was my life: hanging out at Rose and Tweet's, being with Lester; going to work at Walmart, where Delilah always asked me if I was all right.

"I'm going to look out for you, 'Lil Sis. I messed up once, but I'm not going to again. You mean the world to me."

"You don't have to worry," I told her. "I'm fine. Everything's fine. Really."

I thought it was—thought I was on the road to being where my mother had always dreamed I'd be. I made a call to the community college and signed up for GED classes, classes I'd never attend. I had every intention. I wish I could convince my mother of that now. She said later I shouldn't have let what happened stop me. *You have to take care of yourself, Laney.*

It wasn't that I didn't want to, but I was still learning how to stand on my own. Before I could go to my first class, Lester disappeared, and without him, I was lost.

MISS BABY

I kept checking my rearview mirror all the way from Deep Ellum back to Denton, convinced that sooner or later, I'd see Slam's black Suburban bearing down on me.

"He won't come after us, will he?" Donnie asked.

I said I was afraid he might. He was a dangerous man, and there was no telling what he'd do. My heart was pounding in my chest. I took a few deep breaths and curled my fingers more tightly around the steering wheel. It took everything I had to keep my eyes on the highway stretching out ahead of me.

Donnie said, "I won't let him hurt you. I promise you that."

"Oh, Lord." I felt the tears coming to my eyes. "What's going to happen to Pablo now?"

It was after midnight by the time I pulled into my driveway. A light was still on in Emma's house, a little glow that showed through the diamond pane of glass in the front door and told me she and Pablo were in there waiting. When I tapped on the door—such a mousy noise, so afraid I was to deliver my news—the light inside the house went out. I knew Emma was looking out the peephole, making sure it was all right to answer the door.

"Emma," I said. "It's Baby."

The dead bolt shot back, and the door opened, and Emma said, "Miss Baby, Lord-a-mercy. Get in here."

So Donnie and I stepped inside—what else could we do?—and I waited for Pablo to come to us and ask for the money.

The house was quiet, no one but Emma to be seen. She switched on a tea lamp on a table by the picture window. The only sign of Pablo was the rounded toe of a loafer sticking out from the hem of the drapes. One of his shoes had gotten pushed back beneath those drapes and made it look now as if he might be hiding behind them. Mami used to chew him out good for leaving clothes strewn around the house. He'd come home from school and just start a trail from the front door to his bedroom—jacket dropped on the couch, sweater wadded up on the coffee table, shoes kicked off in the hallway. "Careless," Mami said to him one day. "You're a careless boy." He gave her a smirk. "Aren't you one to talk?" he said. She asked him exactly what he meant by that. "Where were you last night?" he asked her. "Who were you with?" Then he said the worst thing he could say: *"Puta."* He called Mami a whore, said it in a low, even voice, and once it was said, there was no way in the world to take it back. Such was the history of our family, a story of hurt hearts, of wounds so deep nothing could heal them. The Watershed song from Club Dada was still in my head. It would be for a long, long time. *Mi familia.* We were experts at breaking the skin, at knowing just where to stick the needle to cause the most pain. In a way, it became the only way we knew we still mattered to one another at all.

"Where is he?" I asked Emma. "Where's Pablo?"

She put a finger to her lips, signaling me to be quiet. Then her bony fingers wrapped themselves around my wrist, and she said, "Miss Baby, he's gone to sleep. He's back there in the bedroom sleeping."

It sliced me open, the thought of Pablo sleeping in the still night, trusting that eventually I'd be there and I'd have just what he needed. I remembered nights when I was still a *niña* and Mami was gone, he'd come to my bed and he'd lie down beside me and tell me not to cry. He'd say he was *mi hermano,* and he wouldn't let anything bad happen to me.

No matter what might happen with Mami or our *abuelita,* he'd be there. The two of us. Forever.

Now he was dreaming whatever dreams a man like him had. Here he was at the worst point of his life—time, for all he knew, running down to *nada*—and he gave himself over to sleep. He trusted himself to the Otherworld, where fairies come out to push our lives along to wherever they want them to go. I longed for that power, the magic to wake Pablo and tell him everything was fine, to give him a new life, one where he and Carolyn would come back together and live long and happy. He wouldn't have to be afraid. He wouldn't have to pay for the bad he'd done. I'd just wipe it away. I'd give him that.

But the truth was I was standing in Emma's house, and I knew I'd have to go down the hallway to that bedroom, and I'd have to wake Pablo and tell him what had happened in Deep Ellum. Everything had gone wrong. I didn't have the money. Slam Dent had chased after Amos, and I didn't know what that meant. Did Amos have the money on him, or had he been taking us to where the money was? Maybe he'd gotten away, and Slam Dent was still after the cash, still after Pablo. The only thing I knew for certain was I didn't have the money I'd gone to Deep Ellum to get.

"Miss Baby?" Emma said, and I knew she was asking what had happened. I thought of her, years back, waiting those nights for her husband to come home from the Carousel Club. She must have wondered how long their luck could last. How many nights could they keep from falling into harm's way? Did the Mister know anything about what Jack Ruby was up to and whether it was part of a plot to kill the president? I asked her once. Point-blank. "Emma, what do you know?" She looked at me for a long time. She licked her lips, took a breath. I was sure she was about to tell me something she'd carried with her so long she couldn't help but wish it on someone else. "I know I loved a man," she finally said. "Loved him a good long while." She put her hand to her breastbone.

"That's what I know in here, Miss Baby. What it was to have a life with my Mister."

I put my hand on the small of Donnie's back and nudged him forward. "You tell Emma what happened," I said. Then I went down the hallway to wake Pablo and do the same.

In the bedroom, a small television on the dresser was playing CNN, but Pablo had given up on it. He'd slipped out of his shirt and pants and had fallen asleep on top of the bedspread. He still had on his white briefs, the kind he'd worn since he was a boy. He slept on his back with his hurt arm in its sling across his stomach.

I sat down on the edge of the bed, and still he didn't wake. I was about to reach out and touch him. My hand was in the air just above his face, still bruised from Slam Dent's beating. One moment more, and I'd lay my hand to his cheek, feel the heat of his skin against mine, and he'd open his eyes and find me there.

Then I heard it. I heard the name. At first I thought my mind was playing tricks on me. I looked to the television, and there he was. Lester Stipp, my Donnie. His picture was on the screen just to the left of the news anchor's shoulder, and the anchor was saying why.

Lester Stipp had been missing since September from his home in Mt. Gilead, Illinois. Now he was wanted, a suspect in a murder case. After months of dead ends, finally a break in the investigation—the murder weapon found. Lester Stipp. His picture disappeared and a news video ran behind the anchor: shots of a wood-frame house with a porch on the front; a town population sign that said NEW HOPE; the front of a Walmart in Mt. Gilead where a young woman had been arrested. They showed her picture, just a skinny-Minnie of a thing with curly brown hair.

There it was on the television, the world my Donnie had stepped out of, a world darker than any I would have dared imagine. Wanted for murder. Surely there was some sort of mistake. I'd known Donnie nearly three months, and outside the times he got frustrated because he couldn't remember something, he'd always been sweet and kind. I knew he was in the living room now telling Emma as gently as he could what had happened in Deep Ellum and what it meant. How could he possibly be the one the police were after?

But he was. I couldn't wipe that fact away. Not even if I was to turn off the television. What I'd heard and seen wouldn't leave me. Murder, this girl, my Donnie. And, finally, this: a reward for anyone who had any information about where he might be. Enough money to make things right between Pablo and Slam Dent, and plenty left to boot.

"Betts." Suddenly Pablo reached out his hand and I took it. "Tell me you got it. Please. Tell me you got the money."

I thought about what I'd just seen on CNN—my Donnie, this Lester Stipp—wanted for murder. I wanted to tell Pablo yes, I had it, the cash he'd promised Amos would give me when I met him in Deep Ellum. I wanted to throw it on the bed, bills and bills that would cover Pablo with all the money he needed to get him out of trouble with Slam Dent. I didn't have it, but I knew I could tell Pablo about the news report, tell him that all we needed to do was make a call to the police and say we had the man from Illinois that they were looking for. Surely, I could do that much, couldn't I? Give up on Donnie, this man I'd sworn came from the Otherworld, this magic man I thought was meant for me. I sat there on the bed, the moonlight washing over me, and I wished I could go to sleep and not have to make this choice.

"Slam," I said, figuring I'd start there and then see what might happen. I couldn't stay tongue-tied forever, not with Pablo waiting, and Donnie—I mean, Lester—out in the living room with Emma. He couldn't know what I'd seen on CNN. He'd be waiting for me to come out and tell him what was going to happen next when it came to Pablo and the fix he was in. Lester Stipp didn't have any idea that the drama he was in the midst of—Pablo's trouble—now had everything to do with him.

"That son of a bitch," Pablo said, catching on to what I was trying to tell him. "He got to Amos."

"Before we could get the money," I said.

"Son of a bitch," said Pablo again, and I know I should have been thinking the same thing about Lester Stipp. If the television was telling the truth, he was a bad man, and maybe he'd come here playing innocent, pretended to love me all because I'd invited him to, and now I wondered whether he'd sucker-punched me, let me believe that he was a man without a memory, when all along he was playing me for a fool, pretending he didn't know a thing about who he was or where he'd come from, all for the sake of trying to escape arrest. Lordy Magordy.

And yet there was a part of me that couldn't give in to that story, that wanted there to be another tale instead. Call me a fool and you'd probably be right, but as I watched Pablo jump up from the bed and pace about the room, I couldn't help but hope that the television was wrong, that this Lester Stipp hadn't had a thing to do with that murder case, and once we could get to the bottom of the story—once we could sit down with the police and straighten it all out—he'd still be the man I'd taken in and then fallen in love with. It didn't matter to me what his real name was, only that he'd still be there with me every day of my life.

"I'm a dead man," Pablo said. He stopped pacing and pointed his finger at me. "You're looking at a dead man."

I felt accused, as if somehow what had happened in Deep Ellum had been my fault.

"You could go to the police," I said. "You could turn yourself in. Wouldn't that be better than letting Slam Dent get hold of you?"

"I'm not doing time. I'm not, Betts." He grabbed a bag from the closet and started throwing clothes into it with his good arm. "Trust me, I'd rather end up dead."

That was what did it, made me decide I couldn't let my brother take off again. I switched off the TV, and I said his name. "Pablo," I said. *"Mi hermano."* Blood runs to blood, my *abuelita* always told me, and here at the moment of decision, it turned out to be true. I chose my brother over whatever cockeyed chance at love there might have still been for me.

When Pablo heard me call him my brother, something about the

Spanish tongue touched him—I could feel it myself, the intimacy in the way those two words came from my mouth—and he stopped what he was doing and straightened up and looked at me, waiting.

It was like we were children again, our *mami* gone away and the two of us left to fend for each other.

"Don't go," I said. "I can help you."

He shook his head. "It's too late, *mi hermana*."

"No, Pablo. I don't think it is."

What I thought about as I told him the story was this: It's never too late for the things that matter. Never too late for love, for faith, for family. Never too late to do what's right. So to save him from Slam Dent, I told him everything about what I'd seen on CNN, told him about Lester Stipp and how there was a reward out there just waiting for us to collect it.

"Betts." He took both my hands in his, squeezing them with a pressure that made me understand how frightened he was. "You know I need the cash." I told him yes, I knew. "You have to make the call," he said. "I can't be involved. If I am, the police will snag me. You have to get the reward and then get it to Slam Dent."

I knew all that. In my head, it all made sense. I had to leave Lester Stipp with Emma and go over to my house to make the call. I could see myself doing it, but then I stepped out into the living room, and there he was. He and Emma were sitting on the couch, and she was patting his hand. His head was bowed, but when he heard me come into the room, he looked up, his eyes wide, his mouth open—that gap between his front teeth making my heart go again, the way it did the first time he looked at me like that, looked at me as if he were waiting for me to save him.

"Baby?" he said. "Is everything going to be all right?"

"It's going to be fine," I told him. "Just fine."

But I knew in my heart it wasn't.

LANEY

It was our night off—the first time Lester disappeared—a Saturday at the end of January. We were going to drive to Vincennes, have something to eat, maybe go to a movie. Maybe we'd get a room at the Executive Inn and stay the night, he said. He was shy when he suggested it, but still, there it was, the idea. "How'd that be, Laney?"

I wasn't sure. We'd gotten pretty hot with the kisses and the hugs, but we hadn't done the down-and-dirty yet, and though I didn't know how to break the news to Lester, I didn't intend to, not anytime soon. I wasn't even on the Pill; I'd never had a reason. And there was so much I didn't know. Frankly, the idea of sexing it up with Lester scared me to death. What if I ended up pregnant like Rose?

I didn't say anything for a long time, and when I finally did, I was very firm. "I'm not like that. I'm not a skank."

Lester said he was sorry. "Gee, Laney. I didn't mean... well, gee, Laney... come on, we'll go, and we'll have some fun."

Fun, I could handle. I was all over that. But no funny business, not until I was sure Lester was the one, with a capital "T-H-E." "You'll have to be a gentleman," I said, and he told me of course, absolutely, nothing but.

So when he didn't pick me up at the appointed time—when it got so late, I knew something was wrong—I thought he'd written me off. A nice girl, that Laney, but not the woman he needed.

"Grow up," Rose said when I went looking for a shoulder to cry on. "What'd you expect? You didn't give him what he was after."

My mind was racing. I drove to Lester's house, but he wasn't there. Not a sign of him. No light on inside. No truck parked in the driveway. He didn't show up for work the next week. He was gone. Days went by and there was no word, and I swore it was my fault. I'd driven him away by being too inexperienced, too afraid.

"No, it's not like that," Delilah said. "It's Rose."

"What in the world would Rose have to do with it?"

"Laney, what if it's the next part of the hex? She's a greedy woman. She can't stand for anyone else to have love."

Rose said good riddance when I came crying to her again about Lester. "Honey, he's nothing to get out of sorts about. You're better off without him if you ask me."

At the time, I thought she was just trying to make me feel better, but it didn't work. In fact, it made me hurt more, and I couldn't help but hate Rose a little for that. I burst into tears, and she said, "Oh, come on, Laney. Did you really think you'd keep him?"

"What's that mean? You think no one could ever love me?"

"I'm just saying you're not the first girl to get her heart broke."

There we were again, getting our backs up, and as much as it saddened me, I decided that this time I wouldn't back down. I think back on it now, and I realize it was the start of our final coming apart, even though we'd go on awhile pretending otherwise.

"You should know," I said. "The way you stole Tweet."

She shook her head, and her voice went hard. "That woman, that Delilah Dade. I don't know how you can be friends with her."

But I *was* friends with her—sisters again. Delilah never told me I was better off without Lester. No, she took me to the Dairy Queen and treated me to a Hot Fudge Brownie Delight. Then we went driving in the country, a Lucinda Williams CD playing, and we sang along with all those heart-sore songs, and by the time we were done, I felt like this was all something I had to do, and by God, I'd be the better for it, just like Lucinda, a little tired, a little sad, a little pissed off, a little wiser.

"It only hurts so long," Delilah told me. "Then it just aches when you touch it."

We put our heads together. We read through my book on spells and magic until we found one that we thought might work to reverse the one Rose had spun to take Lester away. After sunset, I was to write his name on a different piece of paper while standing in the four corners of my house. Then I was to put the four slips of paper under my pillow. I was to repeat the writing of the name every night for eight nights in a row, always sleeping on the slips of paper, and that would bring my love back to me.

"All of them?" I asked. "Or just the four from that particular day?"

Delilah reread the spell. "It doesn't say." She thought for a minute. "Better make it all of them," she finally said. "Why take a chance that the spell won't be strong enough?"

So that's what I did. The evening of the tenth day, I came out to Mother's Corolla to go to work. I got into the car and was about to start it, when a voice from the backseat said, "Hey, Laney," and I just about jumped out of my skin.

"Lester?" I spun around to have a look.

"No, it's just me."

It was Poke, just sitting there in the backseat. I felt my heart sink. "You're a wicked boy. You scared me half to death. What are you doing?"

"Thinking." On the corner, the street signs were twisting in the wind. "It's quiet here."

"Did you ever stop to think that you're trespassing?"

Poke shrugged his shoulders. "The doors were unlocked."

"You could have come inside the house."

"I didn't want to bother you. Looks like you've got trouble. Laney, what've you been doing with those pieces of paper you've been writing on?"

So he'd been peeking in my windows, watching me go from one

corner to another, writing down Lester's name. I felt ridiculous. "Do you think everything's your business?"

"It's something magic, isn't it?"

"No. I don't know. Just never mind, Poke. Now, get out. I've got to go to work."

"Can I go with you?"

"It's going on eleven o'clock. You ought to be in bed."

"I know it."

I started the car. "Come on. I'll drop you off at your house."

At his grandfather's driveway, he got out of the car. Then he leaned back in through the open door. "Whatever you're up to," he said, "I hope it works."

It did. Toward morning, I looked up from my register and there he was, Lester. He'd been gone a little over two weeks. "Hey, Laney," he said, like nothing in the world was wrong.

I was working the express checkout, and there was a woman with a can of hair spray waiting to pay. "I've got customers," I said.

"Okay," said Lester. "I just wanted you to know I was back. They won't let me work here anymore."

He didn't tell me where he'd gone or why. When I asked, he said he'd had business to take care of.

"Why didn't you let me know?"

"Well, you see, Laney. That's where I was an asshole."

What was I to do with such honesty? There was that grin again. I knew I'd forgive him—already had, in fact—but I tried to be tough like Delilah. I said, "Lester, you son of a bitch," in a way I knew would tell him everything was going to be all right. It was coming up on Valentine's Day, and he was back.

"Lord," Delilah said when I told her. "It worked. That spell worked." She had such a look on her face, like light was filling her body, and I knew I'd brought that to her. I got such a feeling then, a feeling that lifted me up and let me believe I was more than I really was. She wrapped her arms around me, and it felt so good. We were together now with no thought of where our road was leading us. Nothing that was in the future mattered—not the GED classes, not college, not what I might do with my singing, none of it—at least not to me. What mattered more than anything was that I'd carried that light to her, that she had a thrill in her voice when she whispered in my ear, "Do you see what this means?" I let her say it. I knew as long as she believed in me, she'd be mine. I swore I'd hold faith in me, too. "Laney," she said, and she hugged me harder. "You can do magic."

ONE AFTERNOON LESTER told me the truth about why he'd disappeared. We were at his house, sitting at the kitchen table, each of us with a cup of tea. He had an upset stomach, so I'd brewed a pot of licorice tea to help soothe it. The steam from his mug curled up over his face, and he said, "It happens sometimes. I forget who I am, and I just take off."

He could remember getting ready to drive out to New Hope that Saturday evening to pick me up for our date—he could even remember the name of the seventies cover band, Back to Back, we'd talked about seeing at the Executive Inn in Vincennes; that was one of the first things he remembered when he woke up one morning, days later, in a LaQuinta Inn in Gainesville, Texas. Everything else was a blank. "Lots of space out there," he said. "Open range and sky, enough to swallow a man up and make it like he never existed."

I set my own mug down on the table and studied him. "You're joking, right? Really, Lester, do you expect me to buy that?"

He kept stirring his tea, his head bowed over the mug. "It's the truth, Laney. Sometimes I slip into what the doctors call a fugue."

A dissociative fugue, he explained, is a state of amnesia where he forgot his name, his identity. Sometimes he came out of it in a few hours and was fine. Sometimes, if the fugue lasted too long, he packed up and hit the road, imagining there was somewhere else he was supposed to be, some other life he'd slipped away from where people who loved him were waiting for him to return. He could go awhile, as he had those two weeks he was gone, thinking he was in the right place. Then it would be like he was waking up from a dream, and he'd remember who he was and where he belonged. He'd remember the way home.

He took a sip of his tea, and I waited for him to go on.

It all started, he said, after that wedding party in Iraq. That was what put him over the edge. He kept trying to forget it, the way he'd put his rifle to the heads of those wedding guests and pulled the trigger. He kept trying to get away from the memory of that, but it kept coming back. He lifted his face and looked at me, and I saw that lost look in his eyes that told me what he was saying was true. I felt my heart go out to him. "Laney," he said. He reached his hand across the table, and I took it and held it until his fingers stopped trembling. "I was afraid to tell you about the fugues," he said. "I thought you wouldn't want anything to do with me."

"You don't get off that easy." I took his hand again. "You're the only man who's ever loved me. You, Lester Stipp. I'm not letting you go. You remember that."

HE STAYED THROUGHOUT the winter, and little by little I stopped worrying that he'd take off again. He'd lost his job at Walmart when he'd been gone those two weeks, but soon he went to work for a house painter. A lot of days, he had the keys to people's houses. They gave them to him so he could come and work while they were gone to their own jobs. He spent his days alone in strangers' houses, painting walls and ceilings. Sometimes the phone rang, and he overheard someone leaving a message.

"Call me," a woman's voice said in desperation once. "Goddamn it, you call me."

Sometimes he couldn't resist poking around a little, opening drawers, looking in closets.

"Lester, you shouldn't do that," I told him.

He said he never stole anything. "I just get curious. That's all. Besides, who's ever going to know?"

Then it was spring, and sometimes on my way home from work, I stopped at Rose's to see how she was doing with the baby, which she was due to have in May. One morning, I found her alone in the house. Tweet was jockeying a car to Champaign. Rose was washing the breakfast dishes, the sun shining through the kitchen window above the sink. A radio on the counter was tuned to the local station, and a man's voice was reading the hospital news—admissions and releases—in a drowsy monotone. Soon he'd read the deaths, with all the information about the visitations and the funerals. All the come and go in Mt. Gilead and vicinity: news of the ill, the well, the dead, followed by the weather and the farm market reports. Such was the morning chronicle of all matters of importance. I knew it was silly, but ever since I'd been a little girl, I'd taken comfort from that voice on the radio. It belonged to Jimmy Bascombe, a humpbacked man with hair dyed black and a string tie—my fifth-grade class had taken a tour of the radio station once, and he'd given everyone a red pencil that had *WMTG, The Voice of Southeastern Illinois,* embossed in gold letters, along its length. Jimmy Bascombe, who kept everyone up to speed and did so with such a calm that I couldn't help but feel, no matter what bad news he had to deliver, that everything would be all right. I took a breath and let it out with a sigh. Rose smiled at me and said, "Isn't it nice sometimes when there's no men around? When it's just us girls?"

"Oh, I don't know. I've always thought a man is just about the best company there is." I realized as soon as I spoke that it sounded like I'd always had a man in my life when the truth was I'd only had the one, Lester, and I knew with Rose he was suspect. "You know why Lester took off that one time, don't you?" Before I could stop myself, I told her about the fugues, even though I knew it was something Lester wouldn't want me to tell.

"And you believe that?" Rose wrung out the dishrag with her strong hands. "I told you once, Laney, back when he took off and left. I told you, good riddance."

Still no sympathy from her. When it came to Lester and what I felt for him, she was hard-hearted.

Jimmy Bascombe was reading the traffic accident report. Bernard Goad of New Hope had run his pickup truck into a ditch on the County Line Road, escaping with only minor injuries. A passenger in the truck, Libby Raymond, suffered a broken arm. The county sheriff issued Goad a ticket for driving too fast for conditions.

"That's Mr. Goad," I said. "He drives the mail truck."

"Sounds to me like he's driving Libby Raymond," Rose said, and then laughed.

Too fast for conditions. Exactly, I thought. Too many people living carelessly. Too many people outside the realm of good sense.

ROSE AND TWEET came into the Walmart that night when I was working checkout and Delilah was working at the jewelry counter just behind me.

"Hey, Laney," Rose called to me as she and Tweet pushed their cart past my checkout line, and I gave her a little wave.

They went on down the aisle, past the greeting-card display and the book racks. Tweet was pushing the cart. Rose slipped her arm around his and for just the briefest moment laid her head against his shoulder, and I thought, There they are. There's Rose and Tweet, in love.

I glanced over at the jewelry counter, and I saw Delilah take note of the way Rose clung to Tweet. No one would have thought a thing about it unless they had it on good faith, like I did, that Delilah had once persuaded herself of a life with this man, this Tweet, only to have it vanish from her. *He was the one,* she'd told me more than once. *I would've bet on it.*

If anyone knew about her broken heart, they would've noticed right away how Delilah saw Rose and Tweet all lovey-dovey and how she bowed her head and fiddled with the lock on the jewelry counter case even though she didn't have a customer and had no reason to be so fascinated with that lock. I knew she was trying with all her might to keep her face turned from the sight of Rose strolling arm in arm with Tweet, the father of her baby, the man Rose was going to spend the rest of her life with, and there was Delilah, getting a little older and living in that trailer in Bird Town.

When three a.m. rolled around and the two of us were alone in the break room, I said, as I'd heard her say so many times before, "Another gravedigger. Enough to bury us."

Delilah was sitting at one of the fold-up tables, eating a taco salad out of a plastic bowl. "Bonedigger, bonedigger," she sang softly. "Dogs in the moonlight."

She said it like she was worn out, like she barely had a breath left in her body, and though I didn't know where she'd come up with that (I'd recall it later from an old record Daddy used to play—a song from Paul Simon's *Graceland*), I felt Delilah's pain, raw in my own throat.

I sat down across the table from her. "So you saw them? Rose and—"

"I saw them."

The radio by the coffeemaker was playing some oldies station, and a Cheap Trick song came on, "I Want You to Want Me," and I remembered what it'd felt like being with Lester at that concert in Evansville, clinging to him in the dark. It was that feeling—that comfort of having someone to be with you always—that Delilah surely missed and wondered if she'd ever have again.

"I wish there was something I could do for you."

She put down her fork. She looked me in the eye for what seemed like the longest time. "Maybe there is," she finally said. "I've got an idea. A little surprise for Miss Rose MacAdow." She leaned in close to me and whispered, "Listen, Laney, here's what we ought to do."

The plan, as she explained it, was simple, something to give Rose a scare. It would take a little gasoline. That's all. A little gas and a match. Set a fire in the grass around her house. Far enough away so the house wouldn't burn. A ring of fire to let Rose know someone was onto her, knew exactly the sort of evil person she was. No harm in that, was there, Delilah wanted to know. Just a little fire.

"You're not saying we're going to hurt her, are you?" I asked.

"Shake her up a little." Delilah wrapped her arms around my waist and gave me a squeeze. She laid her cheek against mine. "Jerk a knot in her tail, right?"

"I don't know, Delilah." I knew she was hurting and out for revenge, but I couldn't justify doing anything like what she was suggesting. "I wouldn't want anyone to get hurt."

My head was pounding, and I put my fingers to my temples.

"It's not those migraines coming back, is it, Laney?"

"I hope not. It's probably just spring allergies. Pollen. I bet that's all it is."

But shortly before dawn, that little headache became a full-blown migraine, and it was so bad I had to tell Mr. Mank, and he said I should go on home.

I said I didn't think I could drive. The lights of the store were doing strange things to my vision, and I couldn't imagine being able to hold my eyes open when I had to look into the headlights of oncoming cars.

"Let me drive her," Delilah said, and Mr. Mank said that would be all right.

So Delilah drove me to New Hope in her Malibu. I hated that we'd have to wake up Mother so she could ride back to Mt. Gilead with Delilah and fetch the Corolla, but I didn't know what else to do. I felt the burden that I was to both of them, and a sudden and fierce anger rose up in me over those migraines. I guess it was at that moment, wrapped up in my pain and my fury, that I chose to believe what Delilah was telling me.

"It's Rose, isn't it?" I said to her. "She's brought the misery back to me."

POKE SAID HE wouldn't call it crazy to think Rose was capable of putting a spell on someone. After all, he'd seen her sticking needles into that poppet doll.

"Could be she's wishing bad luck for you," he said. "Could be she's just mean."

At times, I wondered whether that was it. She'd stolen Tweet from Delilah like she had a right. She'd made me feel miserable that time when Lester was gone. Maybe, like Delilah said, she was selfish and couldn't stand to see anyone else happy.

A few days later, when Delilah and I were at the clinic so I could see the doctor about my migraines, Rose and Tweet came in.

"Hey, Laney," Rose said.

Delilah and I were sitting along the wall by the receptionist's window. Thank goodness there were no empty seats near us. The waiting room was fairly full of patients, some of them coughing and sniffling, some of them reading magazines, and a few chatting with one another.

I looked right at Rose and didn't say a word. Just looked at her hard, stared a hole right through her, until she said, "Well, someone's got her panties in a twist this morning." She slipped her arm around Tweet's waist. "C'mon, sweetie. Let's find a couple of seats on the warmer side of the room."

Tweet hesitated. I remembered the time on Christmas Day when he came to my house to see why I'd stopped coming around. *I thought we were all friends,* he said to me. Then he laid his hand on my shoulder, and I felt something give way. I thought maybe he'd do it now, say something to make the hateful moment wither, something to thaw my frozen heart, to make everything seem square, but all he did was lift his shoulders the slightest bit as if he were saying there wasn't a thing in the world he could do about what she was feeling, not a thing at all. Suddenly I hated him for not saying something to me. I grabbed a *People* magazine, shook it open, and pretended to be fascinated by it, all so I wouldn't have to look at him and Rose any longer.

Delilah said, "What's new, Tweet? Has Rose found you a real job now that you're going to be a daddy?"

I heard the rustle of Rose's jacket, and when I let my eyes lift just a bit from the magazine, I saw her drop her arm from Tweet's waist. She was breathing through her mouth—I could hear that, too—breathing hard as if what Delilah had said had punched her in the stomach and left her gasping for air.

"Damn you, Laney." Rose knew I'd betrayed her confidence. "Why would you tell her about our money worries?"

Her voice was sharp, and a woman sitting next to me took notice. She was an older woman with a blue tint to her hair. She had a walking cast on her foot, and she swung it over and tapped it against my leg. She gave me a stern look, but I didn't pay her much mind.

Tweet said, "You talked to Laney about all that?" He cocked his head toward Rose, trying to make sense of what he'd heard. "That's all private. That's just between you and me."

"Now, Tweet." Rose was trying to smooth things out, and I regretted what I'd done. I couldn't stand to think that I was causing trouble. "Tweet, baby," she said. "You know I didn't mean anything."

"Hurts when someone goes behind your back." Delilah's voice was all sweety-sweet, and I knew she was enjoying this. "Doesn't it, Tweet?"

That's when Rose knocked the magazine out of my hands. "You hateful thing," she said, and still I didn't say a word. Cool as could be—though my heart was pounding and I was trembling inside—I bent over and picked up the magazine. The woman with the walking cast on her foot got called back to an exam room, and she gave us all the once-over, shaking her head with disgust before she got up from her chair.

I kept staring at Rose, until finally she and Tweet walked over to the other side of the waiting room, where they sat, not saying a word. Two men in bib overalls had been talking about the weather, but they stopped when Rose and Tweet sat down beside them. I felt the eyes on me, the folks in the waiting room wondering what sort of girl I was. I couldn't have told them. I'm certain of that now. I had no idea who I was as we made the turn toward the end of our story.

Finally, a nurse came out and called my name, and I was glad to get out of there and into an exam room. The doctor wrote me a prescription for Inderal to keep me from getting my headaches as often. When I came out to settle my bill, Rose and Tweet were gone.

When we were outside, Delilah took my arm and turned me so we were face-to-face. "I've got something to tell you."

I waited, startled by the heat in Delilah's eyes, afraid to ask what she was talking about. Finally, I couldn't tolerate the quiet any longer. Even though I didn't know what she had to report, I felt myself drawn into the rage smoldering inside her, not knowing that in just a few minutes it would be mine. That's how close I was to her at that moment, so close I took her anger as my own even before she said what had caused it. I knew it as well as I knew my own name, and though the power of it terrified me, I couldn't stop thinking that as soon as she said what she had to say, my life—Laney Volk's life—would be on fire. It would be—and this thought struck me with a sharp, aching sweetness—it would be like it was for Lester in Iraq. Alive with possibility and risk and consequence. Not mine any longer. A life on the other side of right thinking. I told myself I would understand better then everything that had led Lester up to and away from that moment when he walked among the Iraqi wedding guests, putting his rifle to their heads and pulling the trigger.

"Tell me," I said to Delilah, knowing that in just a few moments I would be someone different than I ever was. "Tell me what happened."

The story was this: As I went through the door to see the doctor, Rose said in a voice loud enough for everyone in the waiting room to hear, "There goes Laney Volk. You know she's sleeping with that boy, that Poke Hambrick. Fifteen years old he is, and her nineteen. Story too sad to tell."

The thought of that being said in front of all those people made my face burn, not so much over what it made me out to be, but more because of how it treated what was true between Poke and me—that two people could be kind to each other and not expect anything in return. Rose, out of spite, had tried to turn that ugly. She needed someone to draw her up short, scare the stuffing out of her, so she'd learn how to treat people. I didn't once stop to question whether what Delilah had told me was true. From where I sit now, I doubt that it was, but that day I believed it with all my heart.

"This fire?" I said to Delilah. "When do we do it?"

A FEW NIGHTS LATER, just after dark, we got in Lester's truck and drove to New Hope. He toted the gas cans, said, sure, all right, he didn't mind giving Rose and Tweet a little scare.

I told myself there was no harm in it. A fire in the grass on an early spring night when there'd been plenty of rain and the ground was soft and there wasn't a stir of a breeze. Not a chance in the world for that fire to skip to the house. Just a little fire in the night to give Rose the whim-whams.

"Rose MacAdow," Delilah said under her breath. "You watch out now."

We moved through the dark, having left Lester's truck along the street in front of my mother's house. No one would think a thing about seeing that truck there. Everyone knew that Lester and I were a match. I thought about Rose saying what she did about Poke and me so all those people in the clinic waiting room could hear, and, again, I burned with how mean that was, how unfair.

"She better watch out," I said. "She doesn't know who she's messing with."

It was so quiet, I could hear the gas sloshing around in the cans. From time to time, they banged against Lester's legs. The three of us slipped around behind Mr. Hambrick's house. The house was dark except for a faint light coming from the living room, and I knew it was the glow of the television screen, that Mr. Hambrick was snugged down in his reclining chair, dozing after supper while the TV played. He wouldn't hear a thing as we cut through his backyard and made ready to cross over into Rose and Tweet's.

"Where you going?"

The voice came out of the dark and Delilah gave a little yelp. Lester said, "Jesus," and I felt my heart in my chest.

It was Poke. He came out of the dark and stood with us. I could smell his supper on his clothes, the smell of hot grease from whatever Mr. Hambrick had fried up. It was a night of no moon, so I could barely make him out, but I could hear him breathing, and I felt the air stir a bit as he stepped up close to us. He bumped a gas can with his foot.

"That's gas, isn't it?" he said.

"Go inside, Poke," I told him.

"Don't worry," he said. "I won't tell."

"Nothing to tell," said Delilah.

Poke bumped the gas can again. "Soon will be."

That's when Lester said, "You heard Laney. Go inside and forget you saw us."

He said it in a mean tone of voice I'd never heard from him. "Lester," I said, "don't do him like that."

"I said, go." Lester's voice was softer now, but it was too late. I knew he'd hurt Poke's feelings.

"You don't want to be any part of this," I said. "Really, Poke."

He didn't say a word to me. He took off running across the yard, and then off into the dark, where he could be alone with his hurt.

I slapped Lester across the arm. "Why'd you have to do that?"

"Jeez, Laney, I just wanted him to go."

"Well, he's gone," said Delilah. "Now, let's get moving."

At Rose and Tweet's, the house was full of light. Light in every window, a light burning on the front porch.

"Lit up like a Christmas tree," Lester said.

"Like they're expecting company," said Delilah.

"Like they knew we were coming." My voice was a whisper. "It gives me the creeps."

For a good while, none of us said a word. Then the music started. Tweet on his saxophone. The windows were open—it was that kind of night, still and warm enough to make folks think of summer on its way—and I could hear the music, something smoky and hot. I knew Rose was in the house listening. Rose and her man, just whiling away the night. Rose, who said the vile thing she did in the clinic waiting room; Rose, who went dancing by a window, and then another, and I could see she wasn't thinking a thing about how much she'd hurt people. She was dancing to Tweet's music, holding the bottom of her bulging stomach, thinking everything in her life was okey-doke.

"I hate her," Delilah said, and neither Lester nor I said a word to disagree.

So with that music playing, and the dancing going on, Lester finally got to work. Crouched low in the dark, he circled the house, walking backwards, trailing gasoline as he went. He had to stop once and come back to get the other gas can. When it was all done, his breath was coming fast. He bent over, his hands on his knees, and waited for his breathing to steady itself.

The smell of gasoline was all around us.

"Okay?" Delilah asked.

"Right," said Lester. He took a box of matches out of his pocket. "I'll just be a tick."

He went off into the darkness, and soon I heard the scratch of the match head, saw the small flame, and heard the puff of ignition as it touched the trail of gasoline. The flames stretched out in each direction, racing along the circle.

Then I heard Lester cry out, and I knew he was on fire.

I ran to him. I pushed him to the damp ground and slapped at his boot and his pants' leg with my bare hands, not thinking at all of burning myself, only thinking that I had to put out those flames.

Finally, I did. Gas had gotten onto Lester's boots while he'd been making his circle around the house, and when he put the lit match to the trail, the flame caught his boots and pants' legs, burning off the gas. Luckily, I got to him before the fire could lick through leather and denim to the skin beneath.

I helped him away from the fire, to where Delilah was waiting, and then the three of us ran, escaping before Rose and Tweet caught sight of the fire.

At Lester's truck, we panted for breath. I realized that my hands were throbbing. Lester opened the door, and in the dome light's glow, he inspected my palms, which were already starting to blister.

"You're burned," he said.

Then I realized Poke was on the sidewalk. I didn't know where he'd come from or where he'd been when we'd been setting the fire at Rose and Tweet's, only that he came to me now, and he said, "Are you hurt, Laney?"

Just like that, he put away the hurt he'd felt when Lester talked mean to him. If only we'd all been able to forgive one another the way that Poke did.

"My fingers," I said. "Did you see?"

He nodded. The fire whistle started to blow, and I knew Rose and Tweet had finally seen that fire and made the call. Soon there would be a pumper truck, and maybe even the county sheriff, and, of course, it would be all over the news, and there I was marked with those burned hands.

"Get out of here," Poke said. "Just go. Don't worry. I'll take care of everything."

BY MORNING—once I'd been to the emergency room at the hospital, where they gave me Silvadine cream for my burns and Vicodin for the pain, and then wrapped my fingers in gauze—the word was out that Poke Hambrick had tried to set fire to that house where Rose MacAdow lived with that man known as Tweet.

Poke had come clean and told the fire chief and then the police how he'd poured gasoline onto the grass and set it ablaze with a match. Why? Just fooling around, he said.

Fooling around? People shook their heads when that story got around town. Wasn't no fooling to it when it came to fire that close to a house and a woman inside it carrying a baby. Lordy. What was that boy thinking?

He wasn't, he told the police. He didn't have a thought in his head that anyone might get hurt. It was just something to do.

Something like that? the police said. Arson? You don't do something like that unless you're out to do some harm.

I heard the story from Mother the next day. What in the world had happened to my hands, anyway? she wanted to know. I'd been at Lester's, I said. He had one of those smooth-topped stoves, the kind where the burners were underneath a ceramic surface, and after supper I'd gone to brush some crumbs off with my hands, not noticing, until it was too late, the red light on the control panel telling me the surface was still hot. "I'm an idiot," I told her, and Mother said, "Well, my gosh, Laney. You need to be more careful. Play with something hot, and you end up getting burned." I suspect she knew right then and there that I'd had something to do with that fire at Rose and Tweet's. "You hear what I'm saying, Missy? You take care."

What Poke didn't know, when he told his lie to the police, was that people in town would start coming forward to say they'd always thought there was something odd about that boy, maybe even something dangerous.

Ida Henline said she turned off her bedroom light one night, ready for bed, and she glanced toward the window and saw that boy, that grandson of Curtis Hambrick, with his face pressed to the glass.

I heard this and more, heard it on the lips of folks coming through the Walmart, heard it when Mother brought the stories home from work. Even the preacher, Luther Gibson, was telling tales. Claimed he sometimes found letters in his mailbox, the envelopes open. He didn't mean to accuse, but one day he'd seen Poke out at the curb, raising and lowering the red flag on that mailbox, and, well, if you put two and two together...

It adds up to four, said Jess Raymond, who, of course, knew his wife was in love with the mailman, Bernard Goad, and had finally worked up the nerve to tell her, All right, then, he's who you want, well, go on, then, and have him, but don't ever come back to this house.

What a sad lot, said Rayanne Fines when she came to see whether Mother might want to tack on to her life insurance policy. Talking about Poke like he'd done killed someone.

He might have, the police said, and it looked for a while like they might send him away to one of those boot camps for troubled teens, one of those places where drill sergeants stripped them down to nothing and either left them so mean the next thing they did would be even worse, or put them so low they'd barely be able to lift their heads in public.

That's when I promised myself to go to the police and tell them

Poke was lying about that fire. I'd own up to it. I'd tell them the whole story. But I let Lester talk me out of it.

"We don't need that trouble," he said. "Just let it be."

So I did, and then Mr. Hambrick begged the police not to send Poke away. He's not a bad boy, he told them. He just has a hard time fitting in. Mercy, what would happen to him in such a place? Mean breeds mean. Wasn't no call for that.

The police said Poke would have to check in with a probation officer from time to time. He'd have to stop looking in people's windows, reading people's mail. He'd have to walk the straight and narrow. One bad move, and he'd be on a bus to the land of "Sir, yes sir," and there wouldn't be a thing Mr. Hambrick could do about it except tell the boy to straighten up and fly right.

Oh, he'd straighten up all right, Mr. Hambrick said. And just like that he put Poke in lockdown. Put him to work as soon as he got home from school. Wouldn't let him slip off at night. Kept the chores coming for him all through the weekend.

I stepped outside one Saturday and saw him running the rototiller in the garden plot. His white T-shirt had ridden up, and I could see his belly shake with the tiller's vibration. Back and forth he went, and when he hit something that didn't give, he had to shut down the tiller and pick up a shovel and dig out a tree root or a brickbat or a rock. He tossed it out into the yard, and then he had to pull on the cord that started the tiller. Sometimes it took a number of tries, yank after yank on that cord, and then one time the tiller toppled over, and Poke sank down on his knees and pounded at the dirt with his fists.

The cornfield between Mother's house and Mr. Hambrick's had yet to be plowed. I strode across the ground, and without a word, I helped Poke put the tiller upright. Then I took the shovel from him. He started the tiller and I was there to dig out whatever I needed to so he wouldn't have to stop and do it himself and then start all over.

My hands were healed, but still tender, so gripping the shovel handle brought me some pain. I wished I'd thought to grab a pair of Mother's garden gloves, but I hadn't, and now I didn't want to go back for them because I wanted to be there whenever Poke needed me.

So we worked that ground, worked it until the plot was turned over and the earthworms were wriggling on top of the dark brown clay. The sun was bearing down, and I wiped the sweat from my face with the sleeve of my shirt. Mother had bedsheets drying on the clothesline, and a wind came up and made them billow and pop. The air smelled of the dirt and the hyacinths in bloom in front of Mr. Hambrick's house. Poke cut off the tiller, and I was glad to have the quiet that settled around us. I could hear birds singing in the trees, the faint sound of a baseball game on someone's radio, and then the clarinet music coming from Rose and Tweet's.

"You didn't have to help me," Poke said. "Didn't that shovel hurt your hands?"

I shrugged. "I didn't mind."

I studied my palms where the newly healed skin was pink and sore to the touch. When I'd worn the gauze, those first days after the fire, I'd imagined that everyone was looking at me and that someone would finally figure out the connection between that fire at Rose and Tweet's and my burned hands, but no one did, no one except Rose, who came through my checkout line one night and said to me, "What's the matter, Laney? Get too close to the fire?"

"It was Lester's stove," I said, telling the same story I'd told Mother. "You know me. Too stupid for my own good sometimes."

Rose set her hands on the conveyor belt and leaned in close to me. "You tell whatever story you want, and you let that boy do the same." She reached over the belt and touched me on my gauzed palm. "You don't know what kind of trouble you're getting yourself into." She gouged a nail through the gauze, dug it into my blistered skin. "No idea," she said, "but keep going, and you'll find out."

In the garden, I recalled the feel of that fingernail gouging me, and I said to Poke, "You want to know why we did it? That fire?"

He kicked some dirt from the tiller's tines. "You can tell me whatever you want. You know that, Laney. You and me, we're tight."

I told him about Rose gouging my hand that night at the Walmart, and then I added the story of what she'd said in the waiting room at the clinic. As much as it embarrassed me to say it, I told him that she'd announced as big as you please that—here I had to stop a moment and gather my breath; I had to look away, back toward Mother's house, so I wouldn't be looking at Poke when I said it—well, there was only one way to do this and that was to come right out and say the ugly thing, to tell him that the folks in that waiting room heard that the two of us were sleeping together.

For a good while, he didn't say anything. Then in a shy voice he said, "No one would ever believe that. Honest, Laney, even if I was your age, there's no way you'd ever want me. I'm nothing like Lester."

I reached out and took his hand. It was caked with dirt and it was too big a hand for a boy his age. It was hard to hold on to, but I did it, anyway, and I told him he had a good heart, and if he were older, well, then, maybe, and I saw a flicker of smile around his lips, and he looked at me dead-on, and he said, "She shouldn't have hurt you like that. Shouldn't have hurt us."

I smiled. "I guess she still needs to learn her lesson."

"I can help."

I wouldn't for the life of me let him fall deeper into our mess, wouldn't let him end up with a hard edge to his heart like the one I felt coming on mine. I swore that then. "No," I told him. "You stay out of this. You're in enough trouble."

"But, Laney—"

"I said no."

A FEW DAYS LATER, Delilah called to say someone had broken into her trailer and left a mess.

"Rose," she said.

I saw the inverted pentagram drawn on the bathroom mirror, and then Lester came home and found the same pentagrams spray-painted on his house.

When a car came up behind me on the highway and nearly blinded me with its high beams, I got spooked. Delilah said I could have been killed. That's when I decided, like I told the police. That's when I gathered her and Lester one night in her trailer, and I scratched Rose's name into a black candle and set it to burn. I called the evil spirits forth, and we watched the candle wax drip and dissolve Rose's name. The fluorescent light above the sink came on, and that spooked us.

Delilah said Rose had put a death hex on all of us, a curse to last until the one who spun it was dead, and I didn't say a word to dispute what she claimed. I let her believe it. I let Lester believe it, too, a man who already had his demons from the war and didn't deserve any more heartache in his life. I did all that, and it shames me to own up to it now.

"I want us to be happy," I told him when we were finally alone that night. "You and me. I want us to be happy a long, long time."

Did I mean it? I'm not sure. I only know at the time, I needed him by me, so I said what I did, not a thought in my head that this might be the thing that would convince him that it was necessary to take a stand so he and I could be safe to plan a life together.

In time Delilah would show him that .38, and he'd say we needed a silencer. We drove out into the country and tried firing that pistol into a milk jug and a pillow to see if we could kill Rose that way without anyone hearing the shots.

Then we got spooked. We called the whole thing off, said we'd been crazy to even think of such a thing, and we swore ourselves to silence.

"Laney, you're the angel on my shoulder," Delilah told me, and I believed her.

The Earth was turning toward May. Soon we'd have the long, sunny days of summer. We'd put our revenge scheme behind us and we'd wait for the days to pass until it'd seem like it wasn't us who'd thought it up, but three other people—crazy people we didn't know at all.

But for a time, I gave Delilah this gift. I let her believe that if we killed Rose MacAdow, then everything in our lives would be good and right and beautiful forever.

MISS BABY

I meant to make the call. I meant to do the thing that would save my brother, no matter what it cost. Then Lester Stipp looked at me. He called me Baby like we'd been together for years. Said it like a prayer, and I felt everything I knew was right fly out the window.

"Miss Baby," Emma said. "I'm so sorry everything's gone wrong."

"Baby?" Lester said again. He was Lester to me now, not Donnie, but he was still the same man who'd turned my life around, who'd come to me with love.

I put my finger to his lips. "Shh," I said. Then I took him by the hand and lifted him from the couch. I led him out into the night, and we walked up the street, away from Emma's house, away from my own house, where the bottles clinked together on the branches of the mimosa tree. We walked deeper into the dark, and I tried not to think about the fact that Pablo was there at Emma's waiting for me to do the right thing.

Lester and I walked all the way to my shop, neither of us saying a word, and when we were there, inside, I didn't switch on a light. We were shadows, barely visible at all.

Then I told him. I said, "The police are looking for you. I saw it on the TV."

I don't know what look came over his face. Maybe I hadn't turned on the light because I didn't want to see, didn't want any evidence that what the TV said was true.

"What in the world?" he said, and I could hear the confusion in his voice. "Baby?"

"They've arrested a girl in Illinois. A skinny little girl with a mess of curly hair."

I reached out for his hand, but I couldn't find it in the dark. "Laney," he said in a whisper, and I felt my heart break.

"You remember her?"

"I remember."

"What else?"

He wouldn't answer. I let the seconds tick by. "Lester," I said. "Lester Stipp. Did you kill someone?"

"No, Baby," he said, turning on a light. "Not me. Not in a million years." He took me by my shoulders. He looked me in the eye. "But I've got to go back."

I knew he would because I believed he was a stand-up sort of man, and once he knew that girl was in trouble with the law, he'd do what he could to help her. What's more, I felt certain he'd never meant to hurt me. He hadn't played me for a fool. He'd truly forgotten his old life, and he'd let me make this new one for him.

"We could go to the police," I said. "Right now. We could make things right."

He took a long breath, and I was afraid of what he'd say. "I've got to go back for Laney."

Lordy Magordy, I could barely get a breath, feeling the life we'd managed to build slipping away. It was so quiet there in my shop. We found each other's hand, and we held on. "Do you still love her?" I asked.

"I remember her," he said. "I remember what we lived through."

"That counts for something, I expect."

He put his arms around me. He pulled me close. "You took care of me, Baby. You found me when I was lost. That counts for something, too."

I felt my hope rise. "I'll go with you. I'll drive you back to Illinois in my car, and I'll stand by you no matter what."

"No, that wouldn't be right. This is about me and Laney. She's in trouble, and you're not a part of that. You've got troubles enough of your own. I just don't know how I'm going to do it. I don't have a car, Baby, and I don't have much money."

A crazy thought came to me. "I'll give you the keys to my car. I'll even give you money out of the till. If you've got my car—if you owe me money—you'll have to come back."

"I can't promise, Baby. I really can't."

"Then you've got to do one thing for me."

"Whatever you say."

"You've got to let me shoot you. Give you a tat. Something to take with you, the rest of your life."

I gave him money. I gave him my car keys. Then I put him in the chair, and I took my time with that tat. I put it on his wrist, so every time that girl, that Laney, reached for his hand, she'd see it. I put it there in bold letters—**Miss Baby**—so each time he saw it, he'd have my name to remind him, and if the years went on and I never saw him again, at least I'd know that from time to time he'd think of me. He'd see that command, Miss Baby, and he would—I convinced myself it was true. He'd miss me and maybe, just maybe, he'd come back.

"It really doesn't hurt," he said. "Not as much as you'd think."

I wanted to tell him it was killing me. I said as much with the loving way I bandaged him, with the way I kissed the back of his hand. I told him how long to keep the bandage on. "Don't peel it back," I told him. "No matter how bad you want to get a peek."

It hurt me to think of the hours he'd be gone and no sight of my name, but I explained how a tat is a wound and he had to keep it bandaged so bacteria wouldn't infect it. I told him how to care for it after the bandage was off. I gave him some A+D Ointment. Then I remembered the day Slam Dent beat Pablo and Lester put his shoulder back into its socket. I imagined Pablo back at Emma's, furious because Lester and I were gone.

I started to tell him there was money on his head, enough to square Pablo with Slam Dent. I was that close to asking Lester to let me turn him in and collect the reward money.

Then he said, "I don't have anything to hide. Really, Baby. I don't."

I felt ashamed because I'd been wanting to make him guilty. "Are you sure you don't?"

"I don't think so. Not that I can remember."

WHEN WE STEPPED outside my shop, Slam Dent was waiting for us. "I want your brother," he said, "and I want him right now."

It was coming on dawn, the sky brightening in the east. The wind was up and the branches of the live oaks were shaking their leaves.

"I suspect you got your money," I said.

"Money's one thing," he said. "Revenge is another."

That's when Lester spoke up. "I want you to leave her alone." His voice was flat and edged with temper. "I want you to stop messing with folks. You've done enough of that."

Slam stared at him awhile. Then he broke into a low, throaty chuckle that was laced with danger. "Mister, you've got no idea what you're getting yourself into."

"Maybe I do," said Lester.

He put him to his knees with a heel kick to the inside of his thigh. When Slam was on his knees, his head bowed, Lester clasped his hands together to make a bigger fist, and he brought it down onto the base of Slam's skull. I heard something crack. It was a sickening sound, one I've never been able to forget, just like I can't forget the way Slam toppled forward, his face smashing into the sidewalk, and Lester bent down to press his fingertips to his throat and feel for a pulse.

"Did you kill him?" I asked.

"No," said Lester, "but I could have if I'd wanted to."

I let him go. Lester Stipp, my Donnie. I let him walk off into the weak light just before dawn, knowing that he'd go back to my house. He'd get in my car and drive east, back to Illinois, back to her. I didn't want to be around when Slam came to, not even as close as the inside of my shop, but I didn't want to follow Lester to my house, either. What would I say as I watched him get ready to leave? What would be the last words between us other than what we'd said just before he left me standing there on Oak Street? "Thank you," he said to me, and I knew that was all that could pass between the two of us now that he'd made up his mind to leave. *Thank you for taking me in. Thank you for loving me. Thank you for letting me go.* I told him to take care. I told him to remember me. I told him not to go into my house and give Pablo a chance to latch on to him. "Just get in my car and drive," I said.

Then I did the only thing I could. I watched him go.

I couldn't bear to be anywhere in the world just then, but I knew I couldn't stay where I was, so I started walking. All the way up Oak, toward the west, away from my house. Every time a set of headlights swept over me from behind, I held my breath, hoping it was Lester in my car, hoping he'd pull to the curb, throw open the passenger-side door, and tell me to get in. Fairy tales can turn out like that, at least the ones I love, but this was my life I was in the middle of, and I made up my mind, as I watched the cars shoot past me, that once I was home, in the glare of day, I'd gather up all my fairies into a trash bag and toss them out for good. It was time to get on with facing the reality of my life. Lester wasn't ever coming back, and there I was, alone.

Once, I turned around to look behind me. The faintest glow of the sun tipped the horizon in the east. Then I just kept walking, heading north, out past the open range where the longhorn cows were beginning to stir from their night's sleep beneath the mesquite trees. The lights along University Drive were ahead of me, and beyond that, on a hill, the dark houses taking shape in the coming light.

Then I realized where I was headed. I was going to someone who'd understand. I was going to Carolyn. In one of those dark houses, she slept, and I hoped she wouldn't mind too awfully much when I woke her and said, "I didn't know where else to go."

SHE LET ME IN. I was cold now, shivering, and she said, "My word, Baby. What's wrong to bring you out here this time of morning?"

I told her everything. I told her about going to Deep Ellum to get the money we needed to save Pablo and how Slam Dent showed up, and now he was laid out on the sidewalk in front of my shop because Lester put him there.

Lester was gone, I told her. He was on his way back to Illinois, although he swore he hadn't killed anyone. His girlfriend had been arrested. He was going back for her sake. "You knew it from the start, didn't you?" I asked Carolyn. "You knew something was fishy."

Her face was slack, her cheek creased with sleep marks. She had a pink chenille bathrobe on over a pair of sweatpants and a T-shirt. This could have been the moment when she asked me what else did I expect, doing a fool thing like I did, taking a man into my house and persuading him we were a couple, but to her credit she didn't. I suppose she knew what it was to hold on to a dream. I imagine she was still hoping there might be a future for her and Pablo.

She put her arms around me. She said, "My goodness, Baby. You're almost frozen to death." She asked me if I loved this Lester Stipp, and I told her I did. "Then it's no lie." She pressed me to her, and I felt the tears start to come. "What you feel in your heart can't ever be a lie."

I was sobbing. I was choking out the words. "I don't know if I'll ever see him again."

"Who's to say, Baby? Look how crazy the world can get."

She was right. No one could predict the wild bounces and turns a life could take, even a life like mine that appeared to be all played out to a most unsatisfying end. Lester Stipp was gone, on his way back to that girl in Illinois. Slam Dent was either still lying on the sidewalk in front of my shop, or else racked up in the hospital, who knows what broken under his miserable skin. And Pablo? I called Emma's house, and she said, "Miss Baby, you better talk to him. He's in a state."

He got on the phone, and the first thing he said was, "How could you let him get away?"

I was wondering the same thing, of course. Why hadn't I put my foot down? Why hadn't I said the only way I'd let Lester have my car was if I came along with it? I knew the answer, of course. Because I wanted him to be the one to say he wouldn't go without me. Because I wanted to hear those words from him to convince me that we were meant to be together. Because I didn't want to be like my *mami,* always chasing after a man.

"I'm tired," I said, and it was true, I was worn to the bone. I was tired of all the ways people could manage to screw up their lives. Me included. I was tired of how needy we all were. I was tired of all the drama, and the please, Baby, please. So much so that I said to Pablo, "It's time we all stand up and face what we have to face. All of us. Even me."

"What do you have to face, Betts?"

"The same thing you do, *mi hermano. Esta pinche vida.*"

Pablo chuckled. "*La vida loca.*"

"That's right," I told him. "As crazy as we've made it. This life. That's what we have to own up to."

So that's what I did. I let Carolyn drive me home. It was daylight, another sunny day, the first day without Lester Stipp, and I did what I'd promised myself. I shook out a big plastic trash bag, and I went through my house throwing away every fairy figurine I had.

Pablo watched. Once he tried to stop me. He took my arm. "Betts," he said, but I shook free and kept at it.

Emma was there, and she said, "Miss Baby, my lands."

"Let her be," said Carolyn. "Let her do what she has to do."

Emma kissed me on the cheek. "You know where I am, Miss Baby, no matter what you need. It's all right that you made up that man, that Donnie. I don't hold it against you."

She went back to her house. Carolyn and Pablo slipped into the kitchen and left me alone. I heard the murmur of their voices. They were talking in low, private tones, the way they must have done countless times when they were married. It was the sort of give-and-take I was sure I'd never have. I was convinced that Lester Stipp had been my last chance, and I was ready to face a life alone. I took fairies off shelves and tables and ledges. No more Otherworld for Miss Baby. No more living in Wonderland. I carried the trash bag to the curb, where the next day the garbage truck would cart it away. All those fairies tossed into the landfill. Good riddance. I was Betty Ruiz, no different from Emma Hart—two women on their own.

When I came back inside, Pablo and Carolyn were waiting for me.

"We've been talking," he said, and she nodded.

I could tell, like me, they'd made decisions. Something was winding down for all of us.

"The thing is," she said. "Well, Baby, even if that horrible man, that Slam Dent, won't bother us anymore, Pablo's still in trouble with the law."

That much was true. He was still a wanted man.

"I've been thinking about what you said, Betts." He gave me a sad smile. "What you said about owning up. I figure it's time." Carolyn took his hand. "I'm going to call the police," he said. "I'm going to tell them I'm here."

But he didn't have to. Just then, someone knocked on my front door, and when I looked out through the glass, I saw that it was the policeman with the red mustache, the man who'd found Lester Stipp's driver's license from which I'd cut his name and address. The policeman had let me keep that cut-up license. He'd said he had everything he needed. Now he was at my door.

"Well, now, that's convenient," Pablo said, and he nodded for me to let the man in.

He was already yakking as soon as I opened the door, and at first he didn't even register Pablo and Carolyn. "Miss Baby, I've come for that sweetie of yours."

"Lester Stipp," I said.

"So you knew his real name?"

"How'd you figure it out?"

"I wrote down that driver's license number," he said. "I made a call to Illinois and found out who had that number. Lester Stipp. Do you know he's wanted?"

I nodded. "Found that out last night, too. Right before he told me good-bye and left. Now, why don't you tell me something I don't know?"

It was like the ends of his mustache sagged a bit more. That's how disappointed he was. Then he puffed up his chest. "How do I know you're telling the truth? I'm going to have a look around."

"Es verdad," Pablo said.

For the first time since he stepped inside my house, the policeman realized who was standing in front of him. "This is quite a day," he said.

Pablo kissed Carolyn. "It's the day they give babies away," he said. Then he stepped forward, his hands held out, ready for the cuffs.

* * *

AFTER THE POLICEMAN took Pablo away, and it was just Carolyn and me in my house, she said, "It's about the saddest thing there is, isn't it, Baby? A house you live in by yourself?"

"It is," I told her, and I understood this was our way of saying we were both sorry for whatever hurt we had caused the other since our story began. What's more, we were saying the future was now ours to own. Pablo would certainly go to jail. His drama would go out of our lives.

A few days later, I'd see two Rangers easing Slam Dent into an unmarked car on Oak Street. Slam Dent with a cane in his hand, a bandage on his head. He'd look at me for a moment and then turn away. I'd feel the relief of knowing he was done with me.

Maybe it was a blessing to have Lester Stipp gone as well. At least in my strongest moments I'd be able to tell myself that. After all, I was guilty. I stole him off the street. I brought him home and spun a life for him. I made him believe that he belonged with me, that we had years to come, all because I was lonely, all for a chance at love, which doesn't excuse what I did.

Standing there with Carolyn that day, about to face the rest of my life alone, I thought back to the woman I was when I saw Lester Stipp on that street corner, and I said to him, "You're Donnie. You're my sweet Donnie." I was ashamed of that woman because she was so desperate, and yet I loved her for that same reason, loved her because she took that chance.

"Whenever my *mami* got all turned around because of some fool thing," I told Carolyn, "she always said, *'Necesitaba hacerlo.'* "

"What's that mean?"

"I had to do it."

Carolyn nodded. "Some things are like that. They sure as heck are."

"She always believed everything would be all right."

I remembered the other thing she always said. *"Me encamina mi corazón a mi hogar."* She had faith that, no matter how reckless or starry-eyed she was—no matter the mess she made of her life—she'd be fine. "Don't be sad," she said to me seconds before she died. *"Mi corazón…"* She didn't have the breath to finish, but I knew the rest. Her heart. Her heart would lead her home.

LANEY

It was Poke who told the police what they needed to know in order for them to come for me at the Walmart that night in December, but really they'd been on my trail for a while—since summer when the two officers had come to talk to Mr. Mank, and they'd asked me a few questions. Wasn't it true that I used to live with Delilah Dade and Rose MacAdow? "Yes," I told them. "We were friends." And wasn't it true that Delilah had pulled a pistol out of her purse at the Boar's Nest up in Dark Bend on Memorial Day? I lied and said I didn't know anything about that.

Delilah was off sick from work the night the police asked me about her gun, but at break I called to warn her. She said not to worry. She'd already talked to the cops.

"But, Delilah," I said, terrified of what they might eventually find out, "you got so mad at Rose that night at the Boar's Nest, you threatened her with your .38. Someone's told the police about that."

"That .38?" Delilah was all la-di-dah. "Now, honey, I might have been a little ticked off with Rose, but point a gun at her? Why, I haven't even had a gun in my house since Bobby May left. That was his pistol. Remember, Laney?" She kept quiet for a while, and when I didn't answer, she said it again. "Remember?" And I knew she was telling me that if the police asked me about that gun again, this was the lie I was to tell them.

"Sure, I remember," I finally said.

"That's a good girl," she said, and then she hung up on me.

Now, facing the police officers the second time, I'd told as much of the story as I could bring myself to say.

The big-bellied officer nodded at the slope-shouldered one, who went out into the hall. When he came back, he had Poke with him. Poke kept his head down, and I couldn't bear to see him with the slope-shouldered officer's hand on the back of his neck, guiding him to the table where I sat.

I could tell Poke was afraid. He sat down next to me. He took off his glasses and rubbed at his eyes. "I'm sorry, Laney," he said, and my heart broke.

"The boy's grandfather brought him in." The slope-shouldered officer sat down at the end of the table and crossed one leg over the other at his knee. It was a relaxed gesture, and seeing it, I let myself believe everything would be all right. If I just told the truth, every bit of it—if I stated the facts calmly and plainly—everything would be fine. Then the officer said, "Seems like the boy was hiding something in his room. Grandpa didn't like what he found, so he did the right thing. He came to us."

"He's not a stupid man." For the first time, the big-bellied officer wasn't snapping or threatening. He was just saying what he knew in a level voice. "He knew he was looking at trouble. Isn't that right, son?"

Poke nodded. He put his glasses back on.

"And you've been doing everything you can to cooperate, haven't you?" Poke nodded again, but that wasn't enough for the officer. He tapped one of his chunky fingers on the table right under Poke's bowed head. "Speak up, son."

"Yes, sir. I've told you everything there is to tell."

"Tell it to the lady." The big-bellied officer had that edge back to his voice. "Tell her what Grandpa found."

For a good while, Poke didn't say anything. He chewed at his bottom lip and looked away from me. I heard the murmur of voices somewhere in the hallway, and I wondered whether Mr. Hambrick was waiting out there. I wished I could reach over and take Poke's hand, just to let him know that whatever he'd told the officers, it was all right.

"He doesn't have to tell her." The slope-shouldered officer uncrossed his legs and rested his arms on the table. "She already knows. Don't you, Laney?"

It was a gun, he said—that's what Mr. Hambrick found in Poke's room. A .38 Taurus Special, a five-shot with a stainless-steel barrel and Pachmayr grips. The state crime lab in Springfield had lifted fingerprints from those grips, prints that belonged to Lester. There were other prints on that gun, the slope-shouldered officer told me. Besides Lester's there were prints from Poke, and then sets that belonged to two other people. The officer felt certain, now that I'd told the story of the day that Lester and Delilah and I test-fired the .38, that some of those prints belonged to me. They'd suspected that ever since they got the crime lab report, and that's why they'd come for me at the Walmart. Because I'd been Lester's girlfriend. Because they didn't know where he was, but they knew how to find me. And those other prints? Of course they were Delilah's, and had the officers known that when they took me from the Walmart, they would have taken her, too.

"You matched a set with Lester?"

I was confused. Had they found him somewhere and taken his prints? Could he be right there at the station? What would I say if I saw him after all the time that'd passed? *Did you run because you forgot who you were, or were you trying to get away?* If he left deliberately, I'd still forgive him. I'd ask if he was all right. I'd ask if he remembered me. Maybe I'd kiss him on the lips and tell him we'd get through this and everything would be all right. I'd tell him I was sorry that I'd brought him into such a mess.

"Military records," the slope-shouldered officer said, and I thought, Of course. "Laney, are you sure you don't know where Lester is? Haven't you heard from him since he left town?"

So they didn't have him. He was still on the loose.

"Not a word." I didn't tell them how I'd worried over him, how I'd wondered if I'd ever see him again, how I felt all hollowed out on the inside without him. "Not one single word," I said.

The slope-shouldered officer glanced at the big-bellied one, who raised his eyebrows in a way that told me he didn't believe it. I kept talking. I told the officers that, all right, it was true for a while we had a plot, a plan for murder, but in the end we'd come to our senses. What happened after the day Lester and Delilah and I were down that oil lease road wasn't my doing. That was the truth.

The big-bellied officer nodded toward the slope-shouldered one. "Get a warrant," he said. "Let's have a talk with Delilah Dade."

DELILAH WOULDN'T TALK. Poke and I waited, always with one of the officers at our side, for hours while they interrogated her. At last, the slope-shouldered officer came into the room and said she wouldn't tell them anything other than what I already had. Yes, for a while there'd been a plot, first to scare Rose and then to kill her, but nothing had ever come of it, at least nothing that Delilah would claim to be a part of. Whether Lester Stipp put that .38 to work after that day down the oil lease road, she really couldn't say.

"So there we are," said the big-bellied officer. He drummed his hands on top of the table. The noise startled me, and I jerked up my head. Poke was looking at me, and I could see his lip quivering. The big-bellied officer narrowed his eyes and studied me. "Boy with a gun, not just any gun, but the .38 that killed those two people. Lots of explaining to do. I can tell you that. Maybe there's something else you might remember?"

"Tell him, Laney," Poke said. "Please. Tell him the truth."

* * *

I BEGAN BY telling the story of how Lester took me home the day we test-fired the .38. I took my time, the way I am now. I told the two police officers exactly how it was. We drove out of that oil lease road, and once we were back at Delilah's, I got in the truck with Lester. He carried me to New Hope, and we swore we'd never speak of the fact that we'd gone as far as to fire that .38 in preparation for using it on Rose.

I told the officers how I finally went into Mother's house and did my best to step back into the life I'd left, that unremarkable life, comfortable now with common sense and decent living. The days and weeks went on. The Inderal the doctor gave me was working, and by the middle of April my migraines had stopped, and I was glad to be Laney again.

Then one morning, Rose caught me in Mother's driveway when I was coming home from work, and she said that she and Tweet had started to lock the house when they were gone and at night when they slept. She said she walked into the living room one day, and Poke was standing there. He'd just walked right into the house, pretty as you please. Said he was looking for Tweet.

"Laney, I know you're fond of him," she said, "but I'd be careful if I was you."

The next night at Walmart, Delilah asked me if I'd do her one more favor. She wanted me to give Tweet a note. She handed me a folded-up sheet of notebook paper, and her fingers were trembling. "I wrote it out," she said. "Everything I want to say. Everything that's in my heart. You can read it if you want."

"I'd never do that," I said. "They're your own personal words."

"No, go on." Delilah's eyes were red-rimmed from crying, and I could tell she was scraped out, that it'd taken everything she had to write that note. "I want you to. I want to make sure I'm not making a fool out of myself."

Her handwriting made me swallow hard: big, round letters and flowing tails and hearts for dots over the *i*'s as if she were thirteen again and writing to her first crush. The words themselves, though, and what they added up to, were blunt and full of grown-up pain:

> *Tweet, I've done my best to put you behind me and imagine my life going on without you in it, but no dice. I just can't swing it. Here's the truest thing I know. We can make things right. You can come back and we can start again, no questions asked. We can pretend that Rose never came along. All I want in my life is you, Tweet, and if I can't have you, I don't know what I'll do. I'm afraid to find out. When you live alone without the true love of your life in it, you get afraid of a lot of things. You get crazy thoughts, but the one thing you always know is what you need, and you keep hoping for a miricle to bring it your way.*

IT WAS THE MISSPELLING in that last sentence, "miricle," that made me embarrassed for Delilah. A word that couldn't hold all that she wanted to fill it with, couldn't hold everything that was in her heart. A word that broke down with the effort.

I folded the paper. I remembered how she helped me get through that time when Lester was gone. "It only hurts so long," she told me. "Then it just aches when you touch it." I didn't realize then that what she was telling me was that it never went away, the pain in the heart when you lose someone you love. That's how you knew it was real, that love. You knew it from the fact that you never stopped hurting, no matter what joy you found from there on.

"Why don't you put it in the mail?" I asked.

She shook her head. "I don't want *her* to get her hands on it. Please, Laney."

"All right."

"But don't watch him read it. I couldn't bear to hear that he laughed at me."

The next evening, I had a night off from work, so I went to the South End. Helmets on the Short Bus were playing, and when they finished the first set and took a break, I saw my chance. I slipped Delilah's note into Tweet's guitar case for him to find.

He didn't see me do it. He was off in a corner with Rose, and I could hear their voices getting louder. "You'd think you didn't want this baby," she said, and he shot back, "Maybe I don't."

I felt bad then about tucking that note into the guitar case. This wasn't the time for Delilah's words to find Tweet. I didn't want to be any part of what might happen when they did. I wanted to open the case and get the note back into my pocket, but just then Tweet turned away from Rose and came back to the stage, and there was nothing I could do.

How could I know that Rose would find it? How could I imagine that she'd come to me a few days later and say, "You tell Delilah to leave Tweet alone."

But I couldn't tell Delilah that. I didn't want her to know the rest of what Rose said. "Tell her Tweet isn't coming back to her. Tell her there isn't going to be any mir-i-cle." She said the word the way Delilah had spelled it, and I couldn't let Delilah know that Rose had read that note, had said, "Jesus, Laney," with a smirk and a shake of her head as if to add, *How stupid can you all be?*

That was as much as I could say to the police officers. I looked across the table at the big-bellied one. "I put Delilah's note in Tweet's guitar case." I lifted my chin. "I did do that."

The big-bellied officer said that was all fine and good, but the one thing he wanted to know was whether I'd ever been in that house—Rose and Tweet's house—with that .38.

I glanced at Poke, who was rocking back and forth now, his hands all twisted up in his lap.

"Don't look at him," the officer said. "Look at me." He snapped his fingers. "Tell me exactly what happened that morning."

So there was this one more thing, and I knew I had to tell it. I imagined that Poke already had—at least some version of it—and now the officers were just waiting for me to confirm his story.

That May morning, the one in question, I turned off the highway onto the New Hope Road, and as I passed their house, I saw the two of them on the porch. Rose had on the oversized tie-dyed dress she'd been favoring the last month of her pregnancy and a pair of flip-flops. She had a backpack in her hand and she was trying to tug it free from Tweet, who was shirtless and barefoot, wearing only his Tweety Bird boxer shorts with the yellow cartoon bird on them.

I pulled to the side of the road, and I could hear Rose screaming at Tweet to let her go. She couldn't stand another minute with him. If he wanted Delilah Dade, she wasn't going to stop him. She'd have a baby to worry over soon, and she wouldn't have time to keep track of Tweet and whose bed he was in. Better to cut the cord right now and have it done, so she could get on with her life.

As much as I'd once held her to blame and wanted her gone, now that she was in misery, I couldn't bear to see it. I pulled into their driveway and walked up onto the porch.

"Tell him," Rose said to me. "Tell him you know all about that note. It's plain what's going on."

I tried to get her to calm down. "It was just a note Delilah wrote. Maybe it doesn't mean a thing in the world to Tweet."

Rose stamped her foot. "I caught them. The two of them. Right here in my bed." She gave a mighty yank on the backpack and it came free from Tweet's hand. She stumbled backward, and I braced her, staggering a little with the weight. "You're stupid, Tweet. You're a stupid man, and I must've been an idiot to have ever wanted you."

That was it, I thought, as I was telling the story to the officers. It was the idiocy of people so starved for love they didn't have a thought in their heads of how easily their lives could spin out of control. That was the story of Lester and me, and Rose and Tweet, and Delilah. A story of want. A story of greed, but under it all a story of fear, which was the same as love when push came to shove, and you found yourself shaking with the thought that you might never find that someone, that you'd always be alone in a world where everyone but you—you'd swear this to be true—was happy.

Tweet's hands were pulling at his wild red hair like he was desperate to arrange those dreads just right. "Rose," he said. "I swear...that woman...I didn't...aw, hell..." I could see he was trying to put a sentence together, something that would bring him what he wanted at this time when everything was about to change. The problem, though—and I knew this as I found myself trying to do the same for the officers—was he didn't know what he wanted. He only knew he wanted to go back to whatever ground he stood on before he and Delilah ended up in bed, so he wouldn't have this unsettling feeling that everything was about to explode. A time before he felt the fear of being without Rose and their baby, who was soon to come. "You can't leave me, Rose," he finally said.

"You watch me."

And with that, Tweet turned and stormed into the house, the screen door popping behind him with a violent slap.

Rose was trembling. I could feel her arms shaking, her chest heaving. It felt like the most natural thing in the world to hug her and rub her arms and tell her, "Shh, shh." Tell her, "Here now, here." Say, "Rose, oh, Rose."

I didn't turn away from her. At a time when it would have been so easy for me to tell her to grow up, things like this happened all the time with men—did she really think she could keep him?—I instead decided to be kind. On that morning, when she was hurting, I stood by her. I treated her with love. I held to the fact of that even as I told the officers the worst of it, the thing I'd kept to myself on account of it was too hard to say. I knew, once I did, there'd be no going back.

Rose said to me, "Let's go, Laney. Let's get out of here." She reached out her hand and waited for me to take it.

That's the moment that still haunts me, the moment when I started to reach for her hand—in an instant, we'd be down the steps and into Mother's car—but then I saw Lester's truck turn down the New Hope Road, and that was enough to make me hesitate because I saw that someone was in the truck with him, and as he came closer, I saw that the other person was Delilah. The truck was slowing down, and I knew that soon Lester would pull in behind Mother's Corolla, and he and Delilah might come up onto the porch, and then who knew what might happen.

"Come inside," I said to Rose, hoping she hadn't seen Delilah in Lester's truck. "Let's wash your face and get you something cool to drink and just let everything calm down for a while."

"I'm not going in there," Rose said, and then I knew she'd spotted Delilah and Lester because she said, "Oh, Jesus, Laney."

Then she fainted.

I couldn't hold her weight, but I was able to ease her down until she was sitting on the porch, her legs out in front of her, her head lolled over to the side.

Lester was making his way toward the porch.

"Go on back," I told him. "Everything's gone to hell with Rose and Tweet, and Delilah being here's only going to make it worse."

He came up the steps. I could tell he was in a state. "She started talking crazy after you left Walmart. Says she's had it with waiting for Tweet to leave Rose. Says it's time to settle this for good." He was talking so fast I could barely follow it all, something about cutting the battery cables in her Malibu so she couldn't drive out here. Then she threatened to tell the police about the plan to kill Rose. "She said she'd tell them it was me who meant to do it, all because Tweet told me to stay away from the band. Laney, I didn't know what to do. Maybe you can talk some sense into her."

Delilah opened the door and got out of the truck. "Quick," I told Lester. "Get Rose inside the house."

He stooped, got Rose under the arms, and struggled to lift her to her feet. I gave him a hand. The jostling was enough to bring her back around, and she said, "What's going on?"

"Lester's going to take you inside, Rose," I said, and she let him lead her into the house.

I went down the steps and across the grass to intercept Delilah. "What are you doing here?"

She had her purse hanging from her shoulder by its strap, and she sort of swung it to get me out of the way. "I've come for Tweet."

I held my ground. "You don't have any business inside that house. Not now."

"Oh, I've been in that house."

"I know you have. Rose knows it, too."

Delilah gave me a smirk. "You think you know everything, don't you?" It came to me then that maybe she'd been lying all along. Maybe she'd made up the story of what Rose said about Poke and me at the clinic that day. Delilah wanted to turn everything to suit her. Maybe she'd ransacked her trailer and painted those inverted pentagrams on Lester's house herself, so we'd start to believe that Rose was evil. "Now, let me by," Delilah said.

I put my hands out to grab her arms, but she took me by the shoulders and shoved me so hard that I ended up sprawled across the grass. "Tweet," she called out. I heard her moving. Before I could get to my feet, I heard the screen door slap against its frame, and I knew she was inside.

So they were in the house, Rose and Tweet and Delilah and Lester, and I was in the yard, listening to the voices as they rose and clamored inside. I wanted to pretend it was just noise from a television turned up too loud, and for a few seconds I was able to do that on account of I couldn't make out the words that they were saying. Their voices were all mixed up and hard to distinguish.

Then I heard Rose say, "You get out of my house. You, too, Lester Stipp."

I could hear everything as clear as day then, like I was inside that house.

"Rose, I want to make sure you're all right," Lester said.

"Tweet," Delilah called. "Tweet, baby."

"Delilah?" Tweet said. "Jesus, what a mess."

I knew I had to go in there. I had to try to talk some sense and get everyone to calm down. I started across the yard. I heard a door slam somewhere inside the house and then Delilah's voice shouting, "Come out here and face this."

Then I heard the first shot.

It rattled the windowpanes. I put my hand to my throat. I told myself to move, to open that door and go inside the house, but the echo of that shot was still in my ears, and I stood there not wanting to accept the fact of it.

Tweet said, his voice higher-pitched than normal, "You're out of your head." Then there was the noise of feet scrabbling over the hardwood floor and the thud of a body hitting a wall.

"That's when I heard the second shot," I told the officers. "That's what I never told."

They wanted to know why.

"Because we were guilty," I said. "We'd had that plan."

The big-bellied officer stood up, placed his hands flat on the table, and leaned over it so his face was only inches from mine. "Who did the killing?" he asked.

"Lester said it was Delilah. She had that .38 in her purse."

He'd stepped out onto the porch, and he'd said, "Jesus, Laney."

I could hear Delilah inside the house moaning and sobbing, saying, "Oh, Tweet. Tweet, baby. Wake up."

It surprised me how calm I felt. How quiet everything was in the aftermath of those two shots. The morning already too hot. Not a breeze anywhere. The sun burning down.

"We can't go to the police," Lester had said. "You know it'll come out what we were planning to do, and then what'll it look like?"

"Like we came here this morning to do it. Like we were Delilah's accomplices."

"That's right. Now, here's what we've got to do to make sure the cops don't get on our trail."

Lester was going to get Delilah out of there, and I was going to go about my business. "Pretend none of this happened," he told me, as if there were any chance of that. I was to go home. Change my clothes. Eat some breakfast. Say good morning to Mother. Just like this was any other morning.

"What about the gun?" I asked Lester.

The big-bellied officer stopped me there. "The .38," he said. "The one Grandpa found hidden in the boy's room."

I nodded. "Lester gave it to me to get rid of."

I walked into Rose and Tweet's house that day, and I saw Rose on the bedroom floor, sort of wedged in between the wall and the bed. I saw her naked foot first. Her flip-flop had fallen off. Her toenails were painted orange. She was on her side, one arm reaching under the bed like she was trying to fish something out, and I imagined she'd been trying to hide from Delilah. I knew right away that Rose was dead. Her face was no longer a face, and her blood was on the hardwood floor, the front of the night table, and the chenille spread where her arm had lifted it so she could try to crawl under the bed.

Tweet was in the bathroom. He was wearing his Tweety Bird boxer shorts. He was on his knees, his torso folded over the edge of the bathtub.

Delilah was kneeling beside him. "Tweet, baby." Her voice was a hoarse whisper. "Tweet."

I couldn't believe what I was doing. I held that .38—the gun that had killed Rose and Tweet—and its weight felt so strange to me. My whole life felt strange at that point. I knew I was moving—I was putting the pistol up under my shirt to hide it; I was starting toward the door—but it seemed like someone else doing these things. The .38 was hot against my bare stomach, but I kept it there, too afraid to move it, not wanting to bring it out and look at it again.

Lester grabbed me by the arm. "Go out the back," he said. "Make sure no one's headed toward this house. Jesus, those shots were loud. Be careful, Laney. Don't let anyone see you get in your car."

Rose and Tweet's house was so far out the New Hope Road toward the highway, it was possible that no one had heard the shots. The one most likely to have heard them was Mr. Hambrick, and without his hearing aids, he was deaf as a post. Mother's house was on the other side of the cornfield, a good hundred yards away, and I hoped she'd had the radio playing, as she often did when she was getting ready for work, and hadn't heard a thing. Still, I took care. I did what Lester told me. I went out the back door, and I peeked around the corner of the house. No traffic on the New Hope Road. No one come running up from town. All quiet at Mr. Hambrick's. I hurried out to my car.

I drove around town for a while, just trying to get my head straight. I drove past Jess and Libby Raymond's, and I met Bernard Goad's truck coming from the other direction. My first thought was he'd somehow heard the shots and was coming to investigate, but then I saw that the truck was going so slowly it was almost standing still. Mr. Goad didn't take notice of me. He was bent over the wheel, staring at the Raymond house with an anxious look on his face.

Ida Henline was watering flowers up by her house with a hose. She had on a bright red muumuu, and she was letting the water run over her petunias while she looked off in the distance at something I couldn't fathom.

Luther Gibson was on his porch, tearing open an envelope. Rayanne Fines was putting up the red flag on her mailbox.

All those people going about their business, not knowing a thing about what I was up to.

I thought about driving out to the park and heaving the .38 into the lake. Then I saw my mother coming down the sidewalk. She waved her arms for me to stop. The .38 was still under my shirt, lying covered in my lap. I rolled down my window, and Mother said, "What are you doing? I need my car."

"Just driving," I said.

"Mr. Hambrick wants you to clean his house today. Have you forgot that?"

Mother got into the car, and I headed toward the house, praying she wouldn't notice the lump in my lap and ask what I had under my shirt. Thank God she was too busy fussing about being late to work. She didn't realize that anything was out of the ordinary.

At the house, I got out of the Corolla, fumbling to keep the gun from falling, and she slid over behind the wheel. "See you this evening," she said.

Then she backed out onto the street and headed toward the highway.

I stood there awhile, clutching the .38 under my shirt, letting my heart slow down and my breath come more easily.

Then Mr. Hambrick came down the street in his pickup truck—the old white GMC, with the letters spelled out across the grille. I prayed he'd keep going, but he pulled up even with me and stopped. He leaned over and shouted out the window.

"You seen Poke?"

I said no, but in such a small voice Mr. Hambrick couldn't hear.

He curled his hand around his ear and said, "What's that?"

"I haven't seen him," I said, and this time he heard me.

"Door's open to the house so you can clean." He put the truck back in gear. "I've got to find that boy."

I don't know that I was capable then of giving any sort of logical thought at all to what I should do. Lester had told me to get rid of the .38, but I still had it under my shirt. When Mr. Hambrick told me he'd left the door to his house open, I walked down there, still with no notion of what I was going to do with that gun. Maybe I was trying to keep from thinking about what had happened to Rose and Tweet and—good Lord, the thought hit me so hard I almost went to my knees—the baby. Later, I'd hear that if only someone had found Rose sooner, even though she was dead, the baby was so close to being born, the doctors might have been able to save her. It was a girl. That was one of the last things Rose shared with me. A little girl. I would have taken her as my own. At least that's the thing I dream about now. Lester and me and that baby, and all our lives ahead of us.

I walked into Mr. Hambrick's house, and it was so quiet. I stood in the entryway, listening to the grandfather clock's ticking in its alcove alongside the staircase. I called out for Poke, thinking he might be there, but no answer came back to me.

Here, the slope-shouldered officer said to Poke, "Where were you, son?"

"I was up at Rose and Tweet's."

He'd gone there, he said, because he'd heard the shots, because he'd seen Lester and me on the porch. He'd seen us go back into the house, and he'd seen me come out and get into Mother's car and drive away. Soon, he said, Lester came out with Delilah. He had his arm around her shoulders, and she was all crumpled up against him, as if she could barely walk. He got her into his truck, and he turned it around and headed back toward the highway.

"And you never said a word about any of this?" the big-bellied officer said.

Poke shook his head. "It was too big to tell."

It would be Mr. Hambrick who would find the bodies when he finally went to Rose and Tweet's to look for Poke. The police would talk to him and to Poke. Officers would come to Mother's house and ask her if she'd heard anything. "Nothing," she'd say. And me? Had I noticed anything unusual when I'd come by Rose and Tweet's on my way home from work? "No, sir," I'd told the officer who'd asked. "Nothing out of the ordinary at all."

It was too big, Poke said again, and that's what I thought, too. It was too big for any of us to tell—so big that Lester and Delilah and I would keep it quiet, so big that Lester would finally try to forget it by slipping into one of his fugues and going away. Now I had to go ahead and say how I climbed the stairs at Mr. Hambrick's house, where I found myself going into Poke's room. His bed was unmade, the covers tossed in a tangle at the foot, but I didn't touch them. I still had that .38.

The closet door was open, and I saw the pile of clothes on the floor and at the back, a hole someone had punched or kicked in the drywall.

I was standing there when I heard footsteps falling hard and fast on the stairs. I knew they belonged to Poke.

He froze when he came through the doorway and saw me in his room.

"Laney, don't tell me how it happened. I don't want to know."

He went to his bed and started straightening out the covers, pulling up the top sheet and the white chenille bedspread, smoothing out the wrinkles, as if finally he'd come to a point where he'd seen too much, and now he thought if he only kept his mind on making that bed, he'd forget what he'd just come upon at Rose and Tweet's.

I had to grab him by the arm and swing him around. "You see what you get? You see what you've got now from nosing around?"

That's when the .38 fell from my shirt. It banged against the floor, and Poke and I stood there, looking at it.

Then he glanced at me, hoping, I think now, that I'd pick it up, but once it was gone from me, I couldn't bear to hold it again.

"I'm supposed to get rid of it," I said. "Poke, I'm so scared."

He nodded. His glasses slipped down his nose a little, and he pushed them back up. Then, without a word, he bent down and picked up that .38. He held it by the barrel.

"Don't worry," he said. "I'll take care of it."

And like that, he gave me one less thing to worry about. He took that .38, and sometime later, when I was going about my business cleaning

Mr. Hambrick's house like nothing was out of the ordinary, Poke stuffed the gun into the hole in the drywall in his closet.

If I'd been a better person, I wouldn't have let him do that, wouldn't have left him open to suspicion. I came clean with the officers. I said, "It was Delilah's .38. Poke didn't have anything to do with what went on at Rose and Tweet's." My voice got small then, ashamed as I was to admit this next thing. "I never deserved Poke as a friend. I was never good enough back to him."

He took off his glasses and slung them down on the table. He covered his eyes with his hands and kept rocking back and forth.

I started to touch him, just to pat his arm, just to let him know I was there, but I didn't think I had the right.

"Girl, you're in a world of trouble," the big-bellied officer said. Then he nodded to the slope-shouldered one. "Get the boy's grandpa. Tell him he can take him home."

MISS BABY

I went to Illinois the same night Lester did. I borrowed Emma's car, and I took off after him. A 1985 Chrysler Le Baron with a plastic Madonna stuck to the dash. A big old boat of a car, and I wheeled it on faith into Arkansas, up through Missouri, and on into Mt. Gilead, Illinois. An itty-bitty town where it was easy as pie to find the police station.

"I'm here about Lester Stipp," I said to the lady officer behind the glass at the counter.

The woman was peeling an orange. She pressed her fingernail into the rind and tore away a strip. She studied me. "You know Lester Stipp?"

"He lived with me in Texas."

She put the orange down on a white paper towel. "You're Betty Ruiz. You're Miss Baby."

"That's right."

"Sugar, we've been looking for you."

While I was on the road those fifteen hours, the police there in Mt. Gilead had been talking to Lester. He'd come to say the truth. He and Laney didn't pull that trigger. It was that other woman, that Delilah Dade. Maybe that was true, but it wasn't the whole story, was it? Lester said no, no it wasn't, and he owned up to it then, the story that would floor me once I heard it all, a story of witchcraft and sore hearts and the belief that one woman, that poor Rose MacAdow, could cast a spell. A story of conspiracy to commit murder, and even if Lester or Laney didn't pull the trigger, they still had plenty to answer to. They knew enough, the lady with the orange told me, to keep them locked up. The police had run a check on my car and found out my name and address. They'd seen the fresh tat on his wrist. They'd put it all together. They knew about Pablo. They knew about Slam Dent. They knew I'd given Lester a place to hide out all those months, and what they wanted to know was how it all came to be. Did I have knowledge of these murders in New Hope? Did I knowingly harbor a criminal?

"He told me he didn't have anything to do with that business here."

"Oh, he had something to do with it all right. More than he let on with you."

I was worn out from the road. I felt my head spinning and my knees about to buckle. Lester had promised me he was innocent. I held to the edge of the counter to keep from fainting.

"He told me he didn't have anything to hide."

The woman laughed. "Sugar, a man who says he doesn't have anything to hide most certainly does have something to hide."

I wanted to laugh at how silly that sounded, but I couldn't. I understood that Lester was in trouble. I understood that I'd have to answer questions. I'd stepped up to him that evening on the corner of Oak and Fry, and I'd said, "Hey, good-lookin'." I had no idea where I was going then, but I knew where I was now. Deep in his real life, the one I tried my best to cover with a lie. Here I was, playing a part in this tale of witchcraft and murder. All along, I thought I was the one inventing a story when really it was already written, cast like a spell, just waiting for me to appear.

LANEY

June 2010

MT. GILEAD, ILLINOIS

I went on trial first. It was summer again, a little over a year since that May morning when Lester came out onto the porch and told me Rose and Tweet were dead.

He told the story again on the witness stand. He answered all the State's Attorney's questions. He spoke in a soft voice, and said, "Yes, sir," and, "No, sir," when need be. I don't harbor any bad feelings toward him on account of he testified against me. Nothing he said was a lie. I closed my eyes and listened to that voice, and it tore me up inside to think of the trouble we were in. We could have gone on being sweethearts. We could have gotten married, had kids, lived a regular life. None of that was possible now.

Was it true, the State's Attorney asked Lester, that he and Elaine Volk had been involved in a romantic relationship?

"Yes, sir."

Was it true that there'd been a plot to murder Rose MacAdow?

I sat at the defense table, my head bowed, my hands folded in my lap, but when I heard that question, I couldn't keep myself from raising my head to look at Lester. My eyes, folks would say later, looked so big. You could hardly believe I'd been involved in such a story. Laney Volk. Always a slip of a thing, I'd nearly wasted away in jail, losing so much weight my face was all eyes. I wore a blue dress with white cuffs on the sleeves and a white Peter Pan collar. A dress Mother had brought for me. "Oh, Laney," she'd said. "What in the world have you done?"

Lester cleared his throat. "I want to tell the truth here. I want to explain how it all happened."

The State's Attorney was a squat man in a gray three-piece suit, the vest of which stretched across his ample stomach. He had neatly combed silver hair, and a friendly face. "That's what we want, too, son. You go ahead when you're ready."

Lester said that, yes, at one time there'd been a plot. "Then Laney changed her mind. We both changed our minds. Even Delilah. She didn't come to Rose and Tweet's that morning meaning to kill them. Things just happened."

That was true, I said, when, despite the resistance of my attorney, I insisted on taking the stand and telling my side of the story. I thought I had to because the girl—the goth girl with the thick black coils painted from the corners of her eyes onto her cheekbones, the girl who kissed me outside the South End on the night Delilah fell for Tweet—had come forward to tell the story of how I'd given the horns-of-the-devil sign that night, and she knew I worshipped Satan.

"I was just singing," I said from the stand. "All I did was give the sign for rock 'n' roll." I held my fingers up to demonstrate. "I can sing," I said in a small voice. My mother was crying, and I knew she was thinking about that talent I had and how she'd encouraged me and I'd never done a thing with the voice God gave me. "You might not think it to look at me," I said, "but, really, I have this gift. I can sing."

The State's Attorney said, "Didn't you already tell the police that you burned a black candle with Rose MacAdow's name scratched into it? Didn't you try to summon the devil?"

I admitted that I'd begun to believe that Rose had put a hex on me. "I started having horrible migraine headaches," I said, "and I knew she had a doll that was supposed to be me, and she stuck pins into its head. Delilah said there was a hex on all of us, a death hex."

"A death hex?" the State's Attorney said.

I nodded. "Yes, sir. A hex to last as long as Rose was alive. The only way to stop it was to kill her. That's what Delilah said."

"We're not talking about Delilah Dade now." The State's Attorney raised his voice. "We're talking about you and what you did in connection with these murders."

"Yes, sir," I said, "and what I mean to tell you is this: I let Delilah believe what she wanted to believe. I lit that candle, and when she said that about the death hex and what we had to do, I didn't say anything to stop her."

Was I present when Lester Stipp test-fired that .38? After the murders, did I let Gerald Hambrick take it from me to get rid of? Before the murders, did I help set a fire at the home that would eventually become the murder scene? Did I own a book of spells? Did I try to practice them from time to time?

I admitted that all of those things were true.

"Are you a witch, Ms. Volk?"

I picked at the buttons on one of my cuffs. I looked down at my bony, jittery fingers, and I swore they belonged to someone else. For a good while, I didn't say a word, and I got to thinking that I could just shut up now and let the rest of my life play out with no help from me at all. I could give in to the future I'd made. Then the judge leaned toward me, and his chair creaked, and I knew I'd have to go on and do what I'd meant to do when I took the stand, which was to take responsibility for everything, to admit what I knew to be the truth: There were all these lives going on in people and they didn't even know it, all these lives festering just beneath the skin. It didn't take much to call them up to light and air. The prick of a needle here or there, and everything you thought you weren't could get out and stain you forever, could ripple out to other people—you could even swear you loved them—and hurt them in ways you never could have imagined. You could be that person you saw sometimes on the news, that person who'd done something unforgivable and could barely face it. *Trust me,* I wanted to say. *It can happen.*

I'd see Delilah only one more time—at her trial, where I'd tell my story again, and my heart would break from the ugly look she'd give me, like I was no one she'd ever cared about at all.

At my own trial, I answered the State's Attorney's question. "A witch? No. I wasn't really anyone at all. I was just a girl, but I knew that the way we were thinking was wrong."

"You could have gone to the police, couldn't you, Miss Volk? All along the line there were multiple chances to tell the police what you knew."

I couldn't deny that.

"What were you afraid of, Miss Volk?"

"Like I said, we had that plot. Who would've believed us if we said we tried to stop it? We did our best to get back to where we were before we cooked it all up."

"But you were guilty, weren't you? You were guilty of plotting Rose MacAdow's murder. You did that, didn't you, Miss Volk?"

I couldn't answer. I could only think of everyone I'd lost. Tweet and Rose were dead, and their baby. Delilah and Lester and I were going to prison. At one time or another, I'd loved them all—still did, truth be told.

"Miss Volk," the State's Attorney said, "did you conspire with Delilah Dade and Lester Stipp to murder Rose MacAdow?"

It was true. Nothing I could do would change that. It would haunt me forever. I'd never be able to forget everything I'd done or hadn't done that might have kept Delilah from killing Rose and Tweet. If that hadn't happened, I might have lived a pleasant life. What good did it do to wonder? Still I'd never be able to stop daydreaming what the years might have been like for me if I hadn't loved Delilah so much that I burned that black candle and let her believe that Rose had placed a hex on us.

"I'm waiting, Miss Volk."

The word I knew I had to say would be both true and not true, but in a court of law only the truth would count. I looked out at my mother and Poke and Lester. I looked at everyone sitting in that courtroom—some of them were people from New Hope who'd known me since I was a little girl. Then I stared a good while at the woman from Texas who'd taken Lester in. I wanted her to know I didn't blame her. I wanted to tell her I was thankful that she'd given him a place to be and loved the same things about him that I'd remember and treasure the rest of my days. I don't know if it got through, but I hoped she could read it on my face.

Then I said it. "Yes," I said. I couldn't turn away from the fact. "Yes," I said again, my voice as steady as I could make it. "Yes, I did."

MISS BABY

September 2010

DENTON, TEXAS

When she looked at me in that courtroom, her stare went all the way to my heart, and I felt what we shared: a desire to be loved. Like her, I knew that anyone's life could change in an instant. I was guilty, too.

Once upon a time, I saw a man on a street corner in Denton, and before I even knew I was going to do it, I told him he was mine.

Lester Stipp. I'll never forget him. He's lost to me now, but I can't say I'm sorry for any of it. Lordy Magordy.

I had to testify at his trial. I said everything as plain as I could even though it embarrassed me to admit how I manufactured a story for the two of us, how I named him Donnie and came to love him, how I never knew a thing about the life he'd lived in Illinois.

"He was Donnie," I said, and that was the truth. He was Donnie, and all I knew about him was what I invented.

Then I saw his picture on CNN, and I listened to the story, the real one, and just like that, everything I'd so carefully made began to tear and come apart. The most painful thing of all was what I saw about myself. Once I heard Laney Volk say what she did on the witness stand, I was convinced she knew it, too. It's a sin to want too much—my *mami* had and so had Pablo. I was no different, nor was Laney or Delilah or Lester. I suspect the same held true for Poke and Rose and Tweet—all these people who now fill me with something I don't even have a name for, as

I go about my days back in Texas. I still run my shop. I drive to Huntsville on Sundays to visit Pablo in prison. Sometimes Carolyn rides along, or Emma Hart. "Lands, ain't it strange?" Emma said the first time she had to pass through security into the visiting area. "It is," I said, and then somewhere along the line, it stops feeling weird, and it's just what it is. It's your life, and there's nothing you can do to change it.

"I never meant for anyone to get hurt," Laney said that day in the courtroom.

The stories started to come out, stories of how she'd never had a boyfriend until Lester. I heard the people talking in the hallway during recesses. They weren't buying for a minute that nonsense about him forgetting who he was and running away. He knew what he was doing when he went to Texas. He played that Mexican gal for a fool. Well, he'll have a good long while in prison to remember exactly who he is. That Laney Volk, too. And Delilah Dade? Look what happens when a woman gets pissed off at a man who did her wrong.

Bernard Goad, still wearing his mailman's light blue shirt, watched the deputies lead Laney back into the courtroom one day. He shook his head. "Women," he said, disgusted.

That wasn't it, I wanted to say. Not at all. Just like a man, I thought, to imagine that it all came down to a broken heart and revenge.

It was more than that. Much more. When Laney looked at me from the witness stand, I tried to set my face in a way that I hoped would let her know I understood exactly how it happened. It was all about wanting to matter to someone, wanting it so badly that you did things you never could have imagined, and you swore they were right, all for the sake of love.

On the day they sentenced Lester, I waited outside the courthouse along with the others, who for whatever reason couldn't bring themselves to leave even though the story was done. Laney's *mami* was there. Laney had been sentenced first, and her *mami* was stony faced as the sheriff's deputies led Lester down the steps. Curtis Hambrick was there as well—I'd made the acquaintance of all these folks as the trials had gone on—and Poke, who crumpled up against his grandfather and cried in the courtroom when the judge read Laney's sentence; like Lester, she'd spend seven years in the Illinois Department of Corrections. And there were relatives of Rose and Tweet, broken-down country folks who showed nothing on their faces, saving their rage for Delilah Dade, whose trial was yet to come. It wouldn't take long, when it finally did, for the jury to find her guilty of first-degree murder. Laney would testify, as would Lester, and the whole story would come out of how she went to Rose and Tweet's with that .38, how she shot Rose in the face while she was trying to hide under the bed, how Tweet got a hold of Delilah's arm and tried to get the gun away from her. They came out into the hallway, Lester said, and before he could try to help Tweet get that gun, the .38 went off. The bullet struck Tweet in the chest and sent him backward into the bathroom, where he slumped to his knees and fell across the tub. Yes, Laney said, that's where he was when she found him, and yes, Rose was on the floor of the bedroom.

So it was over for Laney and Lester—I'd watched with as much jealousy as I felt I had a right to when the two of them caught each other's eyes in the courtroom and I could see plain as day that they still loved each other. Good for them, I finally told myself. Good for whatever it is that keeps people's hearts in sync even when trouble comes.

As for Lester and me, there was just this one moment, the one I'll remember forever. The deputies had him in handcuffs, and they were holding him by the arms as they came down those courthouse steps. I couldn't help myself. I called his name, and for just the briefest instant he looked at me, and I could tell he remembered all those months in Texas. This light came into his eyes, and his face went soft, and I saw the person who hadn't lived through any of this mess in Illinois. Just that one moment before the deputies put him in the car when I could tell that whatever we'd had was real.

That was enough, that ache I got when Lester looked at me. I knew

I'd carry it the rest of my days, a reminder of what might have been, starting the next day when I was heading west, gone from that place, plenty of time ahead of me to think about everything I'd lived through, everything I'd heard about Lester, Laney, and Delilah.

Poke and Curtis Hambrick. Ida Henline. Jess and Libby Raymond, and Bernard Goad. Luther Gibson. Rayanne Fines. Oh, I met all those folks from New Hope. They took me into their homes. They held my hand. They said, *Now, listen,* and then they told me their stories.

If I could talk to Rose and Tweet, I have no doubt they'd do the same. They'd tell a story that'd leave me tingling inside my skin, their words like needles set against my heart—piercing, pulsing, marking me as deep as that. A story of love, no matter how roughed up and ugly and stained. A story I'll call my own. Tomorrow and for always. The truest story I know.

Acknowledgments

I'M GRATEFUL TO John Glusman, Kate Kennedy, Rachel Rokicki, and all the folks at Crown who have worked so hard to bring this book into the world. Thanks, too, to Sarah Knight, who guided this novel through its early draft. As always, I'm indebted to Phyllis Wender and her assistants, Allison Cohen and Susan Cohen, for all they do on my behalf. A special thanks to my colleague, Manny Martinez, for his assistance with the Spanish that some of my characters use. I knew just enough of the language to make me dangerous, and Manny was there to save me. I'm also indebted to The Ohio State University for the support that granted me the time to finish this book. Joe Oestreich and the excellent band, Watershed, were kind enough to allow me to use lyrics from their songs and to give them a cameo in the novel. Many thanks, guys! Keep rockin'! Thanks, too, to Mary McGlasson and Kevin Ryden for all that they generously shared with me.

Finally, I can't say thank you enough to Shaye Areheart for her friendship and her wise readings. Her good sense and sharp eye made every page, every sentence, better.

About the Author

LEE MARTIN is the author of the Pulitzer Prize finalist *The Bright Forever;* the novels, *Quakertown* and *River of Heaven;* a story collection, *The Least You Need to Know;* and three memoirs, *Such a Life, From Our House,* and *Turning Bones*. He has won a fellowship from the National Endowment for the Arts, the Mary McCarthy Prize in Short Fiction, a Lawrence Foundation Award, and the Glenna Luschei Award. He lives in Columbus, Ohio, where he teaches in the creative writing program at The Ohio State University.

About the Author

[illegible] the author of [illegible] Waiting [illegible] National [illegible] Award [illegible]